Murder at Sunny Lake

A Muskoka Murder Mystery

Liz McGillicuddy

Northshore Noir Press
Toronto, Canada
www.northshorenoir.com

Northshore Noir

ISBN: 978-0-9735190-6-8

First printing 2023

For more information visit: www.lizmcgillicuddy.com.

CHAPTER ONE

The surface of Sunny Lake reflected the early morning sunrise, turning the water into a field of blue diamond dust. He was alone, as he liked to be on mornings like this. It was a time for him and his canoe. He was at peace here. No other boats, no jet skis, no swimmers—not yet. He had felt this way about lakes since he was a little boy. He read about water spirits and sea creatures in myths during English classes at school, and he loved them. He paddled out on the lake and let its calm ripple through his body. The sun warmed his arms and his face. His long hair floated around him like a cloud of sun-brightened silver threads, caressing his face. His eyes were closed. He could feel the water beneath his hands and knew that it was the same water that would hold him in its arms if he fell out of the canoe.

The sun burned away the soft grey fog that hung over the lake. He could see the forested hills reflected in the water. It was a sight that tourists and newcomers paid a lot of money to have, but rarely got up early enough to see. The paddle dipped and swung. A song from his childhood came to his lips as he headed to the shore. "My paddle clean and bright," he sang. He stopped himself. Was it clean? Or keen? Keen and bright? He was sure he had sung it both ways at day camp.

The glimmer of light reflecting off the stone drew him closer, revealing a murky blob floating just beneath the surface, struggling against the relentless current. Panic surged within him; he recognized what it was from a distance — someone drowning. The memories of countless summers spent on this lake only intensified the urgency. With the adrenaline pumping through his veins, he desperately turned the canoe towards the jetty, his heart pounding in his chest.

"Hey! Hey dude! Hang on! I'm coming!" he screamed with desperation, his paddle slicing through the water in a frantic rhythm. His mind raced, knowing every second counted. As he approached the scene, he tried to steady the canoe, but his trembling hands betrayed his fear. He knew deep down that he might already be too late.

Finally reaching the drowning person, he fought to control his shaky movements. "Hold on, I'm almost there!" he gasped, his voice quivering with distress. The closer he got, the heavier the weight of despair settled upon him. With trembling hands, he steadied the canoe, but the sight before him sent shockwaves through him.

With a surge of determination, he threw caution to the wind and leaped into the water. The bracing grip enveloped him, but his urgency overshadowed any discomfort. Swimming swiftly, he reached the floating body, praying for a miracle as he turned it over to face upwards.

"I can't lose you. Come on, don't leave me like this," he whispered desperately, clinging to hope as he kicked his legs to propel them towards the shore. His arms strained with the weight, but he refused to give up, channeling all his energy into saving the life before him.

Finally reaching the safety of the shore, he heaved the lifeless body onto the ground, panting and gasping for breath. "Come on, come on! Breathe!" he pleaded, his voice cracking with emotion. He pressed his trembling fingers against the chest, attempting chest compressions despite his limited knowledge of CPR. "Please, please don't let this be the end."

He knew the man was dead and began to tear up.

With a shaky exhale, he gently nudged at the lifeless body. "Dude, I'm so sorry," he stammered, tears welling in his eyes. His cell phone nearly slipped from his quivering grasp as he dialed for help, trying to keep composure in the face of tragedy. The minutes ticked by, but they felt like an eternity.

As he anxiously waited for the emergency operator to pick up, his heart raced, and time seemed to crawl. "911, what's your emergency?" a voice finally answered on the other end. Struggling to compose himself, he quickly explained the dire situation, providing his location and pleading for immediate assistance.

With a trembling voice, he provided all the crucial details he could remember. The dispatcher assured him that help was on the way, urging him to continue CPR while waiting for the first responders.

He put the phone down on the ground and resumed chest compressions. A mix of relief and anxiety washed over him. He knew that help was coming, but he couldn't help feeling the weight of sorrow for the person who had lost their life before he could reach them. He silently prayed for the paramedics to arrive swiftly and somehow reverse the irreversible.

As the sound of sirens drew nearer, relief washed over him, but it was bittersweet. He had done all he could, yet the outcome was certain. Gazing at the lifeless body and the waiting paramedics, he couldn't help but feel a profound sense of responsibility.

"I tried, I really did," he murmured to himself, tears streaming down his cheeks. He felt an overwhelming mix of sorrow, guilt, and hopefulness, knowing that whatever happened next would be out of his hands. As the paramedics took over, he stepped back, feeling a surge of both relief and lingering dread.

It was just moments before the payments stopped their work. "What? What? It is too late, isn't it?" he asked.

"Yes. He's been dead a while. Stay close, okay?"

He nodded then hurriedly dashed back into the water to retrieve his canoe. He dragged it onto the shore, away from the body. Every second felt like an eternity, and exhaustion clawed at him. He grabbed his phone, called his boss to tell him about the incident, and began crying. He had been a camp counselor for years, but had never experienced anything like this.

Detective Inspector Caitlin Murphy drove her Trurok Brawler 4x4 to work every day. The lifted Brawler had a boxy exterior and aggressive styling. Its powerful engine could handle any off-road terrain. She was listening to music her last girlfriend hated, and she savoured it. "Everything you do is murder. Everything! I am sure you only ever listen to murder music," she had said. So Murphy did exactly that: started listening to music by murderers, or about murder. This morning she connected her phone to the Brawler's BlueTooth system, and the sounds of Leadbelly filled the air.

Murphy followed the winding road, flipping the visor down when she drove into the sun. The vanity mirror was open, and she caught sight of herself. Her undercut blonde hair was streaked with grey, the bags under her blue eyes were more pronounced than last year, and the laugh lines were dangerously close to being crow's feet. She put on a pair of sunglasses, looked at herself and then snapped the visor up. "You look great in sunglasses," she said to herself.

Murphy parked, swiped in at the reception desk, and walked up one flight of stairs to the offices of the Homicide Unit. The modern offices were a combination of private and shared spaces designed to facilitate open communication. The space included individual desks, shared workspaces, interview rooms, evidence storage and filing areas.

Each detective except Murphy had a computer with dual monitors. Murphy's office within the office had an older desk that was not large enough to hold two monitors so she settled for a standard PC. The team desks sat on the outer edge of a U-shaped sectional couch which itself encircled a large glass coffee table. There were two unused desks: one for an unfilled Liaison Officer position and one for any guest from another unit or police force.

Nearby were three mobile white boards, used by the team as link boards to hold information about the current homicide. The boards each had a screen that could be quickly pulled down to cover the information if need be.

The work area was to the right of the entrance, and the interview rooms were to the left. Everything was light and bright and clean, meant to disarm suspects and welcome witnesses. Murphy made it her mission to promote a culture of respect and professionalism with co-workers, grieving families, witnesses, and suspects.

As the early morning sunlight filtered through the office window, Murphy found herself sipping a steaming cup of instant coffee, eagerly diving into the overnight reports before her fellow members of the murder team arrived. She crossed her fingers, hoping for a day that wouldn't be swamped with an overwhelming workload, giving her a chance to catch up on the dreaded paperwork.

The Homicide Unit she oversaw comprised a tight-knit group of four, entrusted with covering the vast expanse of the Municipality of Muskoka. Though physically extensive, it was a mosaic of quaint small towns, sprawling rural farmland, and serene lakes that brought a unique set of challenges and mysteries.

Compared to her previous posting in the bustling city of Ottawa, Muskoka offered a refreshing escape from the labyrinth of politicians meddling in investigations and the relentless scrutiny of the media. It was one of the reasons she had made the bold decision to transfer here — to break free from the shackles of political pressure and media stress that had gripped her life before.

She recalled the exasperation of having the mayor breathing down her neck, the frustration of newspapers misquoting her, and the irritation of podcasters unremittingly mocking her every move. It was enough to make anyone want to escape the unceasing spotlight and seek solace away from that all-consuming anxiety.

In Muskoka, she could breathe a sigh of relief, knowing that her team's pursuit of justice would not be overshadowed by political agendas or media sensationalism. Here, the focus was solely on unraveling mysteries and bringing closure to grieving families.

Muskoka had become her sanctuary, where she could embrace the challenge of solving crimes, free from the suffocating pressures that once threatened to consume her passion for justice.

She was absentmindedly stirring the coffee when the phone rang. She read another paragraph of the report in front of her before answering the call. "Detective Inspector Murphy," she replied as she tapped the spoon on the side of the cup.

"Ma'am, we've got a body. Probably murder."

She took a sip of coffee and waited, but the rest of the information was not forthcoming. "Who, what, where, when?" A whisper of an Irish accent came through in her words.

"Unknown male, we can't identify his age yet. Found off shore in Sunny Lake just past the Nature Centre. A canoeist spotted him. The Forensic Unit is already on site."

"Sunny Lake? Go on."

"The body looked kind of fresh, so it hasn't been in the water for long. There is a rope around the neck."

Rope around the neck. Yes, probably a murder, Murphy sarcastically thought to herself. So much for her quiet day. She took another sip of coffee before replying and calmly said, "Call DSS Girard and tell him I'll meet him there." Before leaving her office, Murphy drained the rest of her coffee and finished reading the report on her desk.

Sunny Lake shimmered as a prime fishing spot, cherished by the locals for generations. There had been a big stink raised when Franklin's Fishin' Adventures tried to open a store on the water's edge. Some of the older residents objected to the chain store opening, drawing even more visitors to the area. They wanted to keep the place clear of tourists, outsiders, and all their chaos.

Without tourists and cottagers, the municipal population of just over 500,000 people could never support the massive infrastructure and government system they currently enjoyed. Highways cut through the area, but it would have withered long ago, if not for the support from the ultra rich and their picturesque homes. Sunny Lake remained at a crossroads between embracing new opportunities and fiercely safeguarding its treasured identity, leaving the future of the community hanging in the balance.

Murphy headed out. She eventually turned onto Lake Kelbowek Road and drove on. The road led to Sunny Lake Corners, a small cluster of houses that were next to the single-lane road. There was a United church, a diner, and a country-house hotel cum sports store, of sorts, where they sold lures, worms, and cheap fishing rods. At last, after the bend in the road, a magnificent clear vista of Sunny Lake opened up in front of

Murphy; this morning it was gleaming in all its glory. Sunny Lake was long and thin. The northern end was lightly developed, and the southern end was in a conservation area. The Sunny Lake Nature Centre and day camp were just outside the conservation area.

The paved road ended in a parking lot with an area of grass on one side and a few scattered picnic tables on the other. A noticeboard showed a map with trails and walking routes around the lake, and further down was the Nature Centre. It functioned as a trailhead, day camp and art gallery.

Murphy parked by the noticeboard and changed from shoes to hiking boots before setting off up the path to the centre.

Detective Staff Sergeant Adam Girard had already arrived and parked his car under a tree near the building. He wore his usual suit and tie with polished business shoes, looking out of place among the trees and goose shit on the ground. He was standing next to a pale, lanky man wearing khaki shorts and a khaki Sunny Lake Nature Centre t-shirt. His bright lime trail-running shoes were his only source of colour.

Murphy loved working with Girard. He was a skilled detective, and she adored his family.

"I appreciate your coming here so quickly, Adam, not sure about your footwear, though," Murphy said playfully as she waved her foot at him. "Who do we have here?" she asked.

Girard smiled broadly. "Boss, great to see you. It's been such a long time. At least six, maybe seven, hours." Girard was tall, almost six foot three, with a slender build. His height gave him a unique vantage point when surveying any crime scene. "This is Andrew Short, the director of the Sunny Lake Nature Centre. One of his instructors found the body."

Murphy offered her hand, which Short took reluctantly. "I'd like to speak with the instructor? What's the name?" Murphy asked.,

"Rodney Taylor. He is a bit shaken up."

"Let's give him a moment, then. Adam, can we make out what's happening at the scene from here?"

"No," Girard said. The locals called this Long Lake, on account of it being narrow and long. Even from where they were at midpoint, one could not see from one end to the other.

"This way." Short headed down a trail. It was a long enough walk, pleasant in the summer shade, but Murphy wondered if maybe she'd have been able to drive here and save Girard's shoes.

Short brought them to an open area filled with a rack of old canoes, paddles, lifejackets, and a jetty constructed of concrete. It was the beginning of the day camp. Short's feet dragged along the ground, kicking up dust and tree litter as he walked. He wanted to get the situation resolved quickly and get the hell out of there.

"All good," he muttered, kicking the ground with the toe of his shoe as he anxiously reassured himself. The breeze had dropped to nothing, and the air was hot and close and smelled of baked mud. A young grackle let out a series of insistent screeches.

"You're right," said Murphy. She looked at the line of trees, which stood tall and purposeful down the bank. "All good. It looks like a great camping place. A couple of cabins, some canoes. Probably a great little getaway for kids. That cabin looks pretty old." Murphy walked over. The door was ajar and swung back and forth in the breeze. An old beer can rattled when the door tapped on it. Murphy frowned. "Beer?"

"Every two-week day camp session has one overnight weekend. This is where our campers stay overnight. Just a small area, a few cabins, some outhouses, that kind of thing," Short said. "But teenagers figured out they could sneak in for parties on the weekends we don't use it. It's hard to catch them. It is getting pretty messy up here. Lots of damage to the trees and cabins and whatnot. We don't use this cabin too often."

Murphy pushed open the door with her foot. It didn't take long for her eyes to adjust to the gloom. No one had attempted to clear the mess inside. There was a broken desk, a few chairs tossed around, and a sofa slashed into ribbons and the stuffing pulled out. Caused by animals or teenagers, she wasn't sure which. She noticed every window was broken. The piles of beer cans, alcohol bottles and cigarette butts spoke volumes. She wondered if her victim had been here before ending up in the lake.

"The body is down there," Short said.

Murphy smiled and nodded and glanced at Girard. "Mr. Short, I don't suppose you know when the cabin was last used?"

"We used it a couple of weeks ago, but no one has been here since. We were hoping to let the campers stay overnight next weekend. When we built the Sunny Lake Centre, we tore down most of the existing cabins. Government said get rid of them, the kids were trespassing too much on Crown Land. We didn't want the kids hanging out here, maybe getting hurt or drowning. So, we took a lot down."

"I remember there was a big party August of last year, a big celebration. End of summer, just before school started." Girard said. "Someone saw the lights from the road and called the police. A fire pit and tons of beer. My neighbour's son was among them. I remember he was pretty angry about it. But that's how it goes, eh? I mean, what teenager doesn't love that kind of late August night?"

Murphy nodded. "Call Cleo, find out if there were any related complaints from last night, maybe the night before. Ask her to go through any missing persons' reports from, say, a week ago." Girard nodded and pulled out his cell phone. Murphy looked around while Girard was on the phone, but paid attention when he started speaking to her.

"Boss, Hamilton says she's not too happy that we don't have an age on the body," Girard reported.

Murphy walked over to Girard and leaned into the phone. "Detective work is so hard," she whined jokingly. "Come on DC Hamilton, how many missing men could there be?" She ruined away from the call and spoke with the camp director. "Mr. Short —"

"Call me Andrew," he replied quickly.

Murphy nodded. "Andrew, how deep is the water here?"

"It's around six metres, but there's a big drop-off, and it doubles that in the middle. There's no water level management in place."

"Thanks. We'll see how the forensic team wants to play it," she said to Girard. She couldn't imagine Dr. Chen, the pathologist, out on a boat. He liked the control and predictability of his lab.

"Will you wait here until Dr. Chen is ready for us, please, Adam? I'll see if Mr. Taylor's up to a few questions. Andrew, if you wouldn't mind..." Murphy said as she gestured back toward the Centre. Short seemed at first not to have heard. He coiled up his lanyard carefully and slipped it into his pocket, then straightened his back as though he had just realized something important and walked off, quickly, toward the Centre.

Rodney Taylor was in his late teens. His face was drained of colour, a remarkable feat for someone who spent so much time on the water. He sat on the sofa in the Nature Centre common room, clutching a tea in both hands. There was an untouched cookie on the plate in front of him. He looked up, startled, and some of the tea spilled onto the floor.

"Ooh, are you going to eat that cookie?" Murphy joked, hoping to lighten the mood. It didn't work, and Rodney did nothing more than push the plate toward Murphy. "I'm Detective Inspector Caitlin Murphy of the Muskoka Municipal Police. Here to talk to you about what you saw."

"I'm so glad none of the kids saw it," Rodney said.

Murphy gave a wry smile and thought to herself, you are a kid and you saw it. She asked, "Would they normally be with you?"

"No. I am the water counsellor." He gave a soft laugh. "I don't bring kids out so early in the morning, so far away from shore."

"How long have you been working here? What do you do outside of camp?" She wanted him more relaxed before she started on the tough questions.

"This is my fourth season. I want to do kinesiology at university. Canoeing's my passion. I compete. I'm hoping for an Olympic trial," he said, his hand now steadier as he set down his mug on a low table. He glanced at Murphy, then looked down at the purple patterned carpet and noticed the damp patch on it and nudged it in with his toe. "It's okay here. Andy could do with being a bit more laid back, but as he always says, he's got a lot resting on this place," he said casually.

"Could you take me through exactly what happened?"

"I was out on a practice run, just me and the lake. The water looked so calm and clear, but it's changing with climate change, getting shallower every summer. Anyway, I had gone part of the way, doing my thing, paddling back — just eight minutes up, eight minutes back, that's all. Then, I saw something floating, and at first, I thought it was just some garbage. I was ready to pick it up, you know, because I care about the environment and the lake. But as I got closer, my heart sank. It hit me like a tidal wave — it was a body."

His mind still haunted by the distressing discovery, he shifted uneasily. The weight of the recent events lingered in his thoughts, causing his body to fidget with restlessness. He sat straighter, trying to find comfort that eluded him, as the memory of the lifeless body bobbing in the water continued to gnaw at him.

"God, I couldn't believe it. My stomach just... I had to fight back the urge to vomit. But I pulled him out, I got him to land and tried CPR. It did not work."

"Did you see anyone else? Or anything else you want to tell me about?" Murphy asked.

"No. I called 911. I called Andy. Then I puked. And I came back to the Centre as fast as I could."

"Ok, thank you Mr. Taylor. We will make sure you get home safely."

"So, I can go home? I don't have to ever see that again?" Rodney asked, his voice still shaky.

"Never again. I'll have patrol take you home. A Family Liaison Officer will contact you. Andrew, does the Centre had CCTV?"

"No. Maybe it's time we got some," Andrew mumbled.

The low rumble of the old van engine shook the peace of the afternoon, and Murphy went outside to greet the man. Chen was in such a state that it took him three circuits of the gravel before he could pull up close to the car and stop with a clunk. The tires threw up a small dust cloud as they spun on the gritty road surface. He jumped out, leaving the door open. "DI Murphy!"

"Hi!" she answered, waving her hand to attract his attention. Chen marched toward her with a purposeful, rolling gait.

She thought from Chen's tone that something exciting had happened. The pathologist walked past her, leaned against a tree and lit a cigarette. "I had to buy more smokes. Ahh, smoking is a wonderful addiction," he said as he exhaled a stream of smoke into the air above him, expanding his chest and squaring his shoulders like a soldier at attention. "I know you don't approve, Murphy, but it calms me."

Murphy screwed up her face, watching as he constantly moved from side to side, watching as his hands shook. She wondered how much worse it would be if he did stop smoking. "Let's get back to the scene, shall we? Scene." Murphy asked as she extended a hand in the body's direction. She and Chen went quickly. She joined Girard while Chen joined his forensic team members.

The pathologist glanced at the progress his team was making before turning to Murphy and Girard. A subtle gesture, his hand found its way into his trouser pocket — perhaps a habit picked up from those dramatic television crime shows, Murphy mused. Chen seemed to have embraced a new style, opting for a white linen suit and a Panama hat, having set aside his beloved Hawaiian shirts last year, fearing they might be considered "nefarious signalling."

Chen gave them a quick rundown. "White male found floating in the lake. Recovered by Rodney Taylor, camp counsellor. Paramedics arrived, saw rope and possible stab wounds, and called us. No thoughts yet on age. Short rope around his neck. Large amount of dried blood, what is probably dried blood, on the shore pooled in one area. Possibly stabbed here, then maybe ran or was pushed into the lake. Shore."

With a sharp flick of his wrist, he knocked the heater off the cigarette. Chen blew hard into the filter—he swore it made relighting a cigarette taste better—and put the mostly-smoked cigarette back into its pack. He never revealed to anyone how he disposed of his used cigarette butts.

Chen promised a post mortem that afternoon and said someone from his office would call the Homicide Unit to arrange for a team member to attend. Murphy nodded. "Adam, call Michael and tell him to expect Dr. Chen's call. He can be the exhibits officer for the post mortem."

CHAPTER TWO

Murphy headed back toward the office but detoured to go home to pick up a parking ticket she had gotten a few days ago. She had forgotten it and wanted to get it paid before the seven-day early payment passed.

Murphy lived in a large house turned art gallery with her wife, Delaney Brice, an old, straight, college friend. At thirty-three, Delaney was in a devastating car accident that left her with paraplegia. After years of therapy and rehabilitation, she was now a full-time artist with her own gallery. She wanted in-home personal support care that was far more expensive than she could afford, so she and Murphy married. This gave her access to some very generous medical benefits. Their relationship was pragmatic, not romantic.

Three quarters of the main floor was Del's living quarters, the other quarter was the art gallery. Murphy had the upstairs all to herself. With Del's encouragement, Murphy had set up her own studio in a shed in the backyard and used the space for her own form of art therapy.

The plaster walls and pitched roof of the house were perfect to keep in the heat during winter, but made it oppressive during the summer. From May until September, Murphy constantly had a fan blowing. She had two long windows that looked out on her world, so when she actually had time to look, she could see the green expanse of farmland and a nearby lake that shimmered in the sun.

There was one bedroom, one bathroom, and a living room. A painted stone hearth provided a focal point in her living room. An inset in the hall became her office space on the rare occasions she worked at home. She hung her walls with her father's paintings, though not her own.

Her father had always wanted to go to art school while growing up in Ireland, but became an electrician to put food on the table. The family moved from Londonderry to Canada in 1990 to escape the sectarian violence of The Troubles. He had a family to support and became a licensed electrical contractor, and his artwork now hung on her walls instead of a gallery. They had lived in North Bay and often rented cottages and spent weekends in Muskoka. Murphy moved to Ottawa but eventually settled in Muskoka by the time she was forty.

Murphy stared at a piece titled 'Chicken Eyes, Symmetrical'. The chicken eyes were very asymmetrical, and she was not entirely sure it was actually a chicken. Her father was nothing if not whimsical. She shook her head and said, "Dad, you're a strange old man." She gazed at it for long minutes before grabbing the paper parking ticket and heading out. She had time to pay the ticket before the post mortem results would come in and the team would provide an update.

Murphy parked her Brawler in her designated parking spot and walked into the police station. She headed to her office. "Good morning everyone," she said. Without waiting for a response, she closed the door to her office, and dialled the phone number on the back of the ticket. Murphy glanced into the main office, affectionately called the atelier. Girard was on the phone at his desk, Hamilton was on the computer. Parker was absent, as Murphy had assigned him to attend at the pathologist's office.

Detective Constable 2nd class Michael Parker accompanied Chen to the post mortem, observing from the corner of the room. The pathologist turned on the audio recorder and began speaking about his findings. Chen was delighted to have Parker as an audience and revelled in the retching sounds coming from the corner.

"What bad thing did you do to get the assignment? Bad?" Chen asked. Parker yanked his mask down and vomited into the trash can. For some people, Chen thought, the vomiting was the attraction to the job. "Wonderful. Step up, young man, time to work."

In meticulous printing, Parker bagged and catalogued every item found. Chen carefully unraveled the rope from the neck of the victim, verbally noting that it was yellow polypropylene one-quarter inch twisted nautical rope, the type used for buoy moorings. He plucked a few spiny water fleas from the rope, which further evidenced the body had not been in the water for long. Every bug, leaf and algae were dropped into small bags and bottles held by Parker. The DC would then seal, catalogue and sign the evidence bag, and hold another one open for the doctor.

The autopsy lasted exactly 96 minutes. Chen turned off the recorder and headed to the computer to confirm the automated transcription. "Tell your boss to call me," Chen said as he snapped off his gloves and threw them in the trash. "Take your evidence and get out. Get out. I have more bodies to process." Parker dutifully headed back to the office just down the road.

Parker arrived at police headquarters and walked into the Homicide Unit. "You okay Michael? You look a little peaked," Girard teased.

"I don't know how you get used to it," Parker said. He could still taste the acrid remains of bile and took a swig of the warm sports drink on his desk. "I hope I never do. Ach. Hey boss, Dr. Chen has his preliminary report if you'd like to call him."

"I hope you never get used to the smell either," Murphy said. Becoming used to seeing murder victims was something no one should ever get used to. Murphy walked to the microwave to boil water for her instant coffee. She watched the dark swirl fill the cup as she stirred her drink. She took a sip, walked into the atelier, and sat on the couch. She stretched out and crossed her long legs and rested them on the coffee table.

"Ha, I see you're drinking a cup of instant regret," Girard joked as he sat down beside Murphy. Parker and Hamilton joined them, following the unwritten rule that when Murphy entered the room, you paid attention. "I'm just glad there isn't much of a smell to instant coffee."

"The only thing I smell is a wet corpse," Parker whined.

"Put a menthol lozenge in your mouth," Murphy offered as she pointed a toe at the candy dish full of lozenges on the coffee table. "Everyone ready?" she asked as she leaned forward and pressed an autodial button on the phone.

"DI Murphy, hello, I've been expecting your call. Did your man get back to the office okay? Or is he passed out under a desk somewhere? Somewhere," Chen said as he answered the phone.

"Dr. Chen, you are on speaker," Murphy said as she looked at Parker and rolled her eyes. "Now, sir, what do you have for us?"

Chen confirmed that the body had been in the water for at most two days, probably one. The victim was a young male, aged between fifteen and twenty-five. He was 167.5cm tall. "What is that in people height?" Murphy asked.

She was forty-eight years old, just old enough to have learned both imperial and metric measurements in school as a young child. The long switch to metric had met with significant opposition and confusion throughout the country. While Murphy was comfortable with a mishmash of measurements, she could not picture how tall a 167.5cm person was.

Chen chuckled. "About five foot six. The muscles were not well-defined. Probably not a football player, maybe a pianist," Chen said. "His arms were lean and hard, his hands were long-fingered, with wide palms. Some wear and tear, some character to the hands. Beautiful hands."

"Not helpful," Murphy said. "Who, what, where, when, and how?"

Chen sighed. "Male aged fifteen to twenty-five. 167.5cm, 66.22kg. Brown shoulder length hair, bracelet around the left wrist which DC Parker has catalogued. Found with his neck bound by yellow nylon rope, with sixty-four centimetres of trailing rope. There were abrasions under the rope but no bruising. It did not contribute to his death. Affixed around his neck after death. No wallet, no phone, no identification, no birthmarks. No remarkable medical issues. Two fillings, both look a couple of years old."

"Don't forget the tattoos," Parker said.

"Please do not interrupt me again! I do not like interruptions. Not again. I was about to talk about tattoos with the Detective Inspector." Chen emphasized Murphy's title, showing that he considered this a conversation with the boss, not the team. Murphy made a commission face at Parker. "Parker has the photographs of the tattoos. The body has seven Sasquatch tattoos. Seven. They should help you with identification. One is of particular interest. Not well done, just a Bigfoot face, but freshly tattooed. With a date under it, Friday the fourteenth, just two days ago. Put your team on to calling local parlours. Call the local tattoo shops." Murphy chuckled to herself. Chen sometimes tried to direct investigations, but only ever stated the obvious.

"The young man died from a knife wound to the heart. There was severe damage to the liver and lung. Angle suggests a left-handed killer. The liver first, then the heart. Two quick jabs, jab jab, each about ten centimetres deep, four inches, upward thrust. The wounds were thin and deep. He would have died immediately after the stab to the heart. Heart. The killer then pushed him into Sunny Lake after he was dead. No water in the lungs."

"Pushed off a boat?"

"There were traces of paint, which were analyzed as vehicle, not nautical paint. Get me a sample for comparison. They were in crevices of the clothing, consistent with being dragged into a vehicle and out again. Tox and further reports are forthcoming."

"Thank you, doctor." Murphy hung up and sat back, draining her coffee. She got up and walked to the blank board, grabbed a marker, and addressed the team. "People, here's what we've got so far. Young man, fifteen to twenty-five years old, no ID. Traces of vehicle paint. Stabbed on the beach just outside the Nature Centre. Why?"

"Maybe after he was stabbed, someone thought about taking him to the hospital. Put him in their vehicle before realizing he was dead, then panicked and dumped him in the lake?" Girard suggested.

"Maybe. The killer had stabbed twice; the wounds are just three centimetres apart. The killer pushed or threw the kid into the water. He's been in the water for a day, two at most. Adam, any CCTV or security footage?"

"No. I canvassed everyone on Lake Kelbowek Road. No doorbell cam footage, nothing. And it's the only road into the area."

Murphy paused and glared at Parker, who had been responsible for photographing and cataloguing everything. His head was down, looking at his phone.

"Michael!" she yelled. His head snapped to attention. "Photos on the board."

"Sorry, boss," he mumbled as he got up and began sticking photos to the board.

"Chen said he had seven tattoos. Michael put those up. Yes, seven tattoos and... Here it is. This one is still fresh, dated last Friday. All the tattoos have dates. Cleo, contact tattoo shops in Kettering, Ravensberg, Falkenburg... All of Muskoka. Find out if anyone worked on it."

Murphy paused and reviewed the board. "Yellow nautical rope tied around the neck. Michael, find out if the Nature Centre uses that size and type. Photos indicate the young man was in jeans and a black t-shirt that said 'Godsmack'. Someone find out what the hell that is. He was wearing Nike Air Jordan 1s, so he had a bit of money."

Murphy eyed the photo of the bracelet that was found around the victim's wrist and tapped the charm hanging from it. "All we have to identify him right now is his Sasquatch obsession."

"A heavy metal band," Girard said.

"Sasquatch is a heavy metal band?"

"No, Godsmack is. The t-shirt."

Murphy gave Girard an annoyed glare. Girard's computer dinged with a new email, further annoying Murphy as he turned to read it.

"Chen sent the tox, post mortem and a dental reports boss," Girard said. "We might identify him that way."

"At least we can use it to confirm the identity," Hamilton added. The dental information hadn't been extensive—two small fillings and one extracted wisdom tooth—but if she found a local dental office, then there might be records of the work.

Chen's report showed the toxicology screen was positive for a small amount of THC. There was no alcohol in his blood.

Murphy asked Girard and Parker to search the Internet for young men in the area who were obsessed with Sasquatch. It would keep her team busy, and she always enjoyed keeping them occupied.

She retreated to her office and tried to put the scant pieces of together in her mind, she gazed at her old handmade Talavera cup—a present from an ex-lover who once travelled to Mexico. She thought more fondly of the cup than the ex.

Murphy had enough information to sift through the missing persons reports Hamilton had put on her desk. Each report was a minor human tragedy, only partially told, to be given dignity and a conclusion. She grabbed the top file and said to the photograph in the printout, "And who are you, Elzabet Dimello?" A report on a fifty-year-old woman with depression. Murphy shredded the paper copy since that wasn't her victim.

In Muskoka, there had been over fourteen thousand people reported missing since 1985. Almost one person a day was reported missing in the 'cottage country triangle,' as the media liked to call it. Most that were resolved were runaways, although sadly some were drowning victims, their bodies washing up after days or weeks in the water.

She read over the few other missing persons' reports that had come in over the past week. An elderly man, eighty-three, wandered away from a retirement home. Shredded. A teenage girl who ran away from her foster home. Murphy dropped the report into the shredder by her desk. A blond teenager, a middle-aged man, a young mother of three. No one came anywhere near her victim's description.

She knew many runaways headed either south to larger cities, or north to more remote towns. Others came into the municipality, and there was no telling where this man was from.

With the current missing person's reports finished, Murphy began reviewing applications for the vacant Family and Community Liaison position.

Seven years ago, an MPP police officer shot and killed a First Nations man who was experiencing mental health distress. Two years later, a joint federal and provincial task force initiated a review of the Muskoka Municipal Police Force's interactions with the local Indigenous communities. After three years, they published the 'Hands and Voices In Unison' report, which outlined fifteen recommendations for sensitivity training, mental health awareness, and improved communication with the Indigenous communities regarding police actions.

None of the recommendations were implemented yet. Murphy hoped she could complete at least one of the recommendations and hire an Indigenous Family and Community Liaison to work primarily with the Homicide Unit. The position would be a civilian one, and ideally would be filled by someone who already lived in Muskoka. The position was posted two weeks ago, and was open for another few days. The applications were coming in and Human Resources was already forwarding the more promising ones.

One applicant, Hamlin Goldstein lived in Winnipeg, and nothing on his resume suggested he had ever been to Muskoka. Murphy could not discount any experience he had. Winnipeg had the largest urban Indigenous population of any city across the country.

He had the necessary bachelor's degree in social work, two years working at a homeless shelter, four at a friendship centre, and references, although they would not be checked until after an interview, if she invited him to have one. He appeared to be a great candidate on paper, and Murphy performed a simple Internet search on him.

His ConnectWork profile provided his photograph, but not the same information as his resume. On ConnectWork, he listed providing professional counselling services. It seemed like an odd thing to leave out of his resume. It was a red flag.

Goldstein's name came up on community activist blog posts going back at least five years. There were many reports of him harassing unhoused people on the street, including a photograph of him apparently yelling at a homeless woman. Murphy clicked the link to a video. She watched cell phone footage of Goldstein and another man leaning over a semi-conscious drunk on the ground. Goldstein's words were laced with racial slurs and insults, and the sound of raucous laughter echoed in the background. Murphy felt sick to her stomach and had seen enough.

The rate of homicide involving Indigenous people in the Muskoka area was six times the rate for cases involving those of other backgrounds. A man like Goldstein had no place in her squad. Compassion for the victim and consideration for their loved ones were two of the most important qualities required. And not being a racist dick, she thought to herself.

A knock at the office door interrupted her thoughts. "Boss, we found him. Sort of," said Hamilton.

"Sort of?"

"Come see this," she said.

Hamilton informed the team that she had found a tattoo parlor that had done work for the man they decided to call Sasquatch Doe. "They won't spill any information," she added, gesturing to the photo on the board. "They did this tattoo last Friday at Helter Skelter Ink and Weed—a tattoo shop on Hewitt Street, out past Gull Lake. They have a picture of it posted on their website."

Murphy approached the computer display to get a closer look. The image on the screen was a close-up of the tattoo, so they could not see the face of the person who had it. It was the right tattoo. "What do you mean they won't give you any information?" she asked.

"When I called and explained that I was a detective trying to trace a customer who had visited recently, he replied with an obscenity and a threat. He said, 'Go fuck yourself. Death to pigs. Die pigs die. Helter Skelter.' Then hung up."

Murphy's eyelids fluttered, absorbing the words. "He said 'Death to pigs and Die pigs?'" she repeated, trying to make sense of it. "Did he see the victim as an animal, and that's why he killed him? Or was it meant for you, Hamilton, after you revealed you're a detective?"

Hamilton nodded slightly, confirming her suspicion. "I believe he meant me, boss."

Murphy fell silent, her face turning stern, jaw clenched tight with growing anger.

"Boss, isn't that..." Girard began.

"Yes. Helter Skelter is a reference to the cult murders from 1969. The killers, led by..."

"Led by Charles Manson," Girard said.

"Led by Charles Manson," Murphy uttered, a shudder passing through her as she recalled the merciless slaughter of innocent souls. The killers had scrawled 'Healter Skelter' and 'Death to Pigs' on the walls, the blood-written words a chilling testament to the chaos that ensued. In her mind's eye, she saw the haunting photos from a book she read in her teenage years — scenes of unbearable torture and death.

And now, this despicable individual dared to draw inspiration from such a heinous event for his tattoo parlor? The audacity of it made her blood boil with rage. To think that he had the audacity to threaten the life of a cop only added fuel to the fire of her anger. She couldn't fathom how someone could be so completely divorced from reality.

Murphy stared at the floor. She was about to speak, but stopped herself. Her feelings were chaotic. She felt both furious and wary. He was the last person to see her victim alive. She knew that if she decided in haste, it could jeopardize the case. Finally, she shut her eyes for a moment to gather her thoughts. He had threatened her detective. This was personal, and she was determined to hold him accountable. She knew exactly what to do—arrest him. She knew the charges would never get to trial, unless there was something more to back up the threat.

"Right. Threatening an officer, interfering with a criminal investigation. We have evidence right there," Murphy said as she pointed to the computer screen, "that our victim was at the shop close to or on the day he died. Maybe he's covering up his involvement in the crime. Cleo, get an arrest warrant for every male employee listed on the website.

"Adam, get a search warrant. We're looking for DNA and financial records, customer records, related to our Sasquatch Doe. I want to get their computers and laptops and phones. I want their credit card sales and sign-in sheets. For a week before Sasquatch Doe was found. I want their garbage because it might have Doe's blood. I want tattoo machines and needles; they might have DNA to prove the guy was there. Michael, prepare an ITO for an arrest warrant. Adam can get the warrant once the ITO is done. Cleo, contact the Warrant Squad, ask for a couple of officers to help execute the warrants. Coordinate the timing. The sooner, the better. Document the website. Save screenshots of staff photos and names. Get a screenshot of the tattoo on the website."

Murphy's sour mood was a force to reckon with, and crossing paths with her in such a state was never a wise choice. She would ensure that the message of 'you can't threaten police' was driven home with unwavering resolve.

More than an hour later, Murphy parked her Brawler near the warrant officers who had arrived on the scene first and opened her rear passenger door. She flipped up the back seat and unlocked the storage container underneath, pulling her bullet-proof vest out. She locked the box and slammed the seat down before putting on her vest.

"Detective Inspector Caitlin Murphy," she said, introducing herself to the warrant officers.

"Constable Clifton Dawson," he said as he shook Murphy's hand. "They are Constables Hawthorne and Jackson." Everyone had parked around a bend in the road, out of sight of the tattoo shop. Murphy confirmed the paperwork, the plan and the backup with Dawson, then returned to her Brawler. Behind her vehicle stood her team members, each waiting for direction, each wearing their body armor. Behind them, three patrol cars with officers to help gather evidence and transport anyone arrested. The detectives would stay well back while the warrant officers gained access to the shop.

Murphy felt her body tense as the officers walked cautiously down the road, around the bend and out of sight. She signalled her team, and everyone drew their weapons and crept forward. The area had a vague familiarity for Murphy.

The members of the Warrant Squad walked the dimly lit street to the tattoo shop. The neon sign illuminating the entrance flickered 'Helter Skelter Ink & Weed', its buzzing adding a surreal touch to the atmosphere. They spotted a security camera that was at the entrance. It was standard for pot shops to have an entry hallway with cameras monitoring the front door, and they knew they would have to act fast.

With a decisive nod from Dawson, the police sprang into action. They surged forward, adrenaline pumping through their veins as they cautiously approached the establishment. Each step was deliberate and measured, their senses heightened, ready for any unforeseen danger.

The officer nearest the entrance quickly yanked the door open, and the police burst inside with an authoritative shout. "Police! Police! Don't move. This is the Muskoka Municipal Police!" Dawson's voice rang out, cutting through the shock like a blade.

Confusion and panic filled the air as customers and employees found themselves caught in the sudden storm of law enforcement officers screaming and pointing guns at them. Hands raised in surrender, they cursed and shouted, unsure of the situation they found themselves in. The Squad members expertly corralled them together, separating the customers from staff and any potential threat.

As the situation stabilized, two customers were cleared and released from the tense scene. Relief washed over them, and they hurriedly left the premises, eager to escape the harrowing encounter with the police. "Come back tomorrow to get it finished!" one tattooist shouted after them.

At the rear of the establishment, the police encountered another customer, who had been innocently using the restroom during the commotion. They approached him cautiously, verifying his identity with focused scrutiny. Once assured of his identity, they let him leave, allowing a sigh of relief to escape his lips.

The tension remained palpable, the thrill of the high-stakes operation still coursing through the veins of the police. Every move and decision they made could have serious consequences. As they continued their search, they knew they had to stay vigilant, prepared for any unexpected twists that might come their way. An assortment of knives was laid on the glass countertop, but no guns.

Stepping forward, Dawson announced the men's impending arrest in a tone that was solemn and direct. "You're being detained by the Muskoka Municipal Police on suspicion of uttering threats and obstructing a police investigation. Hands up behind your heads, please," he commanded. Amidst the chaotic scene, a heavily tattooed man took a swing at the officers, his eyes blazing with anger. The nearest cop reacted with lightning reflexes, landing a forceful punch to the man's stomach, momentarily knocking the wind out of him. It was a split-second decision, born out of necessity to protect themselves and others.

With adrenaline pumping through his veins, a heavily tattooed man, clearly high on PCP, attempted to fight the officers. His strength and aggression were intensified by the dangerous drug coursing through his system. The closest cop moved swiftly, using his experience and training to his advantage. As the man lunged forward with rage, the officer skillfully sidestepped, evading the brunt of the attack. In a split second, he delivered a powerful punch to the man's stomach.

The impact caused the man to stagger back, momentarily disoriented by the force of the blow. However, PCP-induced adrenaline coursed through his system, making him resilient to pain and even more determined to fight back.

Working in tandem with his fellow officers, they executed a controlled takedown. One officer applied a joint lock to the man's arm, immobilizing it and preventing further strikes. Another officer swiftly brought his knee into the man's thigh between the hip and the knee, striking the common peroneal nerve. It weakened the man's stance and he fell to the ground.

With a combination of skillful maneuvering and teamwork, the officers successfully subdued the man, managing to handcuff him despite his fervent resistance. They then stepped back, ready to respond to any further challenges, their focus unwavering.

In the aftermath, the adrenaline still surged through the officers' veins, their hearts pounding from the intense encounter. The heavily tattooed man, now subdued and disarmed, lay on the ground, his anger giving way to frustration and defeat. The room echoed with the heavy breaths of everyone present, the tension still lingering in the air.

The other two complied with no resistance, and they were placed in handcuffs. The detectives waited until they had escorted the people out of the shop before they approached.

Once the store was emptied of people, Dawson and his crew cleared the detectives for entry. As the accused were loaded into the police van and driven off, Murphy could not help but feel a sense of gratification. She could be very petty sometimes, and maybe a nighttime raid was a little more than required, but she felt a strong loyalty to her team and a streak of maliciousness.

Murphy gave out orders with enthusiasm: "Gather every piece of evidence associated with computers, customers, and finances. No stone unturned. Put it into bags and bring it to the station. I'm going to talk with our suspects."

CHAPTER THREE

Murphy stepped into the station and ascended the stairs that led to the Homicide Unit. She was alone; Hamilton was arranging to bring the suspects to the Homicide interview rooms and the rest of the unit was cataloguing evidence. She sat at her desk and rubbed her face with her hands, feeling uncertain such a strong response was the right decision. This damn Catholic guilt, she thought. As she waited, she replayed the evening over in her mind and realized that she attended an address on Hewitt Street last year. A drug-addicted mother had given her two-year-old son a pudding with crushed meth mixed in, to stop him from fussing. Samuel Jones, Murphy recalled. He never stood a chance.

Hamilton bounded into the office and straightaway rushed to Murphy. "I believe it was Patrick Lambert who I talked to; he yelled at us during the raid and it sounds like his voice. He is in Interview One. Norman Moreau is another person. He demanded he call a lawyer and won't talk; he spit on Officer Thomas. He has additional charges for assault police and resisting arrest. Dawson thinks he is under the influence. The last one, Christian Bonnet, hasn't requested to talk to a lawyer yet; he's in Interview Room Two."

Murphy accepted the folder Hamilton was offering, and double-checked the Helter Skelter website as the rest of the unit returned. It listed Lambert as the shop owner. The photograph of the Sasquatch tattoo verified he was the one who inked it. Murphy wanted to chat with Lambert first. Moreau was another artist in the shop, and if he hadn't fought back, he might be in his own bed instead of a jail cell. "Let's try Lambert," Murphy said. "Adam, you are with me. Cleo, run a check on Rodney Taylor, the guy who found the body, and see if he has any connection to our victim or this tattoo shop. Michael, ditto for Andrew Short."

Lambert sat in the dimly lit interrogation room, his tattooed arms crossed over his chest and a scowl etched on his tattooed face. He had a black eye, and a bruised cheek. Murphy sat directly across from him, watching him intently. Girard was on her right-hand side.

"Mr. Lambert, what happened to your face?" She waited for an answer, but after he refused to respond, she said, "Are you on any drugs or otherwise impaired?"

He said nothing.

"Are you high?" He shook his head very slightly. "I take that as a no. I understand a detective on my team contacted you and you said 'Die pigs'."

"My name is full colon Patrick hyphen Julius full colon Lambert. I'm a sovereign citizen. I use a full colon and a hyphen in my name, the first full colon, which is full colon Patrick, it means for the person Patrick hyphen Lambert. That's my given name, and it's also my pronoun, because it uses a psychological phrase... Because I use psychological phrases, through punctuation, which are classified as alien hieroglyphics, which makes me a live, l-i-v-e person. If you don't use my pronoun, then you are violating my constitutional rights to punctuate my freedom of movement. I am a live person punctuated with two full colons which modifies the pronoun, where pro means expert and noun means yes. So therefore, I am in fact an expert and in my expert constitutional opinion everything that goes on in these interviews is fiction."

Murphy couldn't help but roll her eyes. Leaning closer, her expression turned serious. "That kind of nonsense won't cut it," she asserted firmly. "Mr. Lambert, you seem to believe you're above the law, but let me assure you that's not the case."

Lambert's scowl deepened. "Your so-called laws don't mean nothing to me. I have nothing to say to you."

Murphy sighed, rubbing her temples. She had dealt with sovereign citizens before, and she knew they could be a handful. Threatening a police officer was damn serious.

"Mr. Lambert, I urge you to cooperate with us. We are trying to get to the truth here, and your cooperation would go a long way in helping us to do that."

Lambert snorted. "The truth? You government agents only care about covering up your own crimes. I won't be a part of your lies."

Murphy leaned back in her chair, taking a moment to study Lambert. She knew he wouldn't easily abandon his act. Nevertheless, she was determined to get to the bottom of this situation, even if it meant handling his antics along the way.

"Full colon Patrick hyphen Julius full colon Lambert. What constitution do you refer to?" She did not wait for an answer before continuing. "Is that the Constitution of the corporation of the United States of America, all capital letters? The foreign corporate country not of Canada? The fiction of the corporation of the all capitals United States of America foreign corporation not a live, l-i-v-e person? Full colon Patrick hyphen Julius full colon Lambert you are pronoun full colon Patrick, so answer the question."

Lambert cleared his throat. "Uh, I full colon Patrick hyphen Julius full colon Lambert demand to have a lawyer present during questioning and I will choose the lawyer of my choosing."

"You don't have a right to have a lawyer present, only the opportunity to contact one. And I understand from DSS Girard," Murphy said as she gestured to her colleague, "you have already made that call. This is Canada, full stop. Cut the crap. You aren't getting out of this with your bullshit." Lambert frustrated her. He was making everything much harder than it needed to be.

"I refuse to answer questions on the grounds that it may incriminate me," Lambert said.

"Again, this is not 'Murica', Mr. Lambert. We do not have the Fifth Amendment here. What we do have is a recording of you threatening to kill a police officer. We have evidence that places a murder victim at your tattoo shop. That includes a photograph of him on your own website. He died shortly after he was at your shop. And your face is covered in bruises, and you are looking very suspicious." Murphy lifted the file folders in front of her and waved it around. Lambert didn't uncross his arms.

"Very well, Mr. Lambert. If you change your mind and decide to cooperate, just tell the officer."

With that, Murphy stood up and left the room with Girard, signaling a uniformed officer to stand by the door. She left Lambert alone to stew in his own defiance. Girard and Murphy went to the next interview.

Bonnet, who specialized in cannabis, hadn't seemed hostile when arrested, which gave Murphy some optimism.

Murphy and Girard walked into the second interview room and sat down. Bonnet was visibly uneasy. His eyes were wide, and his hands trembled slightly. "Christian Bonnet, I am Detective Inspector Caitlin Murphy from the Muskoka Municipal Police. This is Detective Staff Sergeant Adam Girard," Murphy said.

The young man shook slightly, his arms crossed as if he was cold, as the detectives sat across from him. "Call me Chris," the nervous man said. "What's going on? Like, they said I threatened a cop? I didn't do anything. You gotta believe me one hundred percent."

"All right, let's make sure we have this right. Let's start with that phone call you received earlier today. Did you get a call today at work? Did the store get any phone calls today?"

"Yeah. Tons. I mean, Patrick answers the calls. He even walks away from the customer to take a call. But only him. He's the only one who answers the phone, like it's his business, you know?"

Murphy nodded and Girard jotted down some notes. "Did something unusual happen today with a phone call?"

Bonnet told them about Lambert going off on someone over the phone. "He yelled a few choice words and hung up, then laughed it off, saying he'd take on the police if they ever came to the store. I thought he was just showing off for the customers, trying to act tough. He was high. You know he was just fucking around."

"Well, fuck around and find out," Murphy said. "Have you ever seen him be violent?"

Bonnet began talking faster. "He just likes to play the tough guy around some of his customers, okay? He's just showing off. He's being a jerk. He sometimes gets into fights, but he sucks. He got into a fight on Friday night and got the shit kicked out of him."

"All right, let's disregard that for now," Murphy interjected as she pulled a photo out of her folder and placed it in front of Bonnet. "Do you recognize this tattoo?"

"Ha! That's Sasquatch guy. He kept yapping about finding a Sasquatch or something. He was getting on Pat's nerves. But he seemed like a decent enough dude; he bought a dozen Midnight Blueberry Sleep Gummies. Midnight Blues. You know, that stuff will help you sleep. Midnight Blues." He was nervously repeating himself.

"What was his name?"

"I have no clue. I never asked, you know?" Bonnet said.

"What did he pay with?"

"Cash. Even though gummies are legal now, not many people put it on their credit cards. Did he do something wrong?" Bonnet inquired.

"He's dead," Murphy affirmed.

"Oh fuck! Really? He seemed all right. What happened? No way it was the Blues."

"Not an overdose. We're trying to figure out what happened. Did he tell you anything about himself? His first name? Where he was from? Did he have a wallet?" Every query was met with a negative answer. "Is there anything that was memorable about him?"

"Well, the Sasquatch stuff. Oh, and it was a little weird that he had a map book, like, a back road atlas he called it. He said it was for Sasquatch hunting. Ha, he believed that shit, you know? He even signed the guest book with some Sasquatch thing," Bonnet said.

Murphy nodded and noted Bonnet's comment about the guest book. "What did the atlas look like?"

"A big square book, red on the cover. Like, it was pretty beat up because he rolled it up and stuck it in a pocket in his backpack. He said he liked to keep it handy, but, you know, it was like in the pocket for water bottles?"

Murphy gave her head a slight nod and noted the backpack. "How did the young man seem to you? Aside from Sasquatch stuff? Friendly? Angry? Was he on something?"

"Like I said, he was all right. I won't sell to anyone who is already high. Oh! Pat thinks the kid ripped off a tattoo machine," Chris added. "After buying weed, the guy walked out. I mean, I wasn't watching him the whole time, and my shit... sorry, I lock my stock up, right? But Pat looks for his machine and starts screaming 'Where's my gun? Where's my gun?' He meant his machine, not like a real gun. Anyway, he takes off after the guy but doesn't catch him. He was pretty pissed, you know?"

Murphy wrote 'stolen tattoo machine.' She questioned Bonnet a bit more about the backpack, as she had not found it on the scene, and then informed him he was free to leave. Girard arranged for a police car to take him home.

Murphy glanced at the clock and saw that it was already a quarter past eleven. She sent Lambert back to jail without further contact. She then told everyone to go home. She never enjoyed making her detectives work long hours; homicide investigations drained enough energy without having an overbearing supervisor.

Murphy drove home and parked her Brawler in the small parking lot. She unlocked the front door of the residential side of the building and walked in. Del and her personal support worker, Maria, were getting Del ready for bed. "Hey Del. Hi Maria."

"Hey Caitlin, how was your day?"

"Same same," Murphy said as she bent down to kiss Del on the cheek. Murphy and Del chatted while Maria helped Del get ready for bed. Maria joined Del in the bathroom, partially closing the door for a modicum of privacy, setting up Del's night bag and putting leg warmers and wool socks on Del to keep her warm. She massaged Del's legs and feet to ensure a good blood flow. Meanwhile, the women chatted about their day. Del excitedly told Murphy about selling two paintings to someone as Murphy poked around in the fridge. "Hey Maria, can I eat the chicken and beans?"

"Yes, if it's okay with Delaney," Maria replied. Del shouted out her approval, and Murphy grabbed the container and sat at the kitchen table to eat it cold.

After dinner and good nights, Murphy trudged up the stairs, throwing her keys onto the table and setting her phone's alarm before finally collapsing onto her bed. She clicked the remote to turn on TV, keeping it on mute. Grunting, she got up and opened the window, bringing in the warm air from the summer night.

The smell of dry earth yearning for rain filled her room, immersing her in the sparse desire, singing out its sharp mineral siren call. Murphy breathed in deeply. There was a hint of sourness. Inside the smell, each breath seemed to shrink and slow down. The air was filled with calm.

Murphy changed into her pajamas and knelt, child-like, at the side of her bed, clasping her hands and squeezing her eyes shut. "In your hands, O Lord, are humbly entrusted our brothers and sisters. Welcome them into Your paradise, free of pain and worry. Grant these souls eternal rest. Marcus Icke, Stephanie Nielson, Melvyn Middleton, Tyler Allen, Kettering Baby Doe, Samuel Goldstein, and Sasquatch Doe. Amen." Night after night, Murphy would recite the names of all the murder victims whose cases she had worked on. It would sometimes take an entire week to get through the names. Today, she added her latest victim.

She eventually fell into a fitful sleep.

CHAPTER FOUR

At the start of the next day, Murphy drove to the office, arriving before anyone else. One of the most important things a homicide detective needed was time to think. And the best time to do that was when no one else was around. One by one, over the next thirty minutes, the rest of her team arrived.

Parker always arrived at the station sweaty and stinking. He ran or biked to work each day, rain or shine, whether it was forty above or forty below. He would use the shower in the locker room, change into a shirt and pants, then come into the office and immediately enter a group chat with other police officers to post his running route and time.

Parker was an athletic man with a wiry build, standing at almost six feet tall and weighing 144 pounds. He had short, dark hair and a scruffy beard. His skin was tanned from spending time outdoors. Parker was the kind of white guy who wore shorts in winter. He was from the quintessential cop family and his father still worked with the Ontario Provincial Police. He had been on the MMP force for four years and had quickly risen through the ranks, finally joining the Homicide Unit six months ago.

Hamilton was sitting at her desk when her phone rang. After a brief discussion, a uniformed officer arrived at the office carrying a small box of postcards he had picked up for her at a weekend garage sale. "You are going to love these, Cleo," he said as he handed over the box. "There are cards from Hong Kong, Jamaica and Nebraska." She thanked him, repaid him and eagerly went back to her desk to take a few minutes looking at the stamps on each of the postcards.

Hamilton was a quiet Black woman who preferred reading to running. Hints of blonde shot through her brown afro. She was short but had a commanding presence that made others think she was taller. She was always dressed impeccably in professional attire that accentuated her authority. Her sharp, inquisitive brown eyes missed nothing and reflected her unwavering attention to detail. Despite her sharpness and tenacity, Hamilton was also warm and compassionate, and she always took the time to connect with the people involved in her cases. She had joined Murphy's team two years previously after seeking a transfer from a Calgary homicide unit where she clashed with her racist and sexist colleagues.

Girard was the last to arrive. He was the only one with small children, and today arrived with an emoji sticker on his back, courtesy of his son Alan. It was Monday, so he brought in the oat brittle candy pieces his wife sent with him every week to give to Murphy. He held them up for Murphy to see. She gave him the thumbs up and mouthed 'thank you.' He walked out of the office, put the entire thing on the desk of Suzan, the office administrator, and walked back in. The oat brittle would be gone in an hour.

When Girard, a Metis man, joined the unit in 2020, he had insisted Murphy come to his house for dinner. She had tried to decline, but he was insistent. "My wife is very jealous. When she heard I was working for a woman, well, she wants to meet you and kind of cross you off her worry list."

Murphy was out as a lesbian, but that didn't matter to Ruby. She still had to meet the woman with whom her husband would spend so much time. Girard's mother Rose and grandparents Jean and Ayamis lived with them, all staying in a granny flat behind the house, and all joined in the chaos that evening.

Ruby, plump and motherly, pointed out the photographs of the kids on the mantelpiece and the window-sills. "The only time they sat still," she said. The older boy, Steven, was four, with brown hair and freckles on his cheeks. The next boy, Alan, was two, with round cheeks, and black hair. Then there was Ruthie, the infant, ten months, a wild child with crazy hair that stuck out in every direction. She stared hard at Murphy any time she saw her. The two boys cared less about her, but Ruthie was unnerving.

She ushered Murphy into the living room and over to Ayamis and Jean. The stink of cigarette smoke wafting off the couple was eye watering. "Caitlin, this is..." Girard began.

"Bonjour," Ayamis said with a smile. Jean laughed.

"Bonjour, ça va?," Jean said as he stuck out his hand.

Murphy shook his hand and nodded. "Hello"

"Salut. Tu es grand. Plus grand que moi!," Ayamis added as she patted the seat beside her. Both laughed at Murphy's slightly confused face as she sat down. She did not understand French..

"I only speak English and a little French," she said, causing them to laugh loudly.

Ruby walked past where Murphy sat, patting her on the shoulder and said, "They only spoke French for two months when Adam and I first met and I did not know what they were saying. They'll be trash talking you all night long."

Girard laughed. "But they do speak English, too. Parlez Anglais, s'il vous plaît. Sois gentil. Elle est ma patronne."

"Tell me about yourself," Ayamis said.

Murphy began the same well-rehearsed talk she would give the elderly parents of any girlfriend she had when the door creaked open and Rose, Girard's mother, snuck her way in.

"Elle porte une croix. Est-elle catholique?"

Murphy heard the word 'Catholic'.

"The cross? You are Catholic?" Rose asked as she nodded toward the small cross hanging around Murphy's neck. Jean and Ayamis promptly stood up and walked out back.

Murphy immediately wondered if it was an insult and stammered without answering. Girard waved his hand as if to brush away any concerns. "They're going for a smoke," he explained.

But Murphy knew what they were thinking. She knew the justifiable hostility Indigenous people around here felt against Catholics and cops. She quickly decided Girard would not have invited her if this was a problem.

"I come from a Catholic background, with both my parents being devout Catholics. However, I had to make a clear distinction between the institution and my personal beliefs. I don't agree with the conservative teachings of the Catholic church, especially considering the terrible actions some individuals within it have committed. I'm so radical in my views that I even eat meat on Fridays, contrary to traditional Catholic practice," she said with a smile. It was enough for Rose, who grunted approval, and left to join her parents for a cigarette.

Throughout the evening, the kids screamed and ran, Ayamis and Jean talked in different languages and Rose interspersed her conversation with off-key lines from songs from the 1980s. All three of them would frequently head out the back door to smoke.

Girard, Ruby and Murphy ate and laughed and shouted to be heard over the noise.

At the end of the evening, Ruby pulled Murphy aside. "You're all right, ya know," she said as she lightly punched her in the shoulder.

"Mama, come help mimaw and poppa get home," Steven said. She spent the next fifteen minutes guiding her still-boisterous relatives to their granny flat thirty feet away.

"Hey," Ruby said as things settled down. "You'll take good care of Adam, eh? He's a good man. We can't lose him."

"Always," Murphy said, pulling up her sleeve to reveal a long, faint scar. "This scar is from a bullet. A suspect grabbed my former partner's firearm. I grabbed the suspect, and the gun went off. The bullet travelled along here, then whoosh, and it hit a car a few metres away. My team mean everything to me. I'll take a bullet for Adam, for any of them."

Ruby hugged Murphy tightly. Not only was Murphy off the jealousy list, but every Monday, Ruby also sent her husband in with homemade oat brittle for Murphy. And every Monday, Girard would leave the candy with Suzan.

The microwave beeped and turned itself off and Murphy fetched her cup from inside. She dumped a teaspoon of instant coffee into her cup. She sat down while she stirred her coffee and thumbed through her in-tray. She looked out at her staff. Girard was handling his email. Hamilton was leafing through her postcards. And Parker... Murphy squinted her eyes. Was that a penis? she thought. She blinked a few times. Yes, it was a line drawing of a dick and balls, and he was laughing at it.

She tapped the spoon on the side of her cup, got up, and headed quietly into the atelier. Her eyes were fixed on Parker's screen. She stealthily creeped up behind him and casually said, "Michael?"

"Yes, boss?" he said as he turned in his chair. She glared at him and put her hands on her hips. "Uh, yes, boss?"

"Your screen."

Parker turned his head to look at his screen. "Oh no!" he sputtered as he pushed the off button on the monitor. "I'm sorry boss, I... I am so sorry."

"What was that?" Murphy asked loudly. Hamilton looked up and carefully put away her box of postcards. Girard stood up for a better view.

"It's just a joke, boss," he said meekly.

"Turn your monitor on and explain the joke to me. Go ahead, explain the joke."

Parker sighed and turned the monitor on. His face was burning with embarrassment, and he cleared his throat. "This is, um, this is a route one runner took to work today. A group of us at the station run to work and share our running maps. Some of us, uh, have these silly runs and make drawings from our routes," Parker explained.

"Is that the joke? Because I'm not laughing yet. Cleo, Adam, are you laughing?"

"No."

"No, boss."

"So, explain it. This guy takes a map, draws a dick or something on the map and posts it to the group?" she asked. "And that's funny?"

"No, no," Parker said as he clicked on the next few maps. "Here, see? A stick figure. And here, here's a fish. This one is a cat. Not a good cat, but not bad," he said. "You set your running app to track your route, and then you go, taking certain streets to create drawings. It maps your run and saves it to the cloud. It tracks route, speed, start and finish times. Then you download a screenshot, and, uh, post it to the group."

"Which one is yours?"

Parker paused a moment before hanging his head. "The cat," he said.

"Right. And these images are on a chat group for runners at this station? This police station? Police headquarters? On police computers? Look, I'm all for artistic expression, but it doesn't belong."

Murphy leaned into Parker's ear and whispered. "I'll give you and your running mates one day to remove every single rude image. Dump the dicks, keep the cats and fish," she said. "Everything rude has to go. Dicks, tits, asses, racist shit, swastikas, swear words, everything you wouldn't show a kid. Got it?"

"Yes, boss," Parker said dejectedly. "Boss, I only ever did harmless stuff, I…"

"Now! This is your only warning. If I see anything less than kid friendly, I'll tell HR." Murphy snapped as she stepped away from him. "Sweet Jesus," she mumbled as she headed back to her office. She took a big gulp of coffee and stepped back out to the atelier.

Murphy stood in the middle of the room and addressed the team, giving out responsibilities from the Helter Skelter arrests. Parker had the mission of taking the computers and phones to IT Technical Services because the items had been stored overnight in the evidence locker. Hamilton gathered all the papers to look for sign-in sheets and the guest book mentioned by Chris Bonnet. Girard was phoning the Nature Centre to look into any reported found backpacks, wallets, phones or books of maps, as well as to research whether the police had anything in their lost and found items.

It took only a few minutes for Hamilton to uncover the alias 'squatchhunter732' from the guest book of Helter Skelter. She quickly alerted Parker so he could begin a web search. They waited until they had more information before Hamilton advised Murphy.

"Boss, we think we've located our victim—Squatchhunter732," the team member announced.

Murphy glanced up from her screen, her brows furrowed. "Squatchhunter732?" she shouted.

"It's a username. A fake name people use for..."

"I am aware of what a username is," Murphy interjected impatiently. It irritated her that the younger employee thought she was computer illiterate. She joined the team in the atelier.

Parker shouted out that he found a video. "We haven't identified his actual name yet, but this looks like him. I entered 'Squatchhunter732, Sasquatch, Bigfoot' into the search engine, and voila! He goes by Squatchhunter732 on Cryptvids, which is an online cryptozoology video site. He's uploaded over twenty clips talking about Sasquatch and Bigfoot..."

Girard chimed in with, "Aren't they the same thing?" Murphy shushed him and directed his attention back to Parker, who was continuing his explanation.

"Cryptvids is a free online platform, with no requirement to provide any personally identifying information, it looks like. There is no way to track user 'Squatchhunter732', at least from the public interface. His videos typically have fewer than six views, and he has no followers at all. I zoomed through the videos briefly. Most are of him walking through forests and fields, analyzing poop and broken tree branches, deciding whether a Sasquatch was responsible. At least, that's what they look like. I haven't had time to watch every video entirely. The most recent video was uploaded six days ago, discussing the Spalding Conservation Area. We eventually discovered his body in Sunny Lake, which is partly in that area."

Hamilton punctuated the point Parker made by tapping on the area map that hung on the left side of the board.

The detectives then moved to stand around Parker's desk and watched the most recent video that the victim had left. In his hand, he held up an old book he said he'd found at a garage sale, opened it and said, "In the margins of this book I found handwriting that reads, 'Saskwatch sighting Spalding 1972'. They didn't spell Sasquatch right. I gotta go there, it's only a few hours away and I have never heard about this area before."

Bam! Murphy slammed her fist onto the table and yelled, "Hit the pause button! So, we can see him, but we don't have a name?"

"No, we don't have that information yet," Parker muttered. He quickly printed out a screenshot of the person's face and affixed it to the board, using a magnet.

"Excellent work Michael, Cleo. Adam, what about the backpack? Anything?"

"No boss. No one turned anything in."

Murphy said, "Right. I'm off to the scene to do another search for the backpack since we did not know about it the first time. Adam, with me." As she made her way out, she came to a halt suddenly. "Hold on," she said as she spun around and unexpectedly bumped into Girard. She shooed him away with a snort before ordering Parker to replay the video with the victim holding up the book.

The team again gathered around the screen. "There!" Murphy said. She jabbed the screen. "Go back so we can see the spine of the book where he turns it around. Stop!" In the freeze frame was a slightly blurred spine label. The classification numbers were too small to read, but the words 'Bradburn Lib' clearly stood out.

"Bradburn Library," Murphy said with confidence. "Michael, double check with the OPP, see if they have a missing persons report for our guy here. He might be from the Bradburn area. Adam, Cleo too, I'll meet you both back at the scene in twenty minutes."

Murphy was in her Brawler, tapping the steering wheel in time to the music. It was a song by a Quebecois death metal band. She tried signing. Murphy had no idea if she was saying any of the words properly. It did not matter. She had parked outside Winewood Street Flowers, her usual spot for buying flowers, and sighed. The windows were covered and a note from a bailiff was stuck to the front door. She continued to drum her fingers, let down by the sight.

Her eyes were then drawn to the Dog's Breakfast, a nearby greasy spoon where Eric Faircloud was stabbed to death with a broken beer bottle. The investigation had been easy, since the killer remained on scene. Telling Eric's parents had been hard, since his killer was a childhood friend.

She grabbed her phone and tapped the WeSee GPS app. "Weezy, where is the nearest flower shop?"

The app thought for a moment and a digital voice said, "The nearest flower shop is Winewood Street Flowers. Would you like directions?"

"Oh, for fuck's sake I am right in front of it" Murphy scolded. "Weezy, show me the three closest flower shops."

"Here is a list of the three nearest flower shops. Would you like directions?"

"Yes, jerk." Murphy was grateful she could curse and swear at the phone without having to apologize or get into a messy argument.

"Please select a number," WeSee purred in a calm voice.

Murphy chose the second option, put the Brawler into gear, and followed the directions. It wasn't long before she arrived at Sun Flowers on Centre Street. Murphy got out of her Brawler and clocked the rainbow sticker in the window of the flower shop. When she walked in, there was no one in sight, so she rang the silver bell that was placed on the counter. A woman came out from the backroom with a rag in hand. "Hi, may I help you?" she asked cheerfully.

She was wearing a jeans and a crisp dark blue shirt with white polka dots, her long black hair cascading over her shoulders. Murphy turned toward her. Their eyes locked, and In that moment, her heart leaped with exhilaration, 'bang bang bang bang', pulsating with pure excitement. It was love at first sight, an electrifying connection. Standing before her was the most breathtaking woman she had ever seen, a vision of beauty that left her breathless. The only thought that raced through her mind was, Wow, oh, wow, check her out, whoa, whoa, whoa! The encounter was simply thrilling, and she could barely contain herself.

Sunita 'Sun' Kumar, an East Indian woman, possessed a warm and inviting presence that effortlessly made customers feel welcomed and at ease. Her sparkling brown eyes exuded kindness and charm, drawing people in with their captivating allure. Her smile was radiant, lighting up her face with genuine warmth and friendliness. Sun had a graceful and confident demeanor, moving with a natural grace that exuded both strength and approachability. Her lustrous, dark hair cascaded down her shoulders, framing her face like a halo. With an air of natural beauty and a genuine spirit, Sun's presence left a lasting impression on anyone fortunate enough to encounter her. Murphy was falling and fast hard for her.

Sun Flowers had been open for more than a year, owned and operated by Sun. The store was compact. The walls were painted white; the trim, dark yellow. White-painted wood flooring led to a small counter. The flower fridges were hidden from the customer's view. A padded chair sat near the counter, offering a place for any customer to sit while waiting for an order. In the background was a row of shelves that held everything from small stuffed animals to silk plants to bonsai trees. The pleasant aroma drifting from the flowers was all a customer needed.

Murphy blinked twice. This woman is really gorgeous, she thought to herself. Murphy smiled broadly as she quickly scanned the store. "Bzzz bzzzz bzz." Sun turned her head and gave a quizzical smile. Murphy doubled down. "Buzzzz buzz buzz bzzz bzz bzz bzz buzz."

Sun shook her head and opened her mouth to say something, but remained silent. "The sign, the sign," Murphy said as she pointed to an advertisement poster on the wall. The words 'How do you say thank you to bees?' hovered over a wildflower garden. Below that, it read 'Buy Gikayla Seeds.'

Murphy cleared her throat. Her attempt at flirting had clearly failed and would have been embarrassing if Murphy was so inclined. "Detective Inspector Caitlin Murphy, Muskoka Municipal Police," she said as she stuck out her hand.

Sun held her hands up to show Murphy. "My hands are dirty," she said.

Murphy chuckled and winked, saying, "I'm not afraid to get a little dirty." Sun frowned a little, and Murphy realized she really needed to stop flirting. "Right. I need to buy some flowers. Nothing too fancy, something as inexpensive as possible. The shop I usually go to is Winewood Street Flowers."

Sun raised an eyebrow. She was a little taken aback by the detective. Her energy was very intense for someone buying flowers. "So why don't you go to Winewood?" Sun wanted to kick herself. Why would you direct this woman to a competitor? she thought to herself. Especially such a handsome woman.

"The florist is closed. I need a bouquet." Murphy was conscious of the passing minutes and knew she had to go. "I want something with just a few blossoms, no added foliage. Money-wise, ten or fifteen dollars. That's it for today, but I'm a potential repeat customer. I could use a small bouquet about once per week—nothing too elaborate. If you can lower the cost, then I don't mind getting day-old flowers. And I plan on ordering some roses every month."

Sun nodded and handpicked a few colourful Gerbera and Carnation flowers to make her bouquet. She couldn't help but wonder who the recipient was, receiving so much attention from Murphy. She looked at her own reflection in the mirror on the wall and saw a short woman rapidly approaching middle age, with dirty hands and a leaf in her hair. She quickly brushed the greenery away. No matter who the flowers were for, she thought with admiration, that person was extremely lucky.

"No red."

Sun took out all the red flowers and replaced them with a yellow Forsythia. She held up the now yellow, orange, pink and white bouquet, asking if it was acceptable. Murphy showed her approval with a nod of her head.

"Just twine please, no plastic wrap," Murphy said. Sun nodded doubtfully and tied the bouquet with twine.

"This is perfect," Murphy proclaimed. "I'll pay for it with my credit card. I also buy four roses at the end of each month for about five dollars each."

"I'm sorry, but I do not sell roses for that price," Sun replied. "You can get them from a corner store."

"No, no. I got them from the other florist at that price. They gave me a good deal on roses. You can do the same. I need to buy four of them every month at that price, or around there." Murphy handed Sun her business card.

Sun nodded before replying, "I will see what I can do. That will be $17.54, please." Murphy paid for the flowers. As she was about to walk out the door, she turned and asked Sun for her name.

"Sunita. Sun. Sun Kumar. Sun Flowers, I sell flowers and it's my store, so I named it Sun Flowers, get it? Sun. Flowers," she answered, feeling a bit embarrassed by her repetitive response. Something about this detective made her brain go blank. Murphy gave a nod of understanding before leaving with the flowers and throwing them casually on to the passenger seat of her Brawler. Sun watched her drive away, shaking her head before returning to her work.

After twenty-five minutes, Murphy was apologizing to her team for the delay and waved the flowers in her hand. The scene had been released and most of the caution tape had been taken down, though a small piece still clung to a nearby tree. Murphy pulled it off and shoved it in her pocket.

She then walked to the beach, flowers in hand. As Hamilton and Girard stayed back, she solemnly stood at the pool of dried blood. The DI bowed her head and took a few moments of silence before crossing herself and laying the flowers down. The ripples of water lapped softly at the stems. Murphy cast her gaze toward her coworkers.

"If the bag is in there, it could be impossible to locate," Murphy mused.

"We could always hire divers," Girard suggested. "It's about fourteen metres deep. That's a decent range for fish finders, so we might have luck."

Murphy nodded. "Okay, arrange for a unit to come out with sonar. We might get lucky. For now, let's just look around here. Adam, follow the water's edge. Cleo, walk directly from the parking lot into the Conservation Area. I'll explore the area in between."

The detectives started searching their designated areas for the backpack. Since only a small space was initially searched beyond the Nature Centre's camping area when the body was found, they had to widen the search radius. As she trudged through the undergrowth looking for clues, Murphy wondered if she should call for additional help.

It was much more cost effective to send ten Officers onto land rather than five specialists on boats. The sound of her phone ringing cut her musings short.

Parker phoned in. "Boss, the guy's name is Jose Mercado, and he's from Toronto," he said. Murphy shouted out to the rest of the group and they drove back to their headquarters in a convoy. Parker was waiting for them when they got there.

CHAPTER FIVE

"Boss, I think we have our Sasquatch Doe. Look," Parker said, as he posted a missing person's notification to the board. "This is Jose Mercado, out of Toronto. Right height, right age, looks like him. It's the tattoos though, they match," he said. He posted a second printout with images of five Sasquatch tattoos. "His wife reported him missing to the Toronto Police on Sunday night."

"I agree," Murphy said with some relief. "I think we have our man. Is his wife here or in Toronto?"

"Toronto, boss. Her name is Violet Mercado," Parker said.

Murphy nodded. She did not want Violet to make a three-hour drive just to identify her dead husband and then drive three hours home. "We need to find out who his dentist was. Let's go for confirmation that way. Why didn't his name come up earlier?"

"Apparently, the woman had reached out to the Toronto Police, since that's where they are from. They had directed her to the OPP. The OPP refused to take her report. I don't know why. She turned to Muskoka Municipal Police. I had put a flag on the system for any new missing persons," Parker said. "Looks like it was entered this morning."

Murphy nodded. "Adam, you can contact her for death notification and get the dentist information. I'll fly down and speak with her, so tell her to expect me."

"Fine, boss," he lied. It wasn't fine. He disliked being the one who gave a death notification, but it had to be done. "Do you want me with you?"

"Uh, yes, I'll check with Del first, see if she'll fly us down. Otherwise, it's a police helicopter. Dental confirmation should take less than an hour once we have the records. Have them sent to Dr. Chen ASAP," Murphy said. Girard turned to his desk, cleared his throat, and picked up the phone.

"Do we have any information on Short or Turner?" she asked. Parker and Hamilton both provided their findings on the two men associated with the Nature Centre; both had alibis for the estimated time of death. Hamilton also advised that there had been previous reports of teenagers drinking at the cabins, but nothing recently. Parker updated the board.

Murphy walked into her office to call Del, closing her door to allow her to make a speaker call and a coffee at the same time. She used her personal cell phone to make the call. The art gallery phone rang, and it was answered quickly. "Delaney Brice."

"Del! How are things? Are you busy?"

"No, it's a slow day. What's up?"

Del was a licensed pilot with a customized single-engine plane, and she loved to fly. It gave her freedom from her wheelchair. She was always eager to explore the stunning scenery that Ontario offered from the air. "Absolutely!" Del shouted while Murphy began filling in the authorization form to allow Del to fly her and Girard to Billy Bishop Airport in Toronto. "I'll file a fight plan and apologize for the short notice. This is just what I needed today!" Delaney said.

Murphy called Chief Valencia to request permission to fly and was not surprised when he firmly said "No."

"Chief, it costs about half the money to fly, and it saves hours of travel time. Delaney Brice already has flown for us as an authorized Search and Rescue pilot."

"Isn't she your wife?" he asked.

"Yes, that's why she is cheap. Ha, I mean, she's volunteering her time. She just wants gas and landing fees. She is less expensive than driving. And this will help make up for the Marine Unit being called out to Sunny Lake," she said. While that was technically true, flying would save a hundred dollars, whereas using the Marine Unit cost a few thousand. But she did not need to clarify that right now.

"File the paperwork, I'll approve it," Valencia said before abruptly hanging up.

Murphy and Girard drove in the Brawler to the Muskoka Regional Airport. On the way, he confirmed he had spoken to Violet Mercado to tell her that her husband's body had been found, and she had provided contact information for the dentist. He did not tell her he was with Homicide, only that Jose had been found in a lake. "Boss, those calls really weigh heavily on me. They just eat me up inside," Girard confided, his voice tinged with sorrow.

"I'm so sorry you had to deal with that. Is it particularly distressing this time?" she asked with genuine concern.

"Yes, it's heartbreaking, especially when they're so young, you know? He was barely out of his teens," Girard replied, his emotions evident in his tone.

"Okay, I understand. Let's make sure you don't have to handle any more death notifications for now," Murphy assured him, offering compassion.

"Thank you, boss," Girard said gratefully. "It's so tough to face that reality and then go home and look at your own kids. It hits close to home."

Murphy nodded understandingly, acknowledging the emotional toll of such calls on her team. She wanted to support Girard, recognizing the importance of providing compassion and understanding in their line of work.

They arrived at the Muskoka airport, parked and walked to a hangar.

"Hey you two, over here!" Delaney brought Maria with her for a trip to the city. They were already there, and Maria was helping Del into the cockpit of the Piper Cherokee 140, a plane she had purchased years ago with her insurance payout. It took another two years to customize it and learn how to fly with hand controls. She had always had a wanderer's heart, and the accident had slowed her down. First, Del had to get through physiotherapy. Then came the years of self-pity and anger and psychotherapy, followed by a still-unsettled acceptance of her limitations. She had turned her art therapy into a career as an artist, and bought a building on a section of Highway 11 where a dozen other artists had set up galleries to attract the tourist trade. That was how she met The Boys, each one an artist along the same stretch of road.

She had been flying for a few years and loved the freedom. She had even helped with a search conducted by police looking for a young boy, and although they had not found him, it was exhilarating for Del that she had been involved. "Everyone in and settled?" she asked her passengers after Maria had shoved the wheelchair into the back of the plane. After each one confirmed, Delaney proceeded with take-off.

"Tower, this is Piper Cherokee C-MEGO, requesting permission to take off from runway 2," Delaney said.

"Piper Cherokee C-MEGO, this is Tower. Runway 2 is clear for takeoff. Winds are calm, visibility is excellent. Have a good flight."

"Roger that, Tower. Thank you. Cherokee C-MEGO, taking off from runway 2." Delaney contacted Departure Control on frequency 122.8 as directed and advised she was climbing out at two thousand feet, heading southeast. After being cleared to climb to six thousand feet and changing the heading slightly, everyone settled in for the hour-long flight.

As they soared higher into the sky, Murphy marveled at the expansive wilderness that stretched out before her. To the north, the rugged and unyielding terrain of the Canadian

Shield lay like an ancient guardian, with its rocky outcrops and rolling hills creating a mesmerizing landscape. The dense forest canopy below painted a picture of serene greens of all shades, and thousands of small lakes dotted the land like precious jewels, glistening in the sunlight.

As the small airplane continued its flight, the scenery underwent a gradual transformation. The ruggedness of the Shield gave way to the softly undulating countryside of Ontario's farmland. Fields of lush greens and golden hues spread as far as the eye could see, testament to the agricultural abundance of the region. Small villages and picturesque hamlets occasionally punctuated the landscape, adding a touch of charm to the panoramic view.

Approaching the southern stretch of their journey, the landscape changed once again. The quiet countryside evolved into the bustling energy of small towns and thriving cities. Malls and paved roads replaced the tranquility of the rural areas, signaling their nearing proximity to Toronto.

The vastness of the Canadian Shield, the serenity of the farmland, and the vibrancy of the urban landscape all painted a beautiful tapestry of Canada's diverse beauty. Murphy couldn't help but feel a deep appreciation for the land she now called home as she continued her flight towards the bustling heart of Toronto.

"Tower, this is Piper Cherokee C-MEGO, requesting permission to land." Delaney's voice startled Murphy, who had drifted into a peaceful calm by the whirr of the engine. They were close to Billy Bishop airport and seeking to land.

"Piper Cherokee C-MEGO, this is Tower. You are cleared to land on runway 09. Winds are 060 at 5 knots, visibility is excellent. Be advised, there is a Cessna on short final for runway 07, caution wake turbulence."

"Tower, Cherokee C-MEGO, copy that. Looking out for the Cessna and wake turbulence." The plane touched down smoothly, and she taxied to the designated area and shut down the engine. Delaney and Maria had a couple of hours to roam downtown while Murphy and Girard got into one of the taxis at the airport and went to speak with Violet Mercado.

The detectives approached the entrance to the small apartment building in the bustling city, and the sounds of car horns and people chattering filled the air. The building itself was old and worn, with faded paint and rusted stair railings leading up to the second floor. Just before entering, Murphy showed Girard an email she had received from Dr. Chen, confirming the identity of the murder victim.

Upon entering the apartment, they found themselves in a cramped living space. The walls were dark grey, which only made the room seem smaller. A couch sat in the corner, facing a small TV that was mounted on the wall. A small kitchenette was tucked away in one corner of the room, with a mini-fridge, microwave, and two-burner stove. The entire place seemed to have a faint musty smell, as if it had been closed up for too long.

In the centre of one wall was a twin-sized bed with a thin mattress covered in a plain white sheet. There was a small wooden dresser and a bistro table, both of which looked like they had seen better days. Two office chairs sat at the table, showing it doubled as a desk. Dozens of piles of books leaned here and there against the walls.

Despite its modest appearance, the apartment had a certain charm to it. The windows were large and let in plenty of natural light, and though it was small, the apartment felt like a cozy refuge amid the bustling city outside.

Murphy knocked at the door and a woman answered. "I am Caitlin Murphy, this is Adam Girard. From Muskoka Police," Murphy said softly.

Violet's heart felt like a heavy stone, burdened with the weight of sorrow and disbelief. Just hours ago, her entire world shattered when she received the devastating news of her husband's death. As she stood there, her eyes red and swollen from crying, she felt an overwhelming sense of numbness. Emotions swirled within her, each one vying for dominance — grief, anger, confusion, and a haunting feeling of emptiness. Her mind was a jumbled mess of memories and emotions. She had just stayed breathing normally. Now, with the police at her doorstep, the pain was again raw, and the ache in her chest so profound, that even uttering a single word felt like an insurmountable task. She stepped back, and the detectives followed her in.

"I am very sorry for your loss," Murphy said. She sat down where Violet had gestured. Murphy had a thin folder with her, with a few preliminary notes and photographs.

"Please, you sit down," Girard said as he waved off the seat.

Murphy looked Violet in the eyes. "I am very sorry. We have used dental records to confirm that it was your husband Jose who we found."

"I was told he died in a lake? Did he drown? I didn't hear whoever called me. It was hard to hear," Violet said with a shaky voice.

"That was me, ma'am," Girard said. "A canoeist found him in Sunny Lake."

"And he drown? I mean, I don't think he could swim, so what was he doing in the lake?" Violet asked.

"We're trying to find out," Murphy said. "But he didn't drown. We are from Homicide. I am sorry to say, um, he was stabbed…"

Violet's body trembled. The words felt like a physical blow, sending shockwaves through her entire being. Anguish etched across her tear-streaked face as she struggled to comprehend the violent and senseless death. The future they had planned together was now stolen, replaced with a harrowing emptiness the likes of which she had never known.

The realization that she would never see him smile, hear his laughter, or hold him close again was agonizing. The world seemed to blur around her, and the room felt suffocating as she grappled with the unfathomable loss. Murphy put her hand on Violet's shoulder: it was the most comfort she could offer the woman. Nothing could ease the pain of her shattered heart.

Murphy waited for Violet to stop crying before continuing. "We need to know what he was doing in Muskoka. What he was doing in the Spalding Conservation Area, at Sunny Lake. Who he might have seen. And just more about him. His name is Jose? And he's nineteen? And he was staying where? Did he drive up?"

Violet responded to Murphy's questions with a quick nod of the head, and sobbed, "He read the comment in the book, looked up Spalding, found it and figured he would drive up. He drove up to the Kettering Traveller Motel. He was up there to find Sasquatches. He went up Friday and, oh God, he never came back. We talked on Friday night. Jose said he found a bone, and got a new tattoo, and then Saturday morning he texted and said he was going out squatching, and he hasn't, didn't, come back and his phone is off."

Murphy could only guess what squatching was. "He got a new tattoo?"

"Yes. He said he got a tattoo on Friday night, a Sasquatch with a date. He did that every time he had a 'big find'," she said. "He texted me a photo," she sighed as she scrolled through her phone and showed the detective an image of the now-familiar tattoo. Murphy pulled out her notepad and noted the time Violet received the text.

"He got that Friday night at Helter Shelter or something like that. He said the tattoo place looked a little sketchy, but he also bought, uh…"

"He bought some gummies while he was there," Murphy said, filling in the rest of Violet's sentence.

"I mean, that's all legal, right?" Violet asked.

"One hundred percent. There's some good stuff out there," Murphy said. Although Murphy did not use any recreational drugs, so she was only assuming. "Anything else? Drinking? Fentanyl or-"

"No," Violet said, cutting Murphy off. "He was a nerd. He smoked some weed, he ate gummies and 'shrooms, but not drinking, no other drugs. He was all about Sasquatches."

"Can you explain the Sasquatch thing a little more?" Girard asked.

"Jose had this intense passion for Sasquatches. It consumed him entirely. He spent endless hours researching sightings, poring over blurry photos and videos from other hunters, and looking into any scientific studies or conspiracy theories that might prove it's existence."

"Jose took things pretty far if he was travelling to find one," Murphy said.

"Oh, he definitely took it further. Reading about Sasquatch wasn't enough for him. He needed to experience the hunt for himself. Jose was determined to embark on his own quests, like some, I don't know, quest from Star Wars or something. I love him dearly, but I couldn't help but worry about his safety and how much this passion was consuming him. I often told him to be careful, but his fascination with Sasquatch was just too strong for him to ignore," Violet said.

"Did he ever find anything?"

"Yes. I remember he once came back with blurry photos and recordings from the woods, thinking he might have caught something, but it was always inconclusive. Always a 'maybe'."

She explained that, armed with his atlas of back roads and trails, and an obsession, he would set out on a mission to track down a Sasquatch. Jose travelled around the country, venturing into remote wilderness areas where Sasquatch sightings had been reported. He spent days at a time in the wilderness, scouring the terrain for any sign of the creature.

As he searched, he recorded everything he saw and experienced, documenting his journey with a cell phone. He captured footage of the stunning wilderness vistas, the wildlife he encountered, and even the occasional footprint or broken branch he believed might be evidence of Sasquatch's presence. He posted videos to Cryptvids, recording his voiceovers in coffee shops or his car and putting it all together using online software.

He would walk for the entire day, sometimes from dawn until dusk, looking for signs. "He always finds something interesting, though I doubt anyone can walk through the woods for eight hours and not come across something squatchy. Jose will find a pile of acorns and say it was a Sasquatch food stash. Or a bit of fur. It was either Sasquatch hair or fur from an animal it ate. It was kind of jokey. He doesn't really believe it all, I mean he believes in Sasquatches, but not about acorn stashes and things. It was fun. It was supposed... supposed to be fun." Violet took a deep breath and waited until the burning tears went away.

She told Murphy that Jose made the video with the book the night before he left for Kettering.

"Yes, we watched it," Murphy said. "Is that book here?" she asked as she warily eyed the piles of books on the floor.

"Oh my God, Jose would be so excited to know real detectives watched his video," Violet said. "The book is here, somewhere. If you can find it, you can have it." Murphy nodded at Girard and he began looking.

"When did you last hear from him?" Murphy asked.

"It was the text of the tattoo. But he 'Supped me earlier Friday night. He was so so so excited. He said he found this amazing proof. He said it was a leg bone. I mean, he was blabbering on about the most mind-blowing thing he'd ever found, actual proof of a Sasquatch. He was describing how he got there, Sunny Lake I think, and which pictures he took. And he took hundreds. Thousands. He got a little loud because he was so excited. He was in the motel café, having a bite to eat. You know, he'd set up his phone so he could talk and eat at the same time."

After catching her breath, Violet continued to talk, her voice quivering with emotion. "I tried to get him to quiet down, but screw it, he was on to something. Then he reaches into his backpack and pulled out this gross old bone he'd found! I was so psyched! He swore it was part of a Sasquatch leg bone, and he found it poking out from under some leaves and dirt. He said he was going to go back and find more bones. To me, it looked like a dog chew toy, kind of? Well, as soon as he pulled out that thing, some old guy behind him just flipped out." Violet took a deep breath.

"He screams at Jose, saying 'you can't have deer bones in here! There's food here, no deer bones allowed, it was a health hazard,' those kinds of things. Stupid jerk. Jose grabbed his phone and filmed the guy. Well, not film him, but showed me. It was a live phone call, not a video. Anyway, the guy tried to take the bone from Jose! But he wouldn't give it, so he slapped Jose's phone out of his hand, and I couldn't see anything anymore. I thought he was going to attack him! But the waitress, I think it was the waitress, some woman's voice, told the old guy to sit down and leave him alone. Jose was pretty freaked.

He grabbed his phone and said he'd call me back tomorrow, like, Saturday. And I got that tattoo text, but-"

"What is 'Supped?'" Murphy quietly asked Girard, and was told that 'Sup was a video chat app. "Your husband found a bone. He called it a Sasquatch leg bone, in the Spalding Conservation or Sunny Lake area? How big was it? Can you describe his backpack?"

"The backpack was a just a regular black backpack, like kids take to school. Look, the old guy was right. It was just an old animal bone, but he was so mean about it. It's, maybe this big?" Violet held out her hands. "Maybe about ten or fifteen centimetres. The old guy was such an asshole."

"Okay, I have to ask some questions you might find upsetting, but I have to ask again. Did Jose get involved in illegal things? Use illegal drugs?"

"No, I said no the first time you asked. He was a nice guy never got into-" Violet stopped mid-sentence. "Wait, okay, one thing, it was stupid. He stole some guy's tattoo machine. From that Shelter place. Texted me after the tattoo photo. He said the guy was a douche, and he thought it was funny. Jose said the guy chased him out of the store, but he drove away. I mean, he was going to return it, you know? He was just being a goof."

Murphy nodded. The idea that Patrick Lambert might go after him for stealing something was plausible. "And where were you on Friday night and Saturday morning?" she asked.

"I was at work until three on Friday, then I was back on Saturday at seven a.m. Harper's Hamper over on Broadview. Why do cops ask that question? I mean, obviously I was here, right?" Violet said.

Murphy smiled. "If I didn't document where you were, then some defence attorney down the line will try to use it to make it look like I didn't do my job properly. And maybe say you were a better suspect and create reasonable doubt. It's just standard protocol, to avoid that possibility," Murphy said.

"Huh. I never thought of that. Shit, you'll find who did this, right?"

"Yes, yes, the entire team will do our absolute best. We don't give up. Now, do you have someone who can be with you?"

Violet called a friend to stay with her, and the detectives waited until the friend arrived before heading out. Violet had provided details on Jose's family and friends, employment, banking, and social media. Girard had located the library book and the notation inside the book that Jose had held up during the video. It was a young adult book on weather,

Storms and More Crazy Weather. Murphy called Del and let her know to head back to the airport.

During the trip back to Billy Bishop, Murphy emailed assignments to people. Hamilton was to call Harper's Hamper and confirm Violet Mercado's work times, and to get Jose's financial records. Parker was to go to the Kettering Traveller Motel and locate and secure Jose's room and car. Soon enough, Murphy and Girard were clambering into the plane, ready to return home.

During the flight, Del eagerly recounted the wonderful places she and Maria had visited and the items they had purchased during their trip. Her face lit up with excitement as she described the accessibility of every store they had visited, thoughtfully designed to accommodate wheelchairs, making their journey more enjoyable. "Even the change room at La "BelleFemme Boutique" was accessible," Del said.

As Del animatedly shared their adventures, Murphy and Girard listened attentively, each speaking they had the chance to speak of the case. their interest evident in their focused expressions. However, they were acutely aware of the need to maintain confidentiality in front of civilians. Despite their desire to discuss the matter, they held back, knowing that it was essential to protect the integrity of their investigation. They were eager to get back to the office.

"What have we got?" Murphy asked when everyone had gathered in the atelier.

"Harper's Hamper confirms that Violet Mercado worked until three on Saturday morning, and then opened at seven, just four hours later," Hamilton said. "It's an all-night diner, and she runs tables. Brutal split shift." Murphy nodded in agreement, glad at first she did not have those kinds of hours, and then she laughed to herself, realizing she had those kinds of hours.

Hamilton continued. "I contacted Jose's parents and gave them the news. They live in Vancouver with his brother and sister-in-law. I left my number with them in case they have any questions. Jose worked at Briskon and Sons and was on a week's vacation. Financials show he's just a work-a-day guy, regular income, regular expenses, some debt, but nothing of interest there."

"I went to Kettering Traveller Motel, got the Forensics Unit in there. He checked in on Friday afternoon, and since he paid for a room until Tuesday morning, no one has been in. He had a 'do not disturb' sign on the door, so not even cleaning services had gone in. There was a backpack and some kind of bone from something. It's with Dr. Chen. No phone, laptop or tablet. He had left an atlas of backwood roads, a bunch of the

Midnight Blue gummies, some clothes and some leftover takeout. And what looked like a tattoo machine, like you said. I did not find any writing in the atlas. Everything is with the Forensics Unit or Dr. Chen. I asked them to check for any foreign DNA, in case his killer was with him in the room. The Forensics Unit is not holding out a lot of hope for anything helpful. It was a hotel room," Parker said.

"His car was in a reserved parking spot at the motel, behind a closed gate. It's been taken to the Police Garage for analysis."

"Good," Murphy said. "Cleo, check out that library book we brought back. See if you see anything we didn't. Adam, get that Lambert guy, the tattooist, back here. Let's see what he has to say about this machine Jose stole."

CHAPTER SIX

Murphy was used to people lying to her, whether it was an active lie or omitting information. The sin of omission, she called it. She understood why people did it. Almost always, it was something they thought wasn't important, or something they knew would make themselves look bad. Chasing a guy out of your store and then have him turn up dead later would be the latter, not the former. "Mr. Lambert, first, none of this sovereign citizen shit. I don't have the patience, don't piss me off," Murphy said.

"Hey! You can't talk to me like that! I have rights!" Lambert protested.

"File a complaint. Now, you seem to have forgotten to tell me something when we last spoke," Murphy said, as she sat across from her suspect.

"I told you everything about everything," he said.

"What about chasing this guy out of your store after he stole something? It looks to me like you caught up to him, got into a fight, and maybe you won that fight. Is that where you got your bruises?" Murphy pulled out a photograph of Jose his wife had provided. "This is him, Jose Mercado."

"That bastard stole from me! He grabbed one of the tat guns and ran out, so I chased him. But he drove off really fast," Lambert said.

"A tat gun?" Murphy asked as she noted that Jose had the car that night.

"Yeah, not one of my best machines, but he stole it. Bastard."

"Did you report it stolen?" she asked.

"No, I try to avoid cops and handle things myself. If he's telling you I did something, he's lying."

"He's not lying, Mr. Lambert, he's dead. Murdered. The morning after he stole from you. And look at your face, you've been in a fight. Did you fight with him? Flat out, did you kill him?" Murphy asked.

"No, no way. I swear on my mother's life I never touched him!" Lambert then explained to Murphy how he and Norman Moreau had gone out later that night, after the shop closed, to look for Jose. They had driven along the half-dozen nearby streets with hotels and motels, hoping to spot his car. "We smoked some weed, had some beers, and went home. Never found him," Lambert said.

"In that order? You started looking, smoked weed, drank and went home?" Murphy asked. "What kind of weed?" she asked.

"Something mellow," Lambert said.

"And where did you get it?"

"Christian. I mean, I run a tattoo and pot shop, ya know?" Lambert said sarcastically.

"Where were you when you were drinking? Did anyone except Moreau see you? And why the bruises?"

"We had beers in Gull Lake Park, I... There were a couple of old guys in the park. That's where I got into the fight. The guy wouldn't share his vodka. I was pretty wasted by then, and I fell asleep. Woke up. I don't know what time. I didn't ask anyone's name. Gull Lake Park. Around seven, seven-thirty? The sun was already up."

Murphy grew frustrated with the uncooperative suspect. Despite her persistent efforts, the suspect refused to offer any helpful information, leaving her feeling stuck and exasperated. Lambert's nonchalant demeanor only intensified her irritation, adding to the weight of the unsolved case. She ended the interview, sending Lambert back to jail until he was bailed out on the charge of threatening an officer. She gathered up her files and walked into the atelier to stare at the board. She ran through the information with her team.

"So, Friday, Jose Mercado, nineteen, comes from Toronto to Muskoka without his wife to look for a Sasquatch. He goes to Sunny Lake or Spalding Conservation Area before checking into the motel. He mucks about, finds a bone, checks into the motel. He gets a tattoo to celebrate his 'big find'. He eats, video chats with his wife, so he has his phone then. But it's not with his things now. He does a video, upsets some old guys, goes back to his room, we think."

"Yes boss, the motel guest log printout shows he checked in on Friday at 6:32pm, paid for a meal at the motel café just after eight pm, went back to his room by 8:15. Early next morning, Saturday at 7:56am, Jose goes out," Parker said.

Murphy nodded and continued. "Without his car, and he never comes back. Saturday night, his wife tries to report him missing. On Sunday morning, we find Jose in Sunny Lake. Today, Violet Mercado contacts MMP to report him missing. Next steps. We start with tidying up Violet Mercado's story. Michael, we're only taking her word for it she called the other police forces. Contact Toronto Police and the OPP, make sure she called. I will send you some photos I took of text messages between Violet and Jose. Cleo, you can be our point person with Violet so reach out to her tomorrow, introduce yourself. Ask her if she remembers anything else. Adam, we need to follow up with the motel café to find out who the old guy was, check with the motel lost and found for the phone, see if there's any CCTV footage from Friday onward from the motel. And Michael, call the shops near the motel and see if anyone turned in a lost phone, has CCTV from Friday, Saturday, Sunday. Oh, did you follow up on the rope?"

"Yes boss. Sorry. We found similar yellow nylon rope at the Centre and at the cabins where the canoes are docked. I had it sent to the Forensics Unit. We should get an update soon."

Murphy stood in the atelier, drinking her coffee and staring at the board. She grabbed a marker and wrote points under Patrick Lambert's photo 'angry about theft, searched for Jose, weed, drank Gull Lake park 'til morning, verify? Check timeline.'

Under Violet Mercado's photo, she wrote 'alibi checks'. Patrick seemed like a much stronger suspect than Violet.

She finished her coffee and looked at the clock. The bookstore closed in an hour, so if she wanted to buy a new colouring book, she would have to put dinner off for a bit. She locked up her office and headed out. Murphy drove up Highway 11 and over to 118, where the Bookarium sat nestled in a lot just off the highway.

Walking into the Bookarium, customers were greeted with a warm and inviting atmosphere. Murphy loved to browse here. The store had an open floor plan, with bookshelves and display tables filled with a collection of the most popular books of thrillers, romance, horror and mystery. To one side were two shelves for children's books, and beside that, one for true crime books. But what set Bookarium apart from other bookstores was its cozy seating areas, where customers could sit and comfortably read the books they were interested in.

As customers made their way through the store, they were greeted with handblown glass paperweights on the shelves between books. Each small sculpture was slightly irregular and cast a faint but colourful glow on the books to either side. The presence of artwork amidst the books gave Bookarium a personal sense of space, as if you were walking into someone's home.

It was through a cloud of bubbled glass that Murphy saw her walking along an aisle. Sun's body was straight and slender as a vine's tendril. Her eyes were soft and light and glowing as she scanned the books.

Murphy stood still; for a moment her mind knew nothing else. As Sun walked out of view, Murphy's heart skipped a beat, spurring her on to pursue the woman. She walked between customers and down the next aisle when suddenly Sun turned to her and smiled. Murphy wondered at this desire of hers. She did not know why, when she looked at her, she felt the gloom of life lift away.

"Hello," Sun said. The imagined sweetness of her breath drew Murphy in closer.

"Hi. Caitlin," she said, pointing to herself.

Sun's laughter felt like drops of rain on a parched tongue. "I remember from the flower shop. You are...memorable." Murphy smiled, watching as the waving glow of light from a nearby glass sculpture danced across Sun's face. "What have you got there?" Sun asked, stepping a little closer.

"Oh this. It's a, a c-colouring book." Murphy's tongue was tied in pleasure.

"How many children do you have?" Sun asked.

"No kids. This is for me. It relaxes me," Murphy said as she held the book up. She looked at Sun and saw the light in her eyes and the sparks of joy on her lips. "You are beautiful."

Sun's smile did not fade and she did not glance away. Rather, her eyes grew wider and her smile larger. "Oh, thank you," she said as a slight blush rose in her cheeks. "I...think you are too."

They stood in the aisle, watching each other's every movement. Each blink of an eye, each twitch of a finger. Murphy slowly lifted her hand and brushed a strand of hair out of Sun's eyes. Her fingertips lightly grazed Sun's forehead. It felt soft on her fingertips.

"I was wondering if you would like to join me for dinner tonight? I know this great Italian restaurant nearby that has the best pasta and wine," Murphy said.

"I would love to have dinner with you tonight," Sun replied, her eyes shining. They made arrangements, discussing the time and place for their evening dinner date. Sun's hand trembled slightly as she typed the restaurant name and address into her phone.

"I'll give you my number, my personal cell, in case you need to call and cancel," Murphy said.

"I won't. No, I won't cancel. But, yes, please, your number," Sun said.

Murphy felt like singing aloud a tune she had never heard. Something ethereal and heartfelt. "Wonderful. Tavola. Eight o'clock. I'll see you later."

Murphy paid for her colouring book and got into her Brawler. She felt a familiar, uneasy twinge. She was intensely attracted to Sun but knew it was going to be difficult to keep the relationship beyond a few dates. Being constantly on call for her job was bad enough, but being married, well, it was always going to be a hard sell. It's not like she could tell the complete truth about the platonic marriage and risk her job, at least not at first. But she thought this woman might be worth the risk.

Murphy threw the colouring book into the back seat and drove home just a few kilometres away. There, she greeted Maria and kissed Del on the cheek. She used the opportunity to tell her excitedly she had a date.

Del smiled broadly and gave her a high five. After a quick shower and change of clothes, Murphy walked out, saying, "Don't wait up." She got into her Brawler and drove to Tavola. Sun was seated already, a good sign she was interested. The warm lighting, soft music, and pleasant aroma of fresh Italian herbs fill the air.

The waiter offered the two women some tea, a complimentary tasting of Silver Needles organic white tea from Yunnan Province in China, explaining it was new to the menu. "Not for me," Murphy said, but the offer delighted Sun.

"Oh yes, please!"

Without waiting another moment, the waiter headed to the kitchen. "You do not know what you are missing," Sun said excitedly. "It's crafted entirely from the first spring buds in the Menghai and Mengku tea tree groves in the remote, mountainous Yunnan Province of China."

"You love your tea, then?"

"Oh Caitlin, it isn't tea, it's heaven. The tips are taken only on the first day of harvest after the leaf buds reach maturity, but the new leaves haven't even unfurled." Murphy watched Sun's face in awe as it lit up talking about the tea. She had an almost child-like excitement in her voice.

The waiter returned with a clear glass teapot and white bone China cup. "We prepare it in a MingCha tea pot, at 185 degrees. It has been steeping for…" he said, looking at his phone, "three point five minutes. Just another few seconds, please."

Sun was staring at the leaves floating in the glass pot and Murphy was staring at Sun. "And… now," the waiter said. He poured the tea into the teacup for Sun.

Sun inhaled the steam rising from the cup and said, "Oh yes, hints of peach and apricot. Mmmm. Tea like this is as complex as wine. The trees are ancient, and like old grapevines, they yield complexities not found elsewhere." Murphy watched Sun as she licked her dark pink lips, almost in slow motion, before pressing her lips against the edge of the cup. Sun moaned softly as she tilted the cup and let the hot liquid in.

Murphy blinked and swallowed. "I, uh, wow. That looks, that looks fantastic."

"Here," Sun said, waving her hand to bring Murphy closer. "Breathe. Mmm. Can you smell that? Honey, fresh grass, flowering blossoms." Murphy leaned across the table and breathed in. She could smell a warm lusciousness on Sun's breath that caused a shudder through her body and tingling in her fingers. Sun's lips were wet and plump as she relaxed into her pleasure. Murphy willingly followed, taking in a sensation entirely new to her.

"So you like it?" the waiter abruptly interrupted.

"It's orgasmic," Sun said as Murphy leaned back and shook her head to clear it.

"Orgasmic is the best review we've had yet," he said, causing both women to laugh.

The waiter permanently broke the spell by presenting them menus filled with an array of tempting Italian dishes. After some discussion, Murphy and Sun decide to start with a Caprese salad with juicy ripe tomatoes, creamy mozzarella, and fragrant basil drizzled with a balsamic glaze.

For the main course, Murphy chose the classic spaghetti carbonara, while Sun opted for a fresh caught pan-seared trout with a lemon butter sauce.

During the meal, Murphy and Sun engage in lively conversation, laughing easily with each other. Murphy deftly avoided sensitive topics like growing up in Ireland, and work. She explained she could not talk about police matters. Really, she wanted to give Sun space to talk, to listen to the soft notes of her voice. Murphy talked about the art on the wall. Sun talked about the peonies in the bud vase on the table. Soon enough, Sun opened up.

"Twenty-one years ago, my husband Adesh and I took a leap of faith and immigrated to Quebec from Pondicherry in the Bay of Bengal. It was a significant change for both of us, but my ability to speak Tamil, French, and English made the transition a bit smoother for me than for Adesh, who only spoke Tamil when we arrived in Canada." Sun picked up a spear of asparagus and took a crunchy bite.

"We joined his grandparents in Montreal, and slowly but surely, we settled down and built a life here. Two beautiful children later, I applied for and obtained Canadian citizenship. Adesh, on the other hand, never bothered. He despised Canadian winters, the endless snow that seemed to never stop falling. He also faced discrimination at work, something that burdened him with frustration and resentment." Sun took another bite of asparagus and finished the stalk. She poked at her salmon with a fork.

"What hurt me the most was that he seemed to resent me, his own wife, as well. I did my best to support him, but his dissatisfaction seemed to be directed towards me too. I loved him once. I held onto hope that things would improve, that Adesh would find some joy. I realized that was a losing battle," she said with a sigh.

Two years after Sun became a citizen, Adesh moved back to India, taking his grandparents with him and leaving her with the children. She divorced him years ago. Her children Winston and Anna—the Anglicized names were her idea and another reason for Adesh to turn his back on the family—hadn't heard from him in years. She moved the family to Ravensberg five years ago.

Sun said she had dated both men and women over the years, but was never able to find the right person. She struggled with the stigma surrounding her race and her bisexuality. Men expected her to be erotically gifted. "Always asking about the Kama Sutra, I hate that so much," she laughed. Women expected her to provide enlightened criticism of the white heterosexual patriarchy. "That is not very sexy at all."

Being in a somewhat rural area, the dating pool for a someone like Sun was limited, and it was difficult for her to find others who are accepting and understanding of her identities. She tried online dating, of course, and long-distance dating. But she was not, at present, committed to anyone.

Murphy was relieved when Sun told her that her adult children and her flower business were very important to her. It meant she might understand Murphy's deep dedication to her work and the great deal of time and energy spent working on a case. Without fail, it would negatively impact her personal relationships.

A homicide detective's job is especially difficult because of the type of work. Murphy treated her job as a higher calling. These crimes often required a great deal of time, effort, and emotional investment. The workload was unpredictable and included working long hours, weekends and holidays, and being called to crime scenes at all hours of the day or night. This demanding schedule made it difficult for the detective to maintain any semblance of a work-life balance.

Rarely did anyone stick around long enough to merit the 'I'm married, but...' conversation.

After dinner, they decide to each have a glass of wine and share a decadent tiramisu for dessert. As they savoured the last bites of the creamy, espresso-soaked cake, they agreed that their evening at Tavola was delightful.

Murphy and Sun stepped outside the restaurant, feeling satisfied. As they stood under the clear night sky, a slight breeze took hold of a strand of Sun's hair. Murphy brushed Sun's hair out of her face.

Without thought, they stepped closer and shared a passionate kiss filled with the excitement and chemistry that has been building throughout their dinner.

After their kiss, they hesitated for a moment, staring into each other's eyes. Sun gave Murphy her home phone number—so they could plan their next date. They parted ways and Murphy headed to her Brawler. Her legs trembled slightly as she paused to unlock her vehicle. She looked around her and, not seeing Sun, she got in and drove away.

The next morning, Murphy was up and out of the house early. She had hoped for a more complete report from the pathologist's overnight, but it hadn't arrived. She wanted to get an early start on the work and headed to the Goose Gas for a bite to eat.

The Goose Gas was a large, dirty gas station that doubled as a convenience store and diner. Despite its unimpressive exterior, it was a staple in the community and a favourite of Murphy's. They stocked the convenience store with a limited selection of basic household goods, snacks, and drinks. It was utilitarian, with shelves cluttered with products. An outdated cash register sat near the entrance.

The diner was a small area with counter seating and a few booths. Travelers passing through sometimes used it because they didn't yet to know about the terrible coffee and questionable food. The menu was classic diner fare, such as eggs, burgers, and poutine. The coffee was weak, and the food was greasy and leaden in the stomach. Despite this, the detective continued to visit the diner at least once a week for a cheap breakfast and the solitude it offered.

Here, she could poke at her mostly cooked eggs with her burnt toast in peace. For Murphy, the Goose Gas was a place to escape the stresses of the job and enjoy a quiet moment. The slow atmosphere and lack of frills provided a welcome respite from her fast-paced, high-stakes world. And they never complained when she spent most of her time colouring simplistic pictures in her toddler colouring book.

Sun pulled up to the Goose Gas pumps and jumped out to fill her work van. She waved off the old man who always offered to pump her gas for her. It was early morning, the sun just rising in the sky. Sun loved this time of day. It was early and quiet when she headed out with her van every Tuesday and Friday morning to buy flowers at the warehouse. As she stood impatiently waiting for the tank to fill, she spotted Murphy in the diner window, and smiled.

Sun paid for her gas at the pump, pulled her van around the side of the building, and headed into the diner. Murphy's head was bent over as she intently coloured a bunny rabbit's tail a shade of dark green. Sun quietly sat down across the table in Murphy's booth and waited to be noticed. It wasn't until the waitress arrived and flipped over a coffee cup that Murphy looked up. "Sun!" she said, delighted by the sudden appearance of the woman. Her heart raced and she could feel her skin flush.

"No coffee for me, thanks," Sun said, but to no avail. The waitress gave her an indifferent glance as she filled the cup.

"Care to join me for breakfast?" Murphy asked as the waitress stood poised for an answer.

"No, thank you. I have to get going. I just saw you here and thought I'd say hi. I have to get to the flower warehouse," Sun said. The waitress walked away.

"Warehouse?"

"Yes, the wholesaler's. I buy the flowers there and then sell them. At the flower shop. I don't grow them, you know," Sun teased.

"Yes, yes, of course. You're going to buy me some cheap roses, right?" Murphy put her colouring book and pencil crayons into her brown leather bag and turned her attention to the cold eggs and toast in front of her. At least she ate the sausages while they were still hot.

"I don't normally buy on the lower end of the scale," Sun said. "What do you need them for?"

"Mes chères," Murphy said. "My homicide victims. I buy a bouquet of flowers for every new homicide victim. That's usually about one every two weeks. Not all of them are homicides, some are suicides or accidents, but if I get called to a scene, I bring a bouquet. I put roses on the graves of my unsolved cases once a month, four of them. Let them know they aren't forgotten. And once a year, I give flowers to all, well most, of the families. Usually, I take them but some families live further away. I used to work in Ottawa. Last year I reached forty-eight."

Sun blinked back a small tear. "That is a lot. That's very kind, but that's a lot of people," she said. She was also happy to hear it was not for a romantic partner

"It is, but on the other hand, some US cities see that in a month. I try to focus on the people, you know, and do the flower thing. That gets more expensive the more years I work. I need affordable flowers, you see? Especially the year end, that always blows my savings to pieces. I mean, us detectives don't make that much money."

Sun smiled and nodded. "Kind and sensible. I'll see what I can do for you. When do you make the large order?"

"November twenty-first of each year. That's when I started working homicide here in Muskoka."

"You know, there aren't many people who would do such a thing. It shows you have a very kind heart, so thoughtful," Sun said sweetly. She tilted her head slightly and smiled.

Murphy slammed her hand on the table, making Sun jump. "See! I knew you'd get to love me. I'm a great person," she said as she laughed. "Really, I'm not. I..." Murphy's phone rang, so she held up a finger to pause the conversation and answered it. "Murphy. Yes, you sure? Okay, on my way, bye." Murphy hung up. "I have to go. It was great seeing you. Paige? Put it on my tab please! Gotta go. Bye!" Murphy grabbed her bag and sprinted out of the diner without another word and peeled off in her Brawler before Sun stepped outside.

"That sure is dedicated," Sun said out loud to herself as she got into her van.

CHAPTER SEVEN

Girard was waiting for Murphy when she arrived at the office. He had the forensic report on the contents of the backpack and the nylon rope.

"Boss, the rope Parker found at the Sunny Lake Nature Centre is the same type of rope. We need to recheck the ropes themselves, to see if we can find any that match the ends of the ropes used on Jose. There was a dark stain on the ends of the rope around Jose's neck, so maybe it was cut with the same knife as they stabbed him with. I double checked the post mortem report from Dr. Chen. Jose was likely bound after death."

"Why would he be bound after death?" Murphy wondered aloud.

"That is weird, isn't it?" Girard agreed. "Anyway, most importantly, there was that bone, a portion of a femur, a human leg bone. Chen should have the initial tests soon, less than an hour. For the backpack, nothing spectacular. The map book has nothing forensically: there are no notations or markups, no foreign prints, nothing of forensic value. Backpack contained some power bars, Kleenex, baggies and a cloth. The tattoo machine has three sets of fingerprints, from Jose, Patrick Lambert and Norman Moreau. The needle has traces of blood, not much."

"A human leg bone for sure?" Murphy said. "How the hell did he find that? And where? We really only..." Murphy paused as Hamilton walked into the office and stood near the pair. Murphy continued with the summary. "The bone looks to be human. We know from the timeline given by Violet Mercado, Jose likely found it within a few hours' walk of the entrance to Spalding near the Nature Centre. No notations in the map book? No? Okay..." Murphy paused again as Parker arrived. "Jose found a human bone, but we don't know exactly how or where. We don't know why he was there, except for that video showing that library book. Did we check the book?"

"No, boss, not beyond the locating the 'Saskwatch' comment," Hamilton said.

Murphy sighed. "Cleo, follow up. Just check for any more writing. Adam, we need more detail on the bone. Hunt down Dr. Chen and make him prioritize his analysis.

Michael, I want you to go back to the Nature Centre and get samples of all the cut ends of all the yellow nylon rope you can find. Keep an eye out for any possible blood trace nearby. The doctor's report said there is dark staining on the end we have. I am going to find the waitress at the café."

As her staff scattered, Murphy drained the last of her coffee and then headed to her Brawler. She asked WeSee for directions to the Kettering Traveller Motel and headed out to interview the waitress who worked the previous Friday night at the café.

"Detective Inspector Caitlin Murphy, Muskoka Municipal Police," she said walking up to the young man standing at the host station at the café. "Can you tell me who was working Friday night?"

The young man fetched the manager, who then checked the staff schedule. Two women and two men had been working the floor that evening. Murphy spoke to one woman who was there, but she wasn't the waitress who had Jose's table. The manager refused to provide Murphy with the home address of the other woman without a court order, citing privacy reasons. Murphy glared at him for a moment and walked out.

"She lives at Garter Snake Creek Parkocity just across the highway there." Murphy turned to find the young man from the host station standing against the wall, smoking. "Her name is Emily Powell. She was telling me about it on Saturday. She even posted it on her Insta."

"Emily Powell. Do you know which trailer number?"

"Seventeen."

"Thanks," Murphy said as she headed back to her Brawler. If she posted about it on social media, she didn't much care about privacy, Murphy thought to herself as she headed out. Although Parkocity was just across the highway, the roadway was divided, and she had to drive north to loop around to then head south again on the correct side of the road.

She had hoped the trip would be quick, but when she got to the turnoff, Murphy saw there was a blockade. A small group of Indigenous peoples had set up a road blockade protesting a possible taxation of cigarettes on reservations. The protesters were holding signs and banners with slogans expressing their opposition. There was one uniformed police officer and a television crew filming the half dozen cars waiting to pass. She waited in line, moving forward one car length at a time, for just a few minutes before they waved her through.

Murphy arrived at Garter Snake Creek Parkocity, drove past the hedges that hid it from the sight of the highway, and parked her Brawler. Parkocity was a run-down trailer park.

It was a collection of weather-beaten trailers with faded paint and patched-up roofs. The gravel roads that wound through the park were full of pot holes, offering a bumpy and jarring ride to anyone who ventured along them. Tattered flags and weathered welcome signs hung limply, remnants of brighter days now worn by time and neglect.

Scattered around the park were broken-down cars, some propped up on blocks with rust-covered wheels, others abandoned with weeds growing up around them. The trailers themselves had seen better days, their once-vibrant colours now dulled by the sun and wind. Patched-up windows and sagging doors gave a sense of weariness to the homes that had endured many years of weathering.

A sense of melancholy hung in the air, as if the park itself was longing for the days when laughter echoed through its streets and children played freely under the watchful eyes of their parents. The air was thick with the tang of stagnant water, and Murphy heard dogs barking and voices shouting over the hum of traffic. A group of children were playing on a broken-down swing set, while a few people were sitting on folding chairs, smoking and watching the detective's arrival.

Murphy nodded to people staring at her as she walked past, toward number seventeen. Standing in front of the dilapidated trailer, she knocked and waited.

"Who is it?" came a cheerful call from inside the trailer. It was a young woman's voice, and it seemed incongruent to the visual story of despair that Murphy saw all around her.

"Police," Murphy answered. She heard some shuffling come from inside, and then the door popped open.

"Hi! What's up?" said the blonde woman in front of her.

"Emily Powell? I'm Detective Inspector Caitlin Murphy, Muskoka Municipal Police. Do you have a moment to talk?"

"Sure, let's sit here," she said as she gestured toward some filthy plastic lawn chairs to the side of the trailer. "Want some iced tea?" she asked. Murphy shook her head and went to sit in the sturdier looking of the chairs. She saw the chair was so filthy she would have to change her clothes.

"You worked on Friday evening at the Kettering Traveller Motel, didn't you?"

"Yep, in the café."

"Do you recall a young man there, the guy making a video?"

Emily laughed. "Oh, hell yes! That was crazy. This guy started talking on his phone, and he was talking about a Sasquatch at Spalding. Like, he honestly believed it! I thought it was funny, so I started filming him."

"Do you have that video? Can I see it?" Murphy asked.

"Sure. I already posted it on Instagram," Emily said as she pulled up the video. "I started filming before…" she paused as she began playing the video for Murphy. Her unsteady camera work was making Murphy a little dizzy. "Boom!" she shouted as the camera jolted. "This old dude just started yelling at him! Look at that! And bam! He slammed the guy's camera down. What a jerk. I stopped filming before he saw my camera. I didn't want him to break mine too."

"Can I get a copy of that video?" Murphy asked.

"Yep. My Insta is Couleuvre_Vie842, you can download it from there," Emily said.

"Can I get it from your phone? Have my technicians…"

"No way am I giving you my phone," Emily said as she suddenly clutched it to her chest.

Murphy didn't want to press it, so she simply tapped the spelling of the account into her phone. "No problem, Couleuvre_Vie842 on Instagram it is. Did you recognize the man who made the fuss?"

"Yeah. Why? Is that guy going to sue or something? I mean, that old creep cracked his screen."

"No, he's not suing. Do you recognize the older man?"

"Sure, he's a regular. His name is Cornelius something. He used to be a mayor of some shithole around here a long time ago. Him and his buddy, Phillip whatever, they are always there. He orders black coffee, his friend gets a triple triple. Then they sit in my section for an hour or more, every evening, yapping away. They pay cash and never leave a tip. Bastards. I could have real customers with real tips sitting there, but they always want my section and they creepy flirt. It's gross."

Murphy thanked Emily for her help and headed back to her Brawler. Once inside, she emailed Parker and told him to find the Couleuvre_Vie842 video, and to search for any former local mayors named Cornelius. Then she headed home to change before going back to the office.

When Murphy popped her head in; it looked like Del was in the middle of a sale, so she quietly retreated. Murphy headed upstairs and undressed. She saw that both her shirt and pants had dirt and grease on them. She quickly got into identical, clean clothes and threw her dirty laundry in the hamper.

Murphy arrived at the office, made herself an instant coffee, and walked into the atelier for an update from her staff. She was not disappointed.

Hamilton started. "I video chatted with Violet Mercado and got a timeline. She showed me her phone log, sent screenshots. She called a couple of OPP numbers, including one seven-minute call. She called the Toronto Police, just a few minutes long. Lastly, she asked if we could release the car. She needs it for work."

"I retrieved ends from two dozen ropes at the Nature Centre. Three had stains on them. Forensics said one was presumptive for human blood. Luminol showed no traces in the area by the ropes. I asked at stores and shops near the motel. No one had a phone turned in. I have downloaded the video from Instagram. Check this out," Parker said, as he sat down at his computer.

"Right here, it's blurry, but you can see two men behind Jose giving him some looks. This guy," he paused as he opened another tab on his browser, "is Cornelius Price. Here's an article on him becoming the mayor of Bradburn in 1979. They look pretty similar, I mean, for decades apart."

"Parker, good work. That at least gives us a name for one man at the café. Address?"

"Yep, he's in Ravensberg. Seventeen Old Brown Road."

"Excellent. Adam, are you going to add to my joy today?"

Girard laughed. "I sure hope so. They still checked Jose's car, nothing of forensic value, and no matches to the trace evidence found on the body. It can be released back to Victoria. Now, the femur, Dr. Chen wants you to call him before he sends the report. He says it's intriguing."

Everyone gathered around Girard's desk as Murphy dialled the phone. "Dr. Chen," she said.

"DI Murphy. Here's an interesting fact for you. The appearance of clouds often gives the illusion of being weightless, like a puff of cotton. Cotton. However, in reality, they are much heavier than they seem. The average cumulus cloud can weigh over a million pounds, and a thunderstorm can carry billions, or even trillions of pounds of water in a small section of the sky."

Murphy and her team exchanged confused looks. "What? Is this about the femur?"

"No, it has nothing to do with that. I said it was an interesting fact, not an interesting fact about the femur. But I do, in fact, have some interesting facts about the femur. Would you like to hear the facts?"

"In fact I do, doctor."

Chen cleared his throat. "My preliminary evaluation puts this femur at fifty to sixty years old. I can't give you a cause of death for the person it belonged to. Now, the important information. Arsenic. There is arsenic in the marrow of the subject femur. Arsenic replaces phosphorus and localizes in the bone so it is detectable." The team heard Chen rustle around his office and drop something metallic.

"Arsenic is a metalloid element and is a naturally occurring element that is found in various minerals such as realgar, arsenopyrite, and orpiment. Weathering of these minerals can cause arsenic to leach into the water supply. Water supply. This can also occur as a result of human activities, such as mining, smelting, and agricultural practices. Inorganic forms of arsenic have a chemical similarity with phosphorus because of their ionic radius and charge. This chemical similarity allows arsenic to substitute for phosphorus in the structure of bone, resulting in the skeletal accumulation of arsenic. Arsenic. I can detect this accumulation using inductively coupled plasma mass spectrometry, which can determine the arsenic content of bone samples. That in turn can then provide a biomarker of exposure to arsenic-contaminated water..."

"Doctor, doctor, doctor," Murphy interrupted. "Please talk to me like I'm five."

Dr. Chen laughed. "Sorry, I got carried away. Arsenic is a toxic chemical that can be formed via certain kinds of industries. If these industries dump chemicals like arsenic, they can contaminate the water supply. When someone drinks water or eats food that contains arsenic, it can enter their body and end up in their bones. In the bones, it can replace an important mineral called phosphorus. Because of this replacement, we can detect arsenic through special tests. Tests."

"The person died of arsenic poisoning?"

"No," Dr. Chen said to Murphy's confusion. "As I said, I can't tell how this person died. This shows low-level chronic exposure. Not high enough to kill, at least not right away. It would take some years at this level of exposure. They would be sickly long before they died. I saw it when I spent time in Ethiopia. Chronic."

"So not a cause of death. Someone with arsenic poisoning from fifty or sixty years ago. Maybe from Ethiopia. Do you have an age?"

"Oh yes, sorry, yes, this was a young person. Young. Likely six to eleven years old, she may have had stunted growth. She was about 125 centimetres tall. And yes, she was a she."

Murphy thanked Chen for the information and asked Parker to search historic police records for cases of arsenic poisoning, including missing persons and cold cases. "Maybe someone killed their family, maybe she was reported missing, she was just a young girl," she said.

Murphy turned and looked at the board. "Opinions please," she said to her team. "We need to find out about this leg bone, but does this have anything to do with Jose's murder?"

"Jose went looking for a Sasquatch, and he spent hours walking around. Got the bone, then what? Hikers in Muskoka find human remains at least twice a year," Girard said.

"If he found a grave, why not take something cool? Like the skull?" Hamilton asked.

"A human skull won't be confused for a Sasquatch, and he was hunting Sasquatches," Murphy said.

"Maybe all he found was that fragment," Parker said. "I've been watching some of his videos on Cryptvids, and he seems to find a lot of things when hiking. He'll find some small pieces of fur or mouse skeleton. That kind of thing. He said the mouse was a snack for a Sasquatch, the fur was from a Sasquatch. We don't even know for sure he found the bone there. He might have brought it with him, and pretended to find it."

"A grave robber from Toronto? Who stole a poisoned Ethiopian's bones? So, unrelated to Muskoka? Except his wife did not know about it until he told her," Hamilton added.

"Lambert had means and motive, and possibly opportunity. Mercado stole a tattoo machine, so he went looking for payback. His alibi is weak, it's just Moreau, and old men in a park," Girard said.

"Right. I know someone who might have been in Gull Lake Park that night. I'll check just in case Moreau or Lambert were seen. Thank God for his face tattoos, people are likely to remember him if he was there. Cleo, I want you to contact Violet Mercado again, sorry. Ask if she has a user ID and password for this Cryptvids site. Maybe Jose has a draft video there. Oh, and find out if he saved photographs to the cloud, he seems like the kind of person who might do that. Michael, you're on the arsenic angle to identify the bone. Adam... What are you doing?"

"I'll head back to Sunny Lake with some uniformed officers and search again for the phone and backpack."

Murphy nodded, and the detectives got to work. She headed out of the office and drove off. A few minutes later, Murphy pulled into Goose Gas to fill up her tank and ask a few questions. No matter the time of day she arrived, Sergei was there. He was a grizzled old man, a veteran of the Soviet-Afghan War who hung out at the gas station. His scarred and tattered face looked like he'd been through more than one war in his life. Murphy used this gas station specifically because of Sergei—he had once witnessed a murder at the Goose Gas and was the only person to come forward with information. He would pump her gas, clean her windshield and watch her Brawler while she went into the store, and she would buy him a sandwich, two litres of pop and a bag of candies for his help.

He was waiting patiently for her as she stepped out of the store and handed the bag to him. "What did you get me today, officer?" he asked her as he looked through the bag. "Tuna, thanks," he said.

"Sergei, you sometimes drink down at Gull Lake Park, don't you?" Murphy asked as she got into her Brawler. "Were you there Friday night?"

"I don't know what day it is," Sergei said. "But I'm there most nights."

"Do you remember recently seeing a couple of young men, one with tattoos all over his face?"

Sergei burst out laughing. "That goat! He can't hold his liquor. What is he saying?"

"He's saying he was there." Murphy did not want to get into specifics, offering to let Sergei tell his story.

"Stupid little man. Goat and his friend come over, already drunk. They have beer, want to trade my vodka for beer. I say no, he says yes. He threw the first punch. He started it. Then he stumbled, right into my fist," he laughed. "Goat thought he could beat me because I'm old. He kept calling me an old man. I am an old man, but also a soldier. I beat his face, he fell down and, I don't know, just fell asleep. He was fine. Woke me up the next morning, early, said he had fun, left his beer for me. I don't think the stupid goat remembered what happened."

Murphy nodded. "Thanks Sergei," she said and drove away. While he did not know which day of the week it was, the story lined up enough with Lambert's to give him a reasonable alibi.

CHAPTER EIGHT

Murphy's phone rang as she was heading back to the station. It was Dispatch. "Murphy," she answered. They advised her of a double death, suspected murder-suicide. An unknown emergency call had come in and Fire Services had been dispatched, then police, then the Forensics Unit.

It took Murphy thirty minutes to find the location. At one point her WeSee GPS system had told her to turn right, and she drove into a beaver pond. Grateful for the four-wheel drive on her lifted Brawler, she retreated and got back to the road. She drove another half kilometre and spotted four police cars and a fire truck at the side of the road, and a Forensics Unit van parked in the driveway. Pulling in behind a cruiser, she parked and walked to the scene.

The dilapidated white clapboard house sat forlornly on a patch of overgrown land, surrounded by tall grass and weeds. The once-pristine white paint on the exterior has long since faded, leaving a dirty, weather-beaten shell of a building in its place. The porch was rotting away in places. The cracked steps that lead up to the porch were uneven, as if they have been walked on ten thousand times.

On the porch itself, dozens of empty beer cans littered the floor, crumpled and rusted signs of a rough life, joined by a few empty bottles and cigarette butts.

There were no flowers or shrubs, no beauty to be seen at the property, only an old, rusted metal lawn chair sitting on its side, looking cast off and forgotten. The property exuded a sense of abandonment and neglect save for the buzz of first responders who had descended on the scene.

"Detective Inspector Caitlin Murphy," she said as she held out her badge to the officer at the perimeter. He nodded and lifted the tape for her to duck under. She took a quick glance at the scene. A dark-haired woman lay face down in the grass, a defect in her back. A dark-haired man lay face up in the grass near her, much of his face destroyed. The area was muddy, so she headed back to her Brawler and put on some boots.

"I'm Constable Blackstone, this is Constable Sayer. The firefighters are Frank Hickson and Jeremy Fields. They were first on scene," one officer said as Murphy approached the first responders. "We have a murder-suicide. This is Beverly Alexander, 28. And the shooter is Matthew Battiste, 30. Looks like they were drinking all day, probably got in a fight and boom! He shot her as she was running away and then shot himself. The Forensics Unit found a Girsan MC28S, common enough."

Murphy looked around. Alexander's body was in a direct line from the porch, and there was a small handgun near Battiste. "Am I clear to walk?" she shouted out to a member of the Forensics Unit. He waved her in. It disappointed Murphy to see it was Wilson and Winslow from Dr. Smith's forensics team. Smith was lax and his staff were idiots. Smith and his team had lost evidence in one of Murphy's investigations and, she was sure, had falsified evidence to secure convictions in at least two assaults.

"How do we know the identities?" Murphy asked. Wilson handed over two clear plastic evidence bags. Inside one, Murphy could see a Status Card with a woman's face—Beverly Alexander. Inside the other bag was a driver's license—Matthew Battiste. "Do we have phones?"

"Yes, we have one phone from the male victim, back right pocket. Nothing found so far on the female. We haven't entered the house yet." Murphy walked slowly to the front porch as Wilson joined and talked to her. Blackstone and Sayer walked up to them.

"Two types of beer cans, this one has blood on it. There is a cut on Battiste's hand," Wilson said as he leaned over and pointed.

Blackstone chimed in. "Passer-by called and asked for medical. Fire beat us here by a maybe five minutes. Said there was a grass fire as well. They had to hose down the scene."

"What?" Murphy exclaimed. "They did what?"

"Disturbed the scene, that's what. Washed away some evidence maybe," Wilson said. "Said they couldn't let the scene burn."

Murphy let out a frustrated sigh, shook her head, and Blackstone continued.

"We've asked around, and no one in the area has doorbell cams. A couple of people said they heard shouting, but that was almost every night. Nobody saw the actual shooting. I was out here a couple of weeks ago for a noise complaint. They were playing their music too loud. They turned it down, I left. But I have been out here other times for domestic. I've arrested Battiste twice."

Murphy spotted Girard, thanked the officer and waved Girard over to the bodies.

Winslow nodded as the detective approached. "Murder-suicide. We turned Battiste over to find the gun. A Girsan. It was under him," he said. "We will bag up some cans and check the house for anything, a note maybe. It's pretty clear he shot her, then himself," he said as he gestured around.

"Adam, run down the gun, check for previous reports of domestic violence. Blackstone! Do we know who next of kin are?"

"Alexander's parents are over there by the tree, they were here pretty quickly. Nothing for Battiste yet."

"Have you spoken with them? Confirmed it is their daughter?"

"No way, that's above my pay grade," Blackstone said.

Murphy hung her head and sighed. She rubbed both her hands over her face and straightened her hair before walking toward the parents.

Murphy could hear the wailing coming from the perimeter, a deep and anguished rhythmic moan. Breath in, wail, breath in, wail. She saw a woman, partially collapsed, being physically held up by those around her. Fuck I hate this, she thought as she headed over. A middle-aged man was clutching at a middle-aged woman as she struggled to stand. Behind them, an older woman with long, grey braided hair glared at Murphy and rubbed the other woman's back.

"Detective Inspector Caitlin Murphy, Muskoka Municipal Police," she announced as she arrived. She recognized the woman with braided hair.

It was Ellen Longboat.

Longboat was originally from the Kahnawake, a First Nations reservation of the Mohawks of Kahnawá:ke on the south shore of the St. Lawrence River in Quebec.

In 1990, at 27, Ellen became an active protester during the Kanesatake Resistance, near the town of Oka. In the land dispute between the Mohawks of Kanehsatà:ke and the town, she was one of the main spokespersons for the Mohawk people, and helped to organize peaceful protests and rallies to raise awareness about their concerns.

Throughout the crisis, Longboat's powerful speeches caught the attention of the media and the wider public audience. Her eloquence and passion earned her the respect and admiration of many, and she quickly became a leading figure for the press. An unknown assailant slashed her across the chest during the Crisis, and the journalist's photograph of her standing defiantly, bleeding, in front of armed soldiers, made her world famous.

Longboat never wavered in her commitment to her people and she fully embraced the Indigenous community when she moved to Muskoka ten years later. She was commanding whether she spoke at a United Nations retreat or a barbeque, and kind when she comforted the mother of a dead child. Clearly, she was here to support the parents. Murphy knew Beverly Alexander's parents were in excellent hands. "What's your name?" Murphy asked the man.

William Alexander introduced himself, his wife Susan and Ellen, their community elder. He explained a family friend who lived further along the street had contacted the family about the shooting. "Is that our Beverly?" he asked. Susan held out her phone in a shaky hand. Her daughter's face beamed out, grinning.

"Yes, I'm very sorry. It's her, I'm so sorry..." Murphy began. Susan wailed again and fell toward Murphy, clawing at her for support. Together with William and Ellen, they navigated Susan to a patrol car to lean against as she tried to stay on her feet.

"And Matthew?" William asked.

Murphy nodded. "We have photo ID for two people. The coroner will have to make an official identification, of course. Is Matthew your daughter's partner? Do they both live here?"

William told the detective the couple had been together for six months, and despite parental efforts to break them up, they had moved in together three months ago. They spent much of their time drinking and fighting, and Matthew had been arrested three times for domestic violence. Both decedents had criminal records for shoplifting and public intoxication. Matthew had been in jail for assault and domestic abuse. Matthew had called William just before the murder, asking for one hundred dollars. William declined, saying he knew it was for drugs.

"Does your daughter have a phone?" Murphy asked.

"Yes, it's got a big black cat sticker on the back. It's got a knife in its mouth, like a pirate," Susan said shakily. "She got it so everyone would know it was hers. Look, my daughter was a good person. She just got mixed up with the wrong people. Matthew was the problem. She was a good person. Can I... can I have her phone? I know she has pictures on it, and I want those." The bereaved mother's voice trembled with emotion as she spoke, her love and pain intertwined in her words.

Murphy nodded. She knew it was painful for the family to answer questions, but was happy she had gotten the information. "I'll see what I can do. It might be a few days, but I can try to get that to you," she said.

Longboat had been quiet the entire time, then said, "Detective, I'd like a word?" The two stepped away from the cruiser and stood under a large maple tree. "This is a murder-suicide, can't you return the phone now?"

"I don't know yet if it's a murder-suicide. We're still in preliminary stages. But I understand the family would like the phone," Murphy said.

"And any cash in the house. Beverly sometimes helped her parents out with groceries and rent."

"I'll see what we can do about releasing the scene quickly, then they can gain access to the house. But it will still take some time. Do you know anything about Mr. Battiste's next of kin?" Murphy asked.

"Dead, I think. I'm not sure. So the grieving mother has to wait? Nice," Ellen responded and walked away.

Murphy nodded and shrugged. Ellen returned to the Alexanders and Murphy went to Girard. "Adam, head back to the office. We need to find Mr. Battiste's next of kin. We also need to know who owns the house." Murphy called Hamilton on the phone and asked her to attend the scene. Hamilton's stamp collecting hobby meant she had a good eye for details, and there were too many things that could be missed with this scene. Girard headed to the office while Murphy waited for Hamilton.

It took Hamilton twenty minutes to arrive. Murphy used her time to scribble down some notes about the Alexander/Battiste deaths. "Boss?" Hamilton startled Murphy when she approached her Brawler and spoke to her.

"Cleo. We have Wilson and Winslow working the scene. I need you to take photos of all the evidence bags, to match up later, and make sure they lose nothing."

"Boss, they're going to hate that," Hamilton protested.

"That's just the start. You're going to be very hated today. Part of the job. The firefighters were first on the scene and hosed the area down. Said it was a grass fire."

Hamilton looked around and asked, "Fire? Where?".

"For you to find out. And why, what the hell were they thinking? Take their statements. These firefighters should have known better. I'll be reporting them to their Chief. Don't tell them that, though. Talk to the person who made the call. Officer Blackstone has the information. Alexander's phone hasn't been found. I'd like you to find it. It has a sticker of a black cat and a knife on the back. Go with the Forensics Unit when they go into the house. Track every single mistake and misstep, take notes." Murphy saw Hamilton's face and added "It's awkward but I trust you, Cleo. We have a grieving family. They deserve more than a rush job."

"Yes boss, of course," she replied and headed into the scene.

Back in the office, Murphy began talking with her team. "Okay, we have an apparent murder-suicide. Beverly Alexander and Matthew Battiste at 14 Little Hawk Lane. Adam, do we have next of kin for Battiste?"

"Yes, he has a Jack Battiste listed from an arrest two years ago. I have called once, no answer. I have the name and phone number for the landlord," Girard said. "We have arrested Matthew ten times. Two drug possession, three domestic violence with previous girlfriends and another one with our victim. There is one theft, one for possession of an illegal handgun and two more for public drunkenness. Beverly had one domestic, two thefts, and one public drunkenness."

"Busy people. Okay, send that to Cleo. She's gathering the evidence. Find out how long until we get the post mortem results. Michael, draw up an ITO and get a search warrant for the house. Head over to the property and give the warrant to Cleo. You might need the landlord to let you in. Help her look for phones. I want Beverly's. You're checking for any suicide note, drugs, cash, all the usual items. Cleo's staying at the scene with uniformed officers.

"Right. Now we still have Jose Mercado. Have we ruled out that the killer followed him up from Toronto?" Murphy asked as she mentally shifted gears.

"Nothing from Toronto police suggests anything like that. But we haven't found his phone. His wife said he should have had his phone," Girard said.

"Why all the missing phones suddenly?" Murphy asked rhetorically. Girard simply shook his head. "Okay, Lambert's alibi turned out to be true. I found the guy he fought with. Said Lambert and Moreau both passed out, slept all night in the park."

Murphy sighed. "So, we lost Lambert and Moreau as suspects. We cleared his wife. Jose's drugs were fully accounted for in the backpack. No wallet, no phone. Maybe a random robbery by someone hanging out at the Nature Centre cabins. Could also be..."

"Random serial killer?" Parker offered.

Murphy chuckled. "Bigfoot as serial killer. Possible robbery at an infrequently used location. What else? Is his murder tied to the bone he found? Except no one knew he found it because he never posted a public video on Cryptvids."

"The people at the café saw it," Girard said.

"I spoke with the waitress, Emily Powell. We still have that Cornelius Price guy, and his friend, Phillip" Murphy said. "I don't see a couple of old men killing someone for making a video phone chat. But, okay, let's talk to them, to Cornelius. We need to find out who the other man is. Phillip somebody. Maybe there is more to it than we've heard so far. Adam, with me."

CHAPTER NINE

Murphy and Girard got into her Brawler and headed out to speak with Cornelius Price. As they drove, they chatted about Girard's family. Steven was at pre-school and picking up the craziest diseases, giving them to Ruby and the kids, and putting Girard's elderly parents at risk of severe illness. "I swear to God I have never been so sick," Girard said. "And it's horrible watching your kids get sick and you can't do anything about it."

"Wait, a second. Are you coming into the office sick? You better not be coming into the office sick. You aren't the only one with vulnerable people at home," Murphy said.

"No no, I feel fine."

"You just said you've never been sicker," Murphy said.

"I meant, as a general comment. I'm fine, do I look sick to you?" Girard said.

"Adam. Adam. You must still have a stash of masks leftover from the mandatory mask policy at the station. You have to wear one when you need one. And tell me, so I can wear one too. I don't want to bring anything home to Del, she is very vulnerable. And she'll kick my ass."

"Agreed. I'll wear a mask next time my kids get sick, and I'll let you know."

"Same. I'll let you know if Del or her PSW is sick. Ha, hard to believe there was a time when this didn't even occur to us. But now we both have families, with vulnerable people in..."

"Your destination is on the right," WeSee said in its soft, purring voice.

Murphy pulled up to the curb outside the stately home. It was a three-story house with a stone exterior and a pitched roof. A large Canadian flag hung on a pole on the welcoming front porch, and a few steps led up to the door. The lush green lawn was neatly manicured. A large red oak tree stood in the middle of the yard with a tire swing hanging off a main branch and it swung gently in the breeze.

The detectives walked up to the door and knocked. Inside, they could hear a TV suddenly go quiet, and then the creaking floorboards as someone came to the door. "Detective Inspector Caitlin Murphy, Muskoka Municipal Police," Murphy said as the door opened. "This is Detective Staff Sergeant Adam Girard. Is Cornelius Price at home?"

"Oh! Detectives? Is everything all right?" Beatrice Price asked.

"Oh yes, we just have some general questions. Things are fine," Murphy said.

"Okay, well come in, detectives. Have a seat, I'll go get him," the elderly woman said in a soft voice.

Murphy and Girard found themselves in a spacious foyer with a high ceiling and a chandelier. The main living area had hardwood floors, elegant moldings, and large windows that let in plenty of natural light. A fireplace with a decorative mantel was the centrepiece of the sitting room she guided them to. Family photos sat on the mantel. Neither of them sat down, preferring instead to peek around corners and survey the house as best they could. Certain habits were hard to break.

"Detectives, how can I help you?" Cornelius said as he walked into the room. He was a strong, confident man with a weathered yet distinguished appearance.

At eighty-three years old, he had wrinkles and age spots, but his physical strength and vitality suggested that he continued to take good care of himself. He had a muscular build, broad shoulders, and a strong jawline, giving him a commanding presence.

Price removed his well-worn cardigan as he walked into the room, handing it to his wife. His jeans were clean and neatly tailored, reflecting his rugged and no-nonsense personality. He carried himself with a certain level of swagger and confidence that comes from a lifetime of experience and authority.

"We'd like to ask you some questions about a young man you saw at the Kettering Traveller Motel Café last Friday evening."

"Hmph," he scoffed.

"You were there with another gentleman," Murphy said.

"Phillip Smith, my neighbour. He lives just across the street, there," Price said.

"Okay, we can speak to him afterward," Murphy said.

"Nonsense, let's talk to him now," he said as he headed out the door. Murphy turned to Girard and raised a quizzical eyebrow.

"You'll have to forgive my husband. He's used to being in charge. He was the mayor of Bradburn for years," Beatrice said as she held the front door open for the detectives.

"No worries. Thank you, Mrs. Price," Girard said as they stepped outside. Cornelius was already at the end of his driveway, calling out to a man stooped over in his flower garden.

"Phillip!" Cornelius shouted. Murphy and Girard hurried to catch up to Cornelius and join him to talk to Phillip.

"They're detectives. They want to talk to us about that kid at the motel café Friday night."

"Oh, yeah?" Phillip asked. Phillip was slightly younger than Cornelius, though his dirty jeans suggested a more relaxed and easygoing personality. "Just getting the soil ready for my perennials," he said. Phillip groaned and reached out for a helping hand as he stood up. "Sometimes I think gardening and old men don't mix," he said with a chuckle.

Phillip Smith was a short, heavy man with a full head of grey hair and a well-groomed goatee. He smiled broadly whenever he spoke. He wiped his hands on his jeans and extended his right hand out toward Girard. "Happy to make your acquaintance," Phillip said.

"Thank you, sir. I'm Detective Staff Sergeant Adam Girard. This is Detective Inspector Caitlin Murphy." The detectives held out their badges but neither man seemed interested in confirming their identities.

"How can we help you, detectives?" Cornelius interjected.

"On Friday evening, you were both at the Kettering Traveller Motel Café, is that right?" asked Murphy as she shook hands with Phillip.

Phillip and Cornelius both nodded. "Every day, for coffee," Phillip said. "Is this about that kid? The one making the video?" Phillip asked.

"Yes, I'm wondering if you can tell us what happened that night at the café," Murphy said.

"That kid is making a complaint," Cornelius said to Phillip. "He's made a complaint, hasn't he?"

"No, no, nothing like that. We're just asking general questions, there is no complaint," Murphy said.

"Then why are you asking?" Cornelius said.

"It's their damn jobs, Cornelius. They're detectives, they're detecting. We go to the café at 7:30. We meet every evening at 7:30 for coffee," Phillip said. As he spoke, Cornelius walked to the front steps and sat down. He gestured for the others to sit, but no one joined him.

"The kid was practically yelling into his phone," Cornelius said. "Some kind of video thing. Going on about Sasquatches. Ha! Sasquatches! I mean, it was a fun idea as a kid, but he should just grow out of it."

"And then that bone!" Phillip added. As if drawn by an invisible force, he rose from the stairs and headed back toward his garden. He deadheaded a flower. "I mean, he seemed so excited about it. Going on about how he found it and had photos and he walked for hours through the..."

"Not on my watch," Cornelius said. "Filthy thing, that deer bone, near my food? Well, anyway, Emily asked me to take care of him."

Phillip balked. "Oh, it wasn't that bad. Kind of funny, really. He was like a little kid. He was so excited." Phillip plucked at another flower head. He was trying to stay interested in the conversation, but the garden was calling.

"Emily asked you to intervene with the man?" Murphy asked. She wanted to hurry the interview along, but Cornelius's statement struck her as odd. Emily Powell had not said she asked for his help.

"Yes. Sweet young thing. I got up and showed this young man the door," Cornelius said.

"Ha! I think you broke his phone," Phillip said.

Cornelius scoffed. "He gathered up his stuff and left right after."

"And the broken phone?" Murphy asked.

"Not broken. I mean, he didn't complain to me. But yes, he took his phone," Cornelius said.

"And this is because of the bone? You saw a bone of some kind?" Murphy asked.

"Deer bone. You could tell from twenty feet away. I grew up deer hunting. I know a deer bone when I see one," Cornelius said.

"And that was the last you saw of him leaving the motel café?" Girard asked. "You didn't see him the next day, around town or near the café again the next morning?"

"No, not at all. I was home all day Saturday, then church with my wife on Sunday," Phillip said.

"All day puttering in the garden," came a woman's voice from inside the house.

"Lucy, come meet the detectives!" Phillip shouted. An elegant elderly woman came to the door and waved.

"I'd rather not come outside. The weather is too warm for me," she said.

"No problem, ma'am. Were you home with your husband on Saturday?" Murphy asked.

"Yes, I was watching telly, and he was in the garden. Went to church on Sunday, chatted a bit with the Reverend. What is this about, anyway?"

"Haha! I guess she was eavesdrop-"

"I played golf Saturday morning. Goldfinch Greens. Then home with the battle-axe. Heh. And church too on Sunday, but the Baptist United, not Phillip's Holy Chapel Pentecostal Church," Cornelius said as he cut off Phillip.

Murphy thanked them for their time and she and Girard returned to her Brawler.

"If he grew up hunting, why does he think this is a deer bone? And why would he say the waitress wanted help? She told me she was interested in what Jose was saying."

"Maybe he's just old, poor eyesight, terrible memory or something," Girard said.

"Hmm," Murphy responded. "Well, I'll drop you at the station and head over to the Goldfinch Greens to check his alibi. See if I can get a round or two in," she laughed.

After dropping Girard off, Murphy was driving happily on Beatrice Townline Road, a narrow and winding road that led to the golf course. 'Slipped Away' by Avril Lavigne was playing. Beatrice Townline Road was the only road in and out of Goldfinch Greens, although there was housing construction underway, which meant more public roads were to come. Up ahead, Murphy saw a small line of cars stopped along the road, and a group of people stretched across the road, barring travel. Another Indigenous protest. Murphy pulled in behind the last car, turned off the engine, and got out.

Walking up to the protesters, she saw Ellen Longboat. As she approached the group, she suddenly found her path blocked by a young Indigenous man with long brown hair and a pocked face. A quiver was slung across his back, but instead of arrows, it held a baseball bat. He spoke with a crooked smile. "We are here protesting the relocation of the Algonquin peoples of the Tiny Flowers Reservation in 1971. You are being asked to wait nine minutes. Here, this has your time of arrival on it. We will let you through nine minutes from then," he said. The man thrust a pamphlet toward Murphy and remained stock still, waiting for her to take it.

Murphy took the pamphlet and looked over his shoulder at Ellen, and said, "Can I just get through? Police business." Murphy didn't understand why Ellen laughed so loudly.

"Police, eh?" the young man in front of her said. "Give me that pamphlet back." Murphy smiled and handed him the pamphlet, but frowned when he wrote COP on it and gave it back. "It's double that, eighteen minutes, for police."

"Are you kidding me? I have important…" Murphy pauses as she noticed Ellen coming her way. "Look, Ellen…"

"Detective," she said as she held up her hand to silence Murphy. "George, scratch out COP. She can go after nine minutes." Dutifully, George grabbed the paper out of Murphy's hand, scribbled out the word, and handed it back.

"I was hoping to get through now. It's police business."

"Police business at the golf club? Unless it's a murder, detective, you can wait. Is it a murder?"

Murphy sighed. "No, not a murder."

"Then take a few minutes in your car and read the pamphlet and you'll be on your way soon enough," Ellen said.

"What's all this for? Blocking access to the golf course?" Murphy asked, as she looked around.

"This was Indigenous land. This was the land of the Tiny Flowers People, forced onto the reservation by the federal government in 1938. In 1971, the feds came in and took over. It was a small group of people, with all this land. They were easy to push around. The government said everyone was sick, so they adopted and fostered all the children under the age of seventeen and then relocated everyone else to a half dozen different reservations up north. We are fighting to get recognition and restitution for the survivors and their descendants." Ellen's speech was well-rehearsed and deeply felt.

"Why the bat?" Murphy asked, nodding her head toward George.

"At a protest yesterday, a car drove through the field to get past and threw a beer bottle at us. A woman was hit, broke her finger. There are no police here today, so we have to protect ourselves."

Murphy nodded her head thoughtfully and walked away. She had nothing to say and did not want to argue. There was no way she would bully her way through the line. She glanced quickly at the time written on the pamphlet, folded the paper in half and slid it into her back pocket. She made a quick call to headquarters to request a police cruiser for security reasons. She had only a few minutes more to wait, and then they waved her through.

Murphy drove past berms and greens, trees and ponds as she headed to Goldfinch Greens. It was beautiful land. It didn't surprise Murphy that the government had expropriated the land. It would have been easy. She worked hard at recognizing and redressing the injustices against Indigenous people, but working hard and being successful at it were two different things. As both a cop and a Catholic, she knew it was work that would never be complete. And she was only one person.

Murphy pulled into the clubhouse parking lot and parked immediately in front of the main entrance. At over 40 years old, the golf clubhouse and grounds had an established and well-maintained appearance, although it showed some signs of age and wear. The clubhouse was a large, two-storey building with traditional architecture, an arched door-way and a peaked roof. The building had large windows that provided views of the golf course.

Murphy looked around and noted a well-manicured lawn and landscaping with ma-ture trees and bushes, and a faded, decorative dry fountain full of leaves and debris. The smell of fresh-cut grass wafted in on the breeze.

Inside the clubhouse, there was a pro shop on the left and locker rooms for both men and women on the right. Further in was a lounge area where golfers could relax and socialize before or after their games. Murphy could hear the soft chatter of voices and clinking of cutlery coming from a small restaurant upstairs.

"Can I help you?" asked a young man in a Goldfinch Greens sweater.

"Can you tell me where your membership office is, please?" Murphy asked.

"Inside the pro shop," he said as he pointed. "Take a left after the cashier. It's at the back of the shop," he said. Murphy nodded and headed into the busy shop. The faux brick interior looked cheap by today's standards, and the rafters lined with gold-painted clubs as decoration looked a little too gaudy. Murphy knocked on the open door to the membership office.

"Detective Inspector Caitlin Murphy, Muskoka Municipal Police," she said, displaying her badge. "I'm just conducting some basic inquiries, just a follow up. Can you provide me with a list of golfers who were here on Saturday morning?" she asked.

"No, I'm sorry, I can't. Not without my manager's approval," said the young woman behind the desk.

"Hmm. What's your name?"

"Carla," she said. Carla was expecting the detective to go full tantrum on her, stomp her feet, throw a fit, and demand to see the manager.

"Carla, could you please contact your manager and get them here?"

"Oh, sure, just a second," Carla said, surprised there was no tantrum. She got up and walked out of the shop to return a few minutes later with the young man who had pointed Murphy into the shop.

"And you are?" Murphy asked.

"Roger," he said. "You're a cop? Can I see your badge?"

Murphy showed her badge and smiled. "Would you like to see my Warrant Card?" she asked. He nodded, and she produced her Warrant Card.

"That doesn't look like a warrant," he said, squinting at the card.

"What? No, it's an ID card that says I'm a cop. That's what a Warrant Card is, not that it's an arrest warrant or search warrant. Those are different things."

"Oh, okay. What can I do for you, officer?" Roger asked.

"Detective Murphy. I'd like a list of names of all visitors to the golf course for last Saturday, the whole day," she said. She was trying desperately to keep the exasperation out of her voice, but it wasn't working well.

"You'll need a warrant for that," Roger said.

"But you just saw her Warrant Card," Carla said. It caused Roger to think for a moment.

"Can I see your card again?" he asked. Murphy nodded and held the ID case open for him to read the card. "It says this is her 'warrant and authority for executing the duties of that office' so I guess so, eh? Okay Carla, print out a list of everyone who signed in on Saturday," he said. Roger straightened his back and smiled. "I always see that kind of stuff on TV, you know, asking for a warrant."

Murphy nodded. As she again explained the difference between a Warrant Card and a warrant for arrest or search, Carla and Roger hovered over the computer discussing whether they should provide the list in landscape or portrait format. They weren't listening, but Murphy knew she would have to document this in her notebook to avoid problems later. She stood and listened as the pair discussed which font to use and whether to print in colour or black and white. She took the opportunity to briefly write in her notebook.

"Here you go," Roger said triumphantly as he handed her a page of names. "Do you need me to sign something saying you got this?" he asked.

"No, there's nothing to sign. Is it possible for someone to come in and shop or go to the restaurant, but not sign in?" she asked.

"Oh sure. We only track people who play golf. If you're here for shopping, you can just come in. But you can't go to the restaurant or the spa without being a member," Roger said.

"Okay, thank you," Murphy said, and walked away. She climbed into her Brawler and quickly scanned the list of names. It was by entry time and not an alphabetical list. Something for one of her detectives, she thought. She folded the list and put it in her pocket just as her phone rang.

CHAPTER TEN

Murphy looked at the caller ID on her phone—it was the office. "Murphy."

"Boss," Parker said, "there's nothing in missing persons or cold cases that matches the bone. But Cleo thinks she had something. I'm switching to the speaker. It's only the two of us at the office."

"Cleo?"

"Boss, I contacted Violet Mercado about the Cryptvids site. She said Jose used a password manager and gave me the name and password to sign in to the manager," Hamilton said.

"That's an app that generates and stores all the websites and passwords you want to save. Then you just use the app to fill in the login information instead of remembering each password," Parker said.

"All the websites? So, access to Cryptvids and any other websites?" Murphy asked.

"Yes boss. If he saved photos online, it will be on the list. His social media, all sorts of things."

"Okay. It's getting late. Cleo, get an email from Violet confirming that she is granting us access to the information manager, all the websites. I need it in writing. Michael, tomorrow you can go through the list, see what comes up. Do not touch the app until we get written permission. Now, Cleo, how is the Alexander/Battiste report coming along?"

"It's coming along slowly, no coroner's report yet. Which one do you want me to prioritize? Mercado or Alexander/Battiste?" Hamilton asked.

"Mercado. Look at giving me the Alexander/Battiste report next Monday. Have you spoken to Battiste's next of kin?"

"Yes boss. I notified his father. He had nothing good to say about his son. They had not spoken in six years," Hamilton said.

"Good, then go home, both of you."

Murphy hung up and drove away. The protesters were gone, and she had a clear path home. When she arrived at the house, she was glad to see the lights on.

"Hey Del," Murphy said as she walked through the door. "Hi Maria." Maria nodded hello.

"Hey you," Del replied. "We're heading out with The Boys tonight for a drink. Want to come?"

Years ago, when Del had first arrived in Muskoka, very few places in Ravensberg were wheelchair accessible. She ended up finding a gay bar with a ramp; the previous owner had installed it as his lung cancer progressed to where he needed a wheelchair to get around. The Sparkling Unicorn was her refuge from the sympathetic looks she received from so many people. Here, she was treated just like one of the boys.

The Boys were Bob, Jens and Thomas, the men who had immediately taken to Del. They were crass, loud, and a hell of a lot of fun. One requirement of her night time personal support worker was to accompany her weekly to The Sparkling Unicorn, and even more frequently during the summer drag show season.

"I have to change. Give me a minute and I'll go with you," Murphy said. She ran upstairs and changed into jeans and a clean white t-shirt, throwing her office clothes into the hamper for Maria to wash overnight.

"Who's driving?" Maria asked, as they headed out to the van.

"You can," Murphy said. She knew Maria loved to drive, and she was more than happy to let her. Murphy and Maria got Del into the van. Murphy sat in the passenger seat while Maria drove into town.

The nightlife area of Ravensberg was mostly contained within a two-block stretch on Centre Street from Franklin Street to Red Road. The dimly lit restaurants that catered to drinkers at night were common yet low-key. Outside the Sparkling Unicorn were groups of older gay men sitting on the patio gossiping over cocktails and martinis. They gave the area a flourish that carried over to nearby bars. This patio buzzed just like all the others but was punctuated more often with intermittent laughing and not bro-friendly bellowing.

The Sparkling Unicorn was the only queer bar in the community.

The club was owned by a couple, Michael and David, who bought it after Zach had passed away. They wanted to create a safe space for the local queer community, where they could come together and celebrate their identities. The place was open seven days a week and offered a variety of events, from karaoke nights to drag shows.

The decor inside was colourful and eclectic, if a little kitschy and dated. There were glittery unicorns on the walls, rainbow and trans flags draped from the ceiling, and a disco ball that sparkled in the centre of the room. It smelled of spilt beer and greasy food.

The Sparkling Unicorn was also a target for egg-throwing young men who turned it into a sport. They would randomly drive by throwing a raw egg or two, hoping to hit anyone sitting on the patio. They would then park and go into a nearby bar. The attacks were unfortunately common enough, and almost always from someone who lived in town. Each time, the club would offer free egg salad sandwiches the next day.

Del, Maria and Murphy walked in and were immediately spotted by The Boys who hooted and hollered to get their attention. Maria pushed aside chairs—some with people in them—to allow Del to move to the table. The men heartily greeted them, after which Bob and Jens sat on one side, while Thomas made space for Maria and Murphy on the other side. Del sat at the end. Tonight, she was dressed to the nines in a sparkling silver top under a stylish brown leather jacket, black pants and knee-high boots.

The server arrived with a round of drinks for the boys shortly after they arrived. "A pint of Blue, sparkling water and a Cosmo," Murphy said as she pointed to herself, Maria and Del.

"Make mine a tequila," Del shouted over the music. "I feel like getting fucking pissed! We're all gonna get pissed tonight, Boys!" exclaimed Del, who drank way more than she was ever supposed to. The Boys raised their glasses and cheered. With that round of drinks downed, they ordered another round of shots.

The vibrant beat of the music reverberated around the bar, infusing the atmosphere with an electrifying energy. Laughter and chatter filled the air as the crowd embraced the lively ambiance. In the midst of it all, Jens, a spirited and witty redhead, raised his glass high, exclaiming, "Here's to us, the fiercest bitches in the house!" His friends cheered in agreement, and the evening turned into a lively exchange of stories and catch-ups.

Taller and older was Bob, whose grey stubble was as sharp as pins. He loved to rub his face against unsuspecting people, even strangers, despite that having once earned him a black eye from an incensed woman's boyfriend. His sense of personal space only came out when it most suited him. He often spoke in cliches and innuendos when he got drinking.

Thomas was jaded and impudent, his watery eyes always casting about, looking for an ass or chest on which to stop and rest. He was swishy but he never minced—not his gestures and not his words. He preferred young men and had mastered a university dating app, resulting in many dates that ended in blow jobs and promises to keep it secret. 'Doesn't matter, had sex,' he would joke after these brief and anonymous encounters.

The drinks were pouring generously, and a carefree spirit swept over the group. Even Maria, who abstained from alcohol, found herself carried away by the infectious vibe. Laughing and linking arms, they stumbled onto the dance floor, forming a tight circle of camaraderie. Bob and Thomas playfully clung to Del's shoulders while swaying to the rhythm of the music. Del, ever the life of the party, skillfully moved her wheelchair with the joystick, blending seamlessly with the dance.

"I love this song!" shouted Thomas, singing at the top of his lungs, and everyone joined in with gleeful enthusiasm. Their voices merged into a joyous chorus, embracing the delightful chaos of the moment.

Murphy's phone rang, and she quickly glanced at the number before signalling to Del and exiting the club to the relative quiet of the parking lot. The caller ID said 'Sun Flowers'.

"Hi Sun," she said with a smile on her face. "How are you?"

"Good, you?" Sun said.

"Good. Come join us. I'm on a rare night out with friends. The Sparkling Unicorn. Come for a drink," Murphy said. She was already doing the mental gymnastics of trying to explain her wife to her romantic interest without causing too much of a scene. This often resulted in the end of the blossoming relationship. But she really liked Sun and wanted her to meet friends and family.

In less than an hour, Sun arrived at the club and hesitantly walked in. She wore a pretty yellow summer dress and sandals, chosen specifically because she wanted to impress Murphy. She scanned the club but could not spot her date. It was Murphy who saw her first and came over to her.

"Sun!" she shouted over the music, giving her a hug.

"Caitlin, hi." Those were the only words she could get out before Murphy kissed her. As their lips met, the world around them seemed to fade away, leaving only the warmth and intensity of their embrace. The passionate kisses were electric, sending sparks of desire coursing through their bodies. With each gentle caress and probing touch, they were lost in the moment, lost in each other. The kisses were a dance, a rhythmic exchange of breath and passion that seemed to go on forever.

Until Thomas walked over. He couldn't resist interjecting, "Well, well, well, look who we have here! A couple of gorgeous souls attempting to create a cosmic connection with their kisses? I hate to break this captivating moment, but how about leaving some of that magic for later, unless you want to ignite some serious sparks in the room. But hey, don't mind us, go ahead and build your own little world right here. We'll just be patiently waiting for an opportunity to join in on the fun."

Sun blushed and separated herself from Murphy, then laughed a little. Once they arrived at the booth, everyone scooted around to make space as people introduced themselves. "Hello! Cheers!" they all shouted together.

"Who do we have here?" Bob asked, extending his meaty hand.

"Sun," she replied as her hand was enveloped by Bob's.

"Hi Sun. I'm Bob. This is Jens," he said as Jens smiled and raised his hand to wave over the server. He murmured a greeting that was drowned out by the pounding music. "You met Thomas already."

Sun nodded as Delaney shouted to be heard. "I am Delaney. Call me Del. They're my Boys," she said. "This is Maria. She's my PSW. And you know Caitlin, she's my wife." Sun cocked her head inquisitively and her eyes widened. Did she hear that correctly?

"Oh bitch, I thought I was your wife! It is all about you, isn't it? My my my, everyone is yours," Jens shouted with a laugh as he responded to his friend. "I'm Jens, her best friend."

"Bullshit! I am!" Bob yelled. A tray of drinks appeared suddenly, causing everyone to sit back in their seats to make it easier for the server to put the drinks down. "You want something? What are you drinking?" he asked Sun.

"I'll have a soda water please," Sun shouted to the server, who nodded and walked away.

"It's a good thing we drink so much to make up for the non-drinkers," Thomas said with a grin. "Do you come here often? You look familiar. Have we met?" he inquired.

"I've been here once or twice," Sun replied.

"You've probably bought flowers from her. Sun Flowers," Murphy said. "That's where I go now that Wildwood closed."

Thomas slammed the table. "Not Wildwood! It's closed? Oh my God, is there ever going to be an end to the loss? Oh, the humanity! When flowers die, there are no petals to be seen; The heavens themselves wail aloud upon the death of pansies," he laughed as he threw an arm over his eyes and feigned despair as he talked in an English accent. He grinned and shouted, "A rose, a rose, my kingdom for a rose!"

"Shut up, Shakespeare," Bob said as he playfully smacked him on the shoulder.

"Ah, fags and flowers," Jens said. "I never understood the thrill. What a waste of money. Here, buy me this expensive thing you could grow for free, and then it dies in a day. Yeah, thanks for that gift." He rolled his eyes to emphasize 'that.' Jens turned to Sun and added, "No offense."

"He's incredibly offensive. Ignore him," Delaney said with a laugh.

"I buy more than enough flowers to make up for these idiots," Murphy said. "Which reminds me, I need two bouquets tomorrow morning." That prompted Delaney to complain that she never received flowers from anyone. "Make that three bouquets then," Murphy said.

"Is that how you met?" Delaney asked Sun. The three Boys bent forward and eagerly, hoping to get some gossip.

Sun's drink appeared before her almost magically, and she was thankful to take a moment for a sip of water. She hadn't been prepared for such a boisterous group. "Yes, she came into the shop," she said.

"So you know she's a cop."

"A homicide detective," Murphy said.

"You know that and you still came to the club? Bold move!"

"It's an all-inclusive date, breakfast included," Delaney added, throwing up a hand to which Bob gave her a high-five.

"It's not like that," Murphy said.

"Not yet," Jens shouted with a laugh. "How many dates is it, then? Two? Three? You better get on it, you don't have much time left. Caitlin, Bob, anyone for another drink?"

Sun gave him a confused frown as the others raised their hands for drinks. You don't have much time left? "Stop it, you're scaring the poor woman," Delaney said defensively, reaching over to pat Sun's hand. She leaned in to speak to Sun, explaining that Murphy rarely made it past the third date. "She's a fantastic woman, she really is. She deserves a good woman, but the detective thing is hard. You will never be more important than the hunt."

"I don't think it's so much that," argued Thomas drunkenly. "I mean, she looks hot with her badge and gun. Not for me, I mean but-"

"Hey, Boys, I'm right here you know!" Murphy grinned as she held up her hands and pointed at herself. Everyone shouted, and Delaney shook in laughter, almost spilling her drink.

"We love her," Thomas added. "She's a good one."

"Enough! I want one of the bad ones on the dance floor. Dance time!"

As the night wore on, Sun and Murphy got bolder, dancing provocatively, their bodies moving in sync as they felt the rhythm of the music. Sun twirled around the dance floor, her dress swirling around her like a whirlwind. They were on the dancing floor in a sea of men who steadfastly ignored the women grinding and grabbing each other.

At various points, the Boys, Del and Maria appeared on the dance floor or in the periphery, not dancing so much as pulsing to the throbbing music. Murphy had stopped drinking long ago, having a one drink limit, and Sun had opted for water so she could drive home that night.

As the hours wore on, Del became tired, and it signalled an end to the evening. The Boys stumbled out into the night, still giddy from the festivities.

"Same time next week?" asked Jens, grinning from ear to ear.

"You know it!" exclaimed Del as the Boys poured themselves into a waiting cab.

Murphy walked over to the cab driver's window and pulled out a card. "If any of these guys gives you trouble," she said as she handed the driver her card, "You call me at the police station and let me know." Murphy did this every time they were together. It was her way of making sure the cabbie knew not to screw around with his fare. She believed it kept the men safe on their drunken ride home.

In the meantime, Maria had helped Del into the van and was waiting to see if Murphy was coming home.

"I'll head out on my own," Murphy said, hoping she would end up with Sun that evening. She leaned into the van and closed the door. "Later Del. Bye Maria!"

She walked over to Sun, and the two women watched as the van drove away. "Your friends are delightful. Wild. Confusing. But nice," Sun said as they strolled back to her car. "It has been a while since I hit the bar scene."

"They are wild. Don't take what they said too seriously," she said. Murphy looked at Sun and could feel the attraction. She could barely walk for the sexual aching in her body, her legs suddenly weak and untrustworthy. The parking lot seemed darker, more secretive, quieter as they approached the van. Stopping beside it, Sun leaned against the door and Murphy all but collapsed into her, kissing and touching her, breathing in her smothering fragrance of roses and wild flowers.

Her fingers tingled the moment they moved from cloth to flesh—just her arm, but Murphy moaned slightly, unintended and raw. Her lips pressed and moved and opened to make way for an inquisitive tongue to slip in, to taste and leave too suddenly. Her heart pounded madly in her ears and she could sense the slight hint of sweat forming on her brow. Murphy pressed herself into Sun, kissed her again and then pushed herself off slightly, with only a whisper of space between them.

"I'm a pretty straightforward person," she said hoarsely. "I'd like to spend the night with you," she said. Her eyes searched Sun's face, looked at her dark eyes flickering playfully in the streetlight. Murphy pressed her body against Sun, moving slightly with the beat of her own heart. She kissed her and whispered, "I want to make love with you all night, tonight."

Sun nodded. "All night," she said with a smile. Murphy pressed her body harder against Sun, kissing her lips, her neck, her shoulders. Her left hand roamed over Sun's dress, squeezing and massaging. With her right hand, she fished the phone out of her pocket. Pausing her passion, she tapped the 'Hotels For Everyone' app, quickly making a booking for a nearby room for the night.

"What are you doing?" Sun laughed as she realized Murphy was using her phone.

"Just booked a room at the Serene Inn. It's about two kilometres from here."

"Wow, you're well organized," Sun said. Murphy responded with a passionate kiss, running both hands over Sun's body. Sun then said softly, "Let's go."

As Sun drove, Murphy put her head back and closed her eyes. She breathed in deeply, and said, "You smell like flowers. Just…" She paused and stretched out her hand before her, holding her thumb and finger just slightly apart. "A little like flowers."

Murphy eagerly unlocked the door with the app and stepped into the room, flicking on the light. She quickly drew the curtains while Sun locked the door behind them. Murphy stepped closer to Sun, drawn by her eyes. Murphy inclined her face down and at first pressed her lips on Sun's. For a long time they stood in an embrace, hands roaming, lips exploring. Breathing deeply, they undressed each other as if their lives depended on it.

She slipped her tongue inside Sun's mouth, demanding and full of lust as the last of the clothes fell to the floor. She could feel herself melting into Sun as they lay on the bed. Sun straddled her as she reached out and clasped her, pulling her closer, making love on the hotel bed. The soft weight of Sun's body on hers was incredible, erotic, and enticing. The blood roared in her ears as Sun caressed her and stroked her skin, setting her on fire. She inhaled Sun's smells of roses and sweat. She wanted more, wanted to breathe her in, to eat her whole. Orgasms flowed through her and she hoped they would never end.

Both women were breathing heavily, sweat dripping down Sun's face. She pulled her hair back and sat up, resting on Murphy's hips.

Murphy reached up, kissing Sun at first delicately, and then fiercely. She pulled her into her arms, on to her body, her hands moving and touching and teasing. Breast to breast, her hand running down Sun's body until, at last, she pushed Sun on to her back.

Sun's eyes were fluttering, as if sending a secret code, a secret map to places of pleasure, encouraging Murphy to continue. The sounds of breath and bliss caressed Murphy's ears, guiding her kisses, directing her lips. She nudged Sun's hips with her nose, urging her to rise, to meet her tongue. She opened her eyes to see the beauty of rapture, soft and open. She needed to bear witness to their unity at this moment. She ran her fingers through Sun's dark triangle of coarse hair and kissed her tenderly until Sun's fingers finally found her face and pulled her up, kissing her lips and sighing softly.

After hours of making love, Murphy fell into a contented sleep, her arms wrapped around Sun.

CHAPTER ELEVEN

Murphy woke up at five-thirty that morning and slipped quietly out of bed. The morning was cool for June and the golden sunrise was lighting up the room through the slit between the thick grey curtains that covered the wide windows. The cream-coloured walls glowed with light and the warm undertones of the oak furniture gleamed with a subtle reddish hue. She dressed quickly, called a cab to the motel, and then sat gently on the side of the bed. Sun still smelled like roses and Murphy yearned to pluck them from her. "Hey, I've got to go." She brushed Sun's hair to the side and leaned in for a kiss.

"What time is it?" Sun asked as she blinked lazily and stretched out her arms around Murphy.

"About five-thirty."

"Crap, I have to get going," Sun said as she quickly sat up. "I see you have the same idea."

"Yeah, my cab will be here in a few minutes."

"I can give you a lift," Sun said with a smile and a kiss. Murphy wrapped her arms around her, kissing her and running her hands lightly over her skin.

"We'd never make it to your car," Murphy laughed when she finally pulled her face away. "Gotta go. This was... this was more, eh?"

Sun nodded. "Yes, more. Bye."

Murphy reluctantly stood up, straightened her hair and left, saying, "Once you leave, the door will automatically lock." Walking through the inn lobby, she wondered how soon they would see each other again. Life in homicide could be all-consuming and unpredictable. Although the murder rate in Muskoka was manageable, it was certainly not slow. Sometimes there would be no active case for a couple of weeks and then bam! A slew of murders would explode in a day or two.

Her homicide unit did not work on every homicide in Muskoka. Depending on where the murder happened, or the victim was found, it might go to the OPP's Violent Death unit. That team investigated anything on provincial highways and lands, and it often caused a jurisdictional squabble with the executive levels of the Muskoka Municipal Police. Murphy never minded handing over those cases, there were always more coming. If a homicide occurred on federal land, the RCMP took over. If it was on tribal land, it was almost always a collection of agencies working together.

Murphy clambered into the taxi, gave the driver the address, and began browsing her email on her phone. She was grateful they had not contacted her overnight, but she still had work to do. On the ride home, she began looking through more applications for the vacant liaison position. She scanned through an application from Brian Dunn. He had completed BA exams and interviews, but did not hold a final degree. Dunn had served three years at a charity and seemed average. Murphy had nothing against average.

She tapped a few more links and was taken to the application from Sarah Hillman. She was currently a counsellor with the Gingham Centre, which offered a range of programs that help young people to address past struggles, including group care treatment, independent living skills, day treatment, and sexual abuse treatment programs. She had a degree.

She impressed Murphy, and she dragged that email into a folder called Possible, then looked at the next application.

The last one was from Nabil Haile, from the Men's, Women's and Family Addiction Treatment Services. She had a master's degree and was a seasoned veteran. Although nothing suggested she worked specifically with the Indigenous communities, Murphy moved her application into the Possible folder.

These applications needed more scrutiny than she could give sitting in the back of a cab, looking at her phone.

The cab pulled up to the Delany Brice Gallery and Studio, and Murphy thanked the driver for the ride. "The tip is in the app," she said as she got out. She walked in to the sounds of breakfast being prepared. "Good morning," Murphy said softly.

"Good morning, Caitlin," Maria replied. Maria worked a split shift for Del. She would arrive every morning at five, cook breakfast and help Del dress and prepare for the day. By seven she would have prepared an easy to eat lunch and snack, and then went home. Maria would arrive back at five in the evening, prepare dinner, clean, help Del with her colostomy bag, administer medications, and then would usually be gone by eleven. While they would normally split the job between two people, Maria and Del had arranged for just Maria, no other support workers. It meant more money for Maria and consistency for Del.

"Del is just waking up. She will eat in about half an hour. Would you like to join us?"

"Yeah, yeah, would love to, but can't. I have to get to the office," Murphy said, grabbing a piece of toast and headed up the stairs.

"I did your laundry last night. It's laid out on your bed. There was a pamphlet in your back pocket, I put it on the nightstand," Maria said. "Sad business," she added.

"Thanks, Maria," Murphy said as she continued up the stairs. Quickly stripping, she jumped into the shower and reluctantly let the scents of sex wash off her body. God, that was good, she thought to herself, and then laughed. In a few minutes, she was drying herself off and walking over to the nightstand. There was the pamphlet about the reservation that she had picked up at the road blockade. "Sad business," she said to herself, repeating Maria's comment. She was about to open the pamphlet when her phone rang. She peeked at the clock. It was now six forty-two. Her phone rang again.

"Murphy," she answered.

It was Parker. "Boss, are you coming in? There's something you need to see."

"Am I coming in? I always come in Michael. What a... yes, I'll be in shortly. I'm on my way," she said. She hung up and dropped the phone. "Am I coming in?" she repeated to herself. "Idiot," she said out loud. Murphy quickly dressed in the clothes Maria had laid out for her. They felt cool and crisp on her skin. Shoving both her phone and the pamphlet in her pocket, and securing her firearm and badge, she bounded down the stairs. "Gotta run," she said, sticking her head into Del's bedroom and blowing her a kiss. The Brawler roared down the highway as she headed into work.

"Michael, what have you got for me?" Murphy said as she walked into the atelier.

"First, I received written permission from Violet Mercado to use the password manager and access whatever sites might be there. It arrived at... four thirty-eight this morning," Hamilton said.

Parker picked up the narrative. "I logged into the app online after we got in this morning, and did a quick look. There are three sites of interest I checked right off the bat. One is Cryptvids, where he posts his Sasquatch videos. There doesn't appear to be any drafts, only the same published videos we've seen." Parker rapidly clicked through a series of screams on his computer.

"The second is online photo storage. It looks like he uploaded his phone photographs on Friday night. The problem is, there are 1,427 images from Friday. At least seventy percent seem to be photos at Spalding. It will take a long time to go through them to look for anything relevant. They have no GPS metadata in the photos, unfortunately."

"But you're looking through them, right?" said Murphy. She had looked over Parker's shoulder and saw a blur of greens and browns, leaves, grass and trees.

Parker held up a finger. "But this," he said, "this is what I wanted to show you. It's 'Mes Errances', a GPS app that tracks your walk!"

"Like that penis app of yours?" Murphy asked with a smile. Hamilton burst out laughing, and Parker grinned, blushing.

"Sounds like a party. What did I miss?" Girard said, walking into the office.

"Look at this," Parker said, as he clicked the computer mouse. "An exact map of every step Jose took on Friday at Spalding and here, his Saturday movements right up to Sunny Lake. Look at Friday with the topological overlay. I've zoomed in."

"Oh wow," Girard said in admiration as he joined the rest of the team around Parker's desk. On screen was a map of whites and greens, and the words Spalding Conservation Area. A long, criss-crossing squiggly red line showed where Jose had walked that day. The screen showed he had walked thirty-one kilometres over the course of seven hours and thirty-two minutes. Also on the map were a half dozen orange rectangles with numbers.

"These are GPS coordinates. And these show the notes for each label. He tagged his app with everything he found of interest," Parker explained as he opened one of the orange labels.

"No way!" Murphy shouted excitedly as she jabbed her finger at the screen. The text read 'Sasquatch bone' and had the exact latitude and longitude coordinates. "He's told us exactly where he found the bone?" Her hands were tightly closed as if the information was something tangible that someone had hid in the darkness for her to find and now, having touched it, she was hanging on for dear life.

"Yes boss. The other labels don't seem to be relevant. It's poop, fur, a footprint, two piles of berries and a tree structure."

"Adam, coordinate with the Forensic Unit, make sure you get Dr. Chen's team. Cleo, coordinate with Search and Rescue. I want a one hundred metre search around the leg bone coordinates. If need be, we can expand the search area. Good work, people, excellent work!"

Murphy turned to look at the board. "Michael, update the map, please. Fantastic." She had a solid plan to move forward, and that brought her new confidence and a sharp feeling of power. She heard the phone in her office ring. "Get on it, tell them to keep me updated," she said as she headed into her office.

The Chief was on the other end of the line. Despite his stature as head of the Muskoka Municipal Police, he was quick to change his nature when he imagined it might improve his political standing. His aspirations to become a mayor or even, if the gods allowed, a member of parliament, were well known. He was shrewd and always prepared to propel his career by looking for the media's interest in every story. Jose Mercado's murder had garnered just one column inch in the local newspaper. He wanted an update on all her open cases.

Murphy was explaining the Mercado murder when he suddenly cut her off. The local newspaper was requesting a quote on drug bust that happened that morning and he brusquely hung up.

Her crew were still getting the Search Unit and Forensics team members to the GPS coordinates, so she had some time to review the murder-suicide case. "Cleo? Let's talk about the Alexander/Battiste case!" she shouted. Murphy microwaved some water for instant coffee and was rhythmically stirring it, mesmerized by the clink, clink, clink as she swirled the spoon. Hamilton walked into her office and sat down, folder in hand. Murphy put her feet up on a small stool she had brought in for exactly this purpose. She used to put her feet on the desk until one day the Chief walked in, and that was the end of that.

"What can you tell me?" Murphy asked.

"At five-thirty-eight a.m., a call came into 911 reporting two people passed out on the front lawn. At five-fifty-one a.m., two volunteer firefighters advised they were on the scene and they found the two deceased. The firefighters were Frank Hickson and Jeremy Fields, the deceased were Beverly Alexander and Matthew Battiste. Police were dispatched. Constables Blackstone and Sayer arrived at six-twenty a.m. Then Forensics arrived at six-forty-eight a.m. Alexander was shot in the back, Battiste under the chin. The coroner has the cause of death for Alexander as homicide, Battiste as suicide. It was the same gun. Only Battiste's partial fingerprint was found on the gun, and Forensics said it was covered in his blood and brain matter. Firefighters Hickson and Fields claimed the grass was on fire, so they hosed the area down, but there's no sign of fire anywhere," Hamilton said.

"No mention of fire in the 911 call?"

"No boss. I don't think there was a fire, but the firefighters are sticking to that story. It was twenty-nine minutes between when the firefighters arrived and police arrived, but only a twenty-five-minute drive. Battiste had a phone, but Alexander did not have hers on her body. We found the phone by the house. Dr. Smith reports Alexander had a blood alcohol level of .32 and Battiste of .4, both very high. The porch had fifty-three beer cans on it, and Dr. Smith tested five beer cans, including one with blood on it. Preliminary DNA matches our victims for saliva on the cans, and Battiste only on the blood."

Murphy pursed her lips and frowned. She wondered what the hell the firefighters were up to. "They watered down the scene at some point. Okay. What was inside the house?"

Hamilton informed Murphy that she had the landlord unlock the home. As she described it, the house was in complete disarray, with dirty dishes heaped in the kitchen sink and takeout containers scattered on the table. In the living room, empty beer cans and cigarette butts covered the floor, giving it a messy appearance. Moreover, she said, she stumbled upon a small amount of weed placed on a coffee table. The bedroom wasn't any better, with clothes strewn about, intermingled with broken glass from a bottle. A stained mattress rested on the floor, surrounded by heaps of garbage in every corner.

"There are some traces of blood, but the Forensics Unit think it is older than three months, possibly a few years ago. The landlord said he has had several problem tenants in the house and he doesn't paint between tenants. The Forensics Unit did a cursory analysis of fingerprints. There are a hundred different prints, probably because it is a rental. No signs of forced entry, no sign of burglary, no suicide note. It is hard to tell what might be signs of a fight, and just, well, the junk. I found a bank statement. Alexander had a debit card. Nothing unusual on the statement. I have contacted the bank to see if there's been any activity on it since her death and there is nothing. One person I spoke to near the scene reported hearing gunfire, but wasn't sure what time it was and didn't look outside. Someone else said they heard shouting, but again, did not look outside."

"We have a couple on the porch drinking. They argue according to neighbours. She storms off, he shoots her, kills himself. Her phone was inside?" Murphy asked.

"No, we recovered the phone outside. It had fallen into the dirt at the edge of the porch stairs. It had only Alexander's fingerprints on it. It did not have a passcode on it, so Michael ran through it. No text messages suggesting anyone was coming to visit. I called everyone she had contacted within the last two days. It all seemed like idle chit chat. One call was to a local pot shop-"

"Not Helter Skelter, was it?" Murphy asked.

"No boss, it was Potassium. Michael called them, but they don't remember her call. They said people call all the time about opening hours, whether they have a particular brand, that kind of thing. The amount of pot we found was small, personal use only. We also checked Battiste's phone. He called Mr. Alexander that night. The call lasted thirty seconds. Mr. Alexander earlier told you Battiste was asking for money and he turned him down. Again, nothing in the text messages to suggest there was anyone coming over, nothing stood out. I went through photos on both phones as well. Nothing from that day."

"Okay then. Neighbours report arguing and gunfire, but no one called 911 until someone on their way to work saw the couple in the grass and called. We have first responders wash the scene down before anyone got there, which might explain the time delay before contacting the police. You said the family said there might be some cash, but you found none," Murphy said. She sighed and rubbed her face. "Have they released the scene? The family wants access to the house."

"Yes, I contacted the Alexanders, and put them in touch with the landlord," Hamilton said.

Murphy dismissed Hamilton, drained the last of her coffee and headed out. She had flowers to drop off.

Murphy smiled at Sun when she walked into the flower shop. She could not get enough of her. She wanted to hold her, kiss her, smell her, taste her again. She leaned over the counter and whispered, "Do you have a few minutes? Somewhere private?" Her voice was strained with desire.

Sun smiled and her eyes softened. "Come," she said, extending her hand to lead the way. Just the single word made Murphy breathless. She led Murphy into the cramped office, with little space between the desk and a table at which Sun ate lunch. Murphy grabbed Sun around the waist and lifted her onto the table, kissing her hard as she did. Her body ached. She wanted Sun, she wanted her soft weight, to watch her face as sweat formed across her forehead and dropped onto her. Nothing but this moment existed as she ran her hands along Sun's breasts and stomach, deftly unbuttoning her shirt and slipping her hand in. She was breathing heavily, hungrily. She rubbed and squeezed and pinched every piece of flesh she felt.

Suddenly, someone walked through the front door of the store, causing the bell on the door to ring out. Sun smiled and pushed Murphy away with a kiss. She clambered off the table, buttoned her shirt and straightened her hair. "Another time," she said to Murphy as she took a deep breath and walked to the front of the store. Murphy cleared her head and tiptoed to the sales counter.

"I need three bouquets, please," she said softly. "The small ones."

Sun looked incredulous. "I'm sorry, what? For, uh, for work?" she asked. Murphy nodded. "Three?" Sun asked. She glanced at the other customer and leaned forward. "You made out with me and you want the bouquets for three murder victims? New victims?" she whispered. "Is that what you were thinking of back there?" Sun was horrified.

"What? No. It's just about the only time I don't think about it, about work," Murphy whispered. Sun gave her a doubtful look, then turned away. She quickly prepared a trio of white and yellow flower bouquets, each wrapped in string.

"That will be $56.95," Sun said as she laid the flowers on the counter for Murphy. With only perfunctory conversation, Murphy paid for the flowers and left, looking back to see Sun helping the other customer. She wondered for a moment why Sun would be so vaguely accusatory. She had asked for the flowers last night.

Murphy pulled up to the house where Alexander and Battiste died. There was a dark blue older model extended cab truck in the driveway, its dents and dings telling the story of rough years. It was palpably different in this neighbourhood, as if despair tainted the air itself, streaking it with a grittiness that cut the teeth.

She parked on the street and grabbed two bouquets to lay for the victims. Hoping not to disturb whoever was in the house, she crossed the front yard to lay the flowers on the lawn, but stopped in her tracks when the front door opened and a loud voice shouted, "Detective!"

Ellen Longboat stepped out onto the porch, holding the door open as Beverly Alexander's parents joined her. "Hello Detective, what news have you got?" she asked.

Murphy smiled and walked toward the porch, flowers extended. "Feel free to call me Caitlin. I would like to give you these flowers and tell you again how sorry I am."

Ellen took the flowers and handed them to Susan, Beverly's mother. "Thank you, Detective. What news have you got?" she repeated.

"Please, call me Caitlin," Murphy said.

"I prefer Detective. And one more time, what news have you got?" Ellen's tone was one a mother would use with a reluctant child as she stood impatiently, hands on hips.

Murphy's mind wandered to a dozen reasons Ellen might be so cold to her, but all quickly slipped away. She did not know Ellen, had no interactions, had never accused a loved one of murder. It was not the first time someone had instantly disliked her, but

Murphy could not quite place the other mood Ellen seemed to carry. Nothing specific had caused it. She had said nothing specific she was aware of. It unsettled her for no other reason than she could not place it.

"There isn't really any news. I came to drop off flowers. The investigation is ongoing," Murphy said. She answered all of their questions vaguely, explaining that Beverly's body would be released soon by the coroner. They had located her phone and the police would turn it over when they were done with it. They found no cash in the house.

"Why is it taking so long, Detective?" Ellen asked. "Is there any help for Susan and William?"

"I... Yes, we have Beverly's phone and should be able to return it to you soon. And, uh, the Alexanders need help with rent. Is that right? They can apply to the Victim Compensation Fund. It's a federal service, you can find it online. And, uh, do you want me to send a Family Liaison Officer? If I can get their address or phone number, I'll have a Liaison contact them, get them Compensation Fund information and help with the application." Murphy wondered why Ellen flustered her so much.

"I know about the Compensation Fund application. We don't need the Liaison. They have always been useless, Detective," Ellen said.

"We have a position open for a new Liaison, you are welcome to apply," Murphy said as Ellen turned to go into the house.

"Me? Work for police? Not my thing. But I hope you hire someone who knows more than a passing knowledge on local Indigenous politics, economics and culture. Someone who can offer more than a pat answer about grief and self-care." And with that, she walked into the house.

Murphy shook her head and walked back to her Brawler. "Yeah yeah," she mumbled to herself. "Some people just don't like cops."

CHAPTER TWELVE

Girard had called her to advise that they found skeletal remains less than two metres from the GPS coordinates listed on Mercado's app. When Murphy arrived, she saw a half-dozen different media people all waiting for information that no one yet had. She quickly checked herself in her visor mirror and exited the Brawler to speak with media. "We are conducting a recovery search in the forest," she said. "When that search is complete, you will be updated with what, if anything, was found in the area."

The atmosphere was intense as reporters gathered closer, eagerly anticipating a chance to question the detective. Cameras were trained on Murphy as microphones and cell phones were shoved into her face.

"Was this a homicide?"

"Any leads on possible suspects?"

"Detective Murphy, can you tell us the victim's identity?"

"What weapon was used?"

"Is the public in danger?"

"How long do you expect the investigation to take?"

The barrage of questions continued, each reporter trying to outdo the other, shouting out their queries and talking over one another in the quest for exclusive information. But Murphy stood her ground, maintaining her silence. Her expression was unwavering, giving away nothing. The clamor around her only grew, as the reporters pushed for answers, hoping to get the scoop.

"An official statement is forthcoming. Excuse me."

The forest seemed vast and indistinct, with trees that towered high above and roots that twisted into the rocky terrain below. The air was crisp and clean, with the smell of pine wafting through the breeze. The path was rough, with boggy sections deep enough to lose a boot if you weren't careful.

Amidst the trees, there was a quiet stillness, broken only by the occasional wisp of a voice carried along the rustling of leaves in the wind. The forest floor was littered with fallen branches and rocks covered by a thick carpet of greenery.

The trees themselves were a wonder to behold. White birch trees stood tall and proud, their paper-like bark peeling away to reveal a smooth, creamy trunk. Thick black spruce trees towered overhead, their branches stretching out like fingers toward the sky. And everywhere there were white pine trees, with their needles shining like emeralds in the sun. Moose and caribou would have roamed the area freely if not for the buzz of humanity brought by death.

In the forest's heart was a small gathering of people, surrounded by a ring of plastic police tape. Girard and Parker stood outside the ring, watching Dr. Chen and his team work the scene. Hamilton stood further away, staring into the woods.

Here, the ground was soft and mossy, with tiny wildflowers peeking up from the ground. It was a peaceful spot, a place of stillness in the thick wildness of the forest. The maple tree roots wove their way through small boulders, arching under and over, creating perfect natural refuges for all manner of small creatures.

The sun was casting a warm glow over everything around her. It seemed like a good place to leave the flowers she had brought with her, away from the calculating gaze of the media, but still close enough to appease her soul. She quietly laid the flowers by a tree.

Dr. Chen was on his hands and knees inside the small cordoned off area, his team standing on the periphery, taking photographs and writing notes.

Murphy's eyes scanned the area, looking for any clues, but the area looked like it hadn't been disturbed for decades, save for a few wanderers like Jose. She crouched near Dr. Chen, careful not to disturb his work, and waited for him to speak. Then finally came one of his peculiar statements. "The beat of the butterfly's wings is proven remarkably powerful. The beat," he said.

"Dr. Chen, what can you tell me?" she asked, ignoring his butterfly comment.

Dr. Chen told Murphy that a small, incomplete skeleton was found in a hollow, with tree roots loosely entwined in the bones. There were small fragments of cloth, remnants of what appeared to be pants and a shirt. At first look, the age of these bones was consistent with the leg bone found by Jose Mercado. "I believe she was placed here as she is head down, so although I have not retrieved her fully, I would tentatively conclude a suspicious death. Head down."

Murphy sighed and nodded, then rejoined Girard and Parker. "Why would anyone take her this far into the forest? Most dumped victims aren't carried into the forest this far," Girard said. "And what are the chances that this could be a body dumping ground?"

"Bite your tongue," Murphy cautioned as she looked around. "I guess we must consider the possibility there are more bodies. Michael, speak to the Search and Rescue lead, have them bring out ground penetrating radar to conduct a search only, say, one and a half, maybe two metres down. Cleo..." Murphy paused.

Hamilton was still standing apart from the group, arms out in a Jesus Christ pose, looking first from her left to her right, and back again. Her mahogany-coloured curls shimmered in the sunlight, her sunglasses glinting as she moved her head. "She looks like an angel," Girard said with a smirk. Murphy chuckled and punched him playfully on the shoulder.

"Boss, over here," Hamilton shouted out, finally relaxing her arms. The team headed toward her. "Look," she said as she gestured from left to right past the scene. Each team member looked around, but then looked at each other in confusion. "This area, about three and a half, maybe four metres wide. Do you see it? Look, the vegetation is different, the trees are different, smaller, thinner." She waited for a moment while the others struggled to see what was obvious to her. "I think it's an old logging road. And maybe the killer's easy way into this area."

"I don't see it, but let's check. Find any old maps from maybe fifty to what, one hundred years ago? This could explain why a body was in the middle of nowhere, but it also opens a lot of potential problems. The killer could have been a logger or just used this road. Gah! Cleo, I appreciate you found this, but you've made our work a lot harder," Murphy said. "Not to worry, though. Let's get to the office and get working. Adam, try tracking down every logging company within twenty-five kilometres of the area that was active between, say, 1970 to 1975. Thanks everyone," she added.

On the way back, Murphy called Chief Valencia's office and arranged an appointment through his administrative assistant. It took more than an hour to drive to the MPP headquarters, and on the drive, she listened to The Tragically Hip, a refreshing change from the murder music she had been listening to. The songs fit the Canadian geography well, and it felt right; the land figured heavily in this latest case.

Murphy pulled into the parking lot and parked. She threw an instant coffee packet into her pocket, changed into her regular shoes, and brushed off her pants to make herself a little more presentable.

Headquarters was a mid-rise building in the centre of town. They designed the exterior of the building with a traditional police aesthetic featuring a prominent entrance, large windows, and a 'Muskoka Municipal Police' sign over the doorway.

Inside was a large reception area, with a front desk staffed by a uniformed officer who sat behind a plexiglass window. There were uncomfortable metal benches for visitors, and a thick metal door separating the police from the public.

Murphy swiped her employee badge through the reader and the door clicked open. It clanged behind her as she walked through and up the stairs to the Chief's office. "Hi Sandra," Murphy said.

"Detective Inspector Murphy. The Chief is delayed. He asked that you please take a seat. He will be another five or ten minutes," Sandra said. Murphy nodded and headed to the large kitchen to boil some water. She turned on the kettle and opened the sleek cupboard door, choosing a plain blue mug for her coffee. She sat in a large, comfortable leather chair near the Chief's office and waited.

It did not take long for Murphy to become impatient. She had little patience for the Chief. She fidgeted a bit before remembering the pamphlet she had previously picked up at the roadblock. She opened the dog-eared and wrinkled pamphlet and read.

The glossy pamphlet was to support reparations for the Algonquin people of the Tiny Flowers Reservation, asking for both a formal apology and financial support. In 1962, a wood processing company, Stockman Timber, went out of business after thirty years, and instead of cleaning up, they buried large amounts of their waste nearby which polluted the groundwater.

In 1971, the Federal Government determined that all fifty-six people on Tiny Flowers Reservation were being poisoned by the water and needed to be moved. Children under the age of eighteen, twelve kids all told, were sent to live in homes with white people where they had access to municipal water. They sent everyone else to various reservations across Canada. Once the people were off the land, the land was appropriated and sold.

Impacted soil was used to create perimeter berms, covered by a metre of clean soil, and they tied a new irrigation system into the municipal lines. The Tiny Flowers Reservation became the Goldfinch Greens golf course.

Murphy shook her head. This was why the protesters were blocking the road to the golf course. She flipped the pamphlet over and kept reading. Of the fifty-six people moved from the reservation, the 'Justice For Tiny Flowers' group said only nine people, four of whom were quite elderly, were still alive, and all of whom continued to suffer from the effects of arsenic poisoning from industry waste.

Murphy froze when she read the words 'arsenic poisoning.' She flipped the pamphlet over again and reread it, wondering if this was what happened to the girl.

"DI Murphy." The Chief's voice boomed, jarring her out of her thoughts.

"Sir," she responded as she quickly stood. She followed him into the office, standing at attention until he invited her to sit.

"You have ten minutes," Chief Wayne Valencia said. "Go."

"Yes sir. Last Sunday, the body of a young Toronto man was found in Sunny Lake, stabbed. We have been following up on an old human leg bone, a femur, found among his possessions. He found it in the Spalding Conservation Area. We have found a skeleton in Spalding that appears to match the femur. It's a child. She appears to have been there for about fifty years. I think a press release is in order, something very broad to let people know we are in the area, but no meaningful details."

"So, someone was just killed after finding the bone of someone who was killed fifty years ago?"

"We don't know how she died, sir. We are still investigating the scene, and we don't actually have a cause of death yet on the skeletal remains. Dr. Chen is working on it. We are using Search and Rescue GPR to check for other bodies in the area. It's possible a seri-"

Valencia held up his hand to silence her. "Do not say serial killer. I don't want to hear about a serial killer from fifty years ago. Have you found any other bodies yet? No? Good. No other bodies. No cause of death? There is not a lot to report, factually. You can't even be sure it relates to the recent murder, can you? Okay, meet with that social media woman, you know, who works with our media relations. Twenty words, tops. Just something basic for our social media accounts. Got it? Schedule your therapist appointment through Sandra. For your entire team."

"Yes sir," Murphy said. She had not bothered the Chief with the details and theories. She simply wanted to make sure he would not be blindsided once word of the search got out. After being dismissed by the Chief, she spoke to his secretary. "Sandra, can you please set up appointments with the police therapist for me and my team?"

It was policy for the Muskoka Municipal Police that any police officer involved in the investigation of the death of a minor child under the age fourteen attend a therapy session. It could be a detective, a search and rescue officer or a beat cop, whether homicide, suicide,

accident, or undetermined. If the dead person was under fourteen, the investigators had
to attend a twenty-minute session.

"Sure thing. I'll email you," she said.

Murphy headed to Media Relations. Tanisha Jones sat at her desk, staring at her
computer screen while she listened to Murphy explain what she was looking for. "Too
much. Chief Valencia wants twenty words you said? Hang on." She typed quickly, her
long nails clicking against the keys. She read the post out loud.

'POLICE INVESTIGATION: Spalding Conservation Area, 3:07 pm. Search and
Rescue unit assisting with a recovery. Unknown circumstances. Investigation remains
ongoing.' That's twenty words. Okay?" Tanisha said.

Murphy agreed and, after a few pleasantries, she was on her way to her own office on
the next floor down. Once sitting at her desk, she called the phone number on the back of
the Justice For Tiny Flowers pamphlet. Murphy laughed when the person answering the
phone said, "This is Justice For Tiny Flowers. How may I help you?" He made it sound
like he was working for an insurance company.

"I'm interested in finding out more about the Tiny Flowers Reservation. I read about
it in a pamphlet. About the people and the arsenic poisoning," she said. "I'm wondering
if I could speak to whomever researched this for you?"

"That's me," the young man said. "Lethabo Zibi. I am the researcher."

Murphy arranged to meet Lethabo at his apartment above a hardware store on Muskoka Road 4 North to discuss his research. With her team working diligently away at the
station, she knew they would come up with great information, but this potential link to
arsenic had to be followed up.

Murphy drove to Muskoka Road 4 North, past small houses on big lots littered
with cars and overgrown bushes. She listened to Drake as she considered several new
possibilities. Did the person who killed Spalding Doe, which she had decided was the
name for the girl, also kill Jose? If so, why hadn't the killer moved her remains? Certainly,
it would have been easier to move a few bones than to murder a young man and dump
him in a lake.

The disposal of Jose's body suggested it was more than just a random robbery. Most of
his items were in the hotel room, and aside from the drugs, had little value. The tattooists
had an alibi, although it was weak. The people at the café had no reason to kill him, and
although there were some inconsistencies, it was nothing out of the ordinary when talking
with older people.

Murphy felt like she was just spinning her wheels, chasing after an old story hoping to shed light on a new murder. The WeSee GPS app instructed her to drive past the cemetery and then, finally, into a parking lot for three stores—a hardware store, gas station and an outfitter. Murphy parked close to the hardware store and was greeted by a short Black man with round glasses and a high bald fade haircut.

"Lethabo Zibi," he said with a smile as he extended his hand.

"Detective Inspector Caitlin Murphy, Muskoka Municipal Police," she said as she shook his hand.

"Ah, police. Come up, come up," Lethabo welcomed her as he opened the door and ascended the stairs. "I'm happy to show you my work."

Murphy walked into his apartment and was greeted by a wall that looked as much like a link board as anything. "Impressive, yes?" Lethabo said.

Lethabo explained he was a PhD student from the University of Johannesburg, studying the relationship between the Canadian Indigenous Truth and Reconciliation Commission and Indigenous survivors of the Sixties Scoop, and its applicability to remedies for historic victims of the apartheid regime in South Africa.

"I have been here for two years, off and on, researching the Truth and Reconciliation Movement and the Tiny Flowers Reservation. Let me say, the Canadian government's model of restorative justice is admirable on paper, but empty in the hand," he said.

He spent ten minutes explaining his research process, the Freedom of Information requests for documents, and tracking the people who had been displaced.

"So you know who those people were?" Murphy asked. "You have names, do you?"

"There were fifty-six people. I have records from the Departments of Indian Relocation and Indian Child Welfare, which are now in the Department of Indigenous Services. I have been able to locate, one way or another, forty of the forty-four adults and eight of the twelve children. Most are now deceased." Lethabo shuffled through some file folders on his table and produced a pile of thick blue folders.

"So, you have a list of names?" Murphy asked hopefully. "And birthdates?"

"Names, not birthdates. But I have their age at the time of relocation," Lethabo replied. "The government paperwork from back then was improperly completed. Very poor indeed. My research shows that employees of the Department of Indian Child Welfare were lax, and based on the notes written in margins of some forms, overtly racist and hostile."

Lethabo showed Murphy the forms for the children. Many had only a single name, an age, and a code for where they were relocated. He apologized for not having decoded the locations, and explained that it seemed to be the work largely of one employee, based on the illegible signature on the bottom of many of the forms. At Murphy's request, he showed her the forms for girls on the Reservation.

"These two, two girls aged ten and thirteen, have you located them?" Murphy asked.

"Let me see," Lethabo said as he turned to his laptop. "Which names?" he asked.

"Buffalo and Horn," she replied.

"Oh yes, the Buffalo family, that was sad. Father George died in 1976, mother Eleanor died in 1982. The son Billy died in 1995. Yes, Abigail Buffalo died in 1996. They sent Abigail and Billy to the same foster home, then they were moved to separate homes."

"And what about Horn?"

"Horn, Horn, Horn," Lethabo repeated as he searched through files and folders on this laptop. "No, I was never able to find her after her placement." Murphy felt her pulse suddenly surge, wondering if she had found the girl still unaccounted for.

"She... Yes, she stayed with the same family as the Buffalo kids. All three sent together to one family, though I don't know which one," he said. "I have not located Horn after her placement."

Lethabo checked both digitally scanned and paper files at Murphy's request, producing DICW438 forms for all three children. They were the foster placement forms and, he warned her, particularly vitriolic. Each form had the 'male' and 'female' checkbox scribbled out, and someone had written in 'brave' and 'squaw'. In the box marked 'Special Consideration', each had the notation, 'dirty, aggressive Indian.'

The checkbox for 'Addl. Funds' was checked, which Lethabo explained meant the foster parents would get double the usual payment. They sent each child to the foster family noted as number twenty-three, and each form had the same employee signature.

"That's it. That's all I have on Horn. The name is Horn. In 1971, she was a girl aged ten, and they fostered her with an unidentified family with the other children, Billy and Abigail, who are now dead. Do not put stock in the 'Special Consideration' box. These kids were suffering from arsenic poisoning. The government knew. That's why they were put into the system. Chronic arsenic poisoning can cause problems for children. Memory, behaviour, coordination, all affected."

Murphy sat for a moment, considering the possibility that her victim was Horn, a ten-year-old girl, suffering from poisoning, ripped away from her family, then gone, possibly dumped into a tree hollow, waiting fifty years to be discovered. "Well, shit," she finally said. "Okay, can I get copies of those three forms from you?"

"Yes, of course. I hope one day they can use my research in a lawsuit against the Canadian federal government for reparations," he said solemnly. "And of course, there is my PhD thesis."

Murphy's head swirled as she drove home from her meeting. She was getting ahead of herself as they did not get have confirmation that these skeletal remains exhibited the same chronic poisoning as the femur. She was at once excited that she had some evidence to work with, and sad at the untimely end of a little girl's life. It would be difficult to wait until morning, when the report was in and other research concluded. As she drove into her driveway, she knew she would need her art therapy tonight.

CHAPTER THIRTEEN

Murphy kicked her shoes off and threw her keys on the kitchen table. "Honey! I'm home!" she shouted.

"In here!" Del shouted back. At the far side of the converted house, closest to the parking, was her art gallery, then behind it, her art studio. Behind that, a wall and a locked door leading to her living quarters—a living room and bedroom, all in one spacious, comfortable place. On the other side where Murphy always entered was a kitchen leading to her living space, bathroom and the stairs leading up. Del and Maria were watching television.

"Hey gorgeous, hi Maria," Murphy said, greeting both women as she flopped down on the couch beside Del. "Watcha watchin'?" she asked.

'Love Stories From Paradise', your favourite," Del teased, eliciting a groan from Murphy. She hated romance reality TV shows. "Good day? You're home kind of early."

"Good and bad. I think it's an art therapy night."

"Today sucked, eh?" Del asked.

"Fucking sucked," Murphy responded.

"Humping sucked," Del replied.

Game on.

Screwing sucked, mating sucked, bonking sucked, banging sucked, shagging sucked, schtupping sucked. Murphy laughed at 'schtupping sucked'. Whoever laughed first, lost.

"Ha! I win," shouted Del with playful delight. "Okay, get outta here. Let me watch my show. Grab a bite, create some art, let your anger make me rich," she said.

With that, Murphy walked into the kitchen, grabbed a leftover sandwich, and headed upstairs to change. With Del's guidance, Murphy had sold her art through Del's gallery, under the name François Dumaine. Del advertised it as a pseudonym for an angry abstract artist she refused to name, and for whom she refused to provide a back story. Last year the local media gave coverage to the mystery painter whose works were produced randomly, and the works occasionally sold.

She changed into shorts and an old t-shirt, threw on some runners, and headed out the back door to a shed in the backyard. Murphy opened the door and flicked on the light, revealing her studio.

The shed was a standard eight by twelve, with large double doors and windows in the front. Inside, she had covered the windows with a clear plastic to protect them from the paint. Murphy used only a few paint colours—black, white, blue, green, red and yellow—kept in five-gallon buckets. Her tools were tossed into a heap on the floor under a window, ready for picking and choosing.

"Lacrosse, hockey. Cricket bat, nice and flat. Baseball bat. Yes, you are all chosen."

She had set the canvases up on three walls and on the ceiling. Each wall had a large canvas roll hung on a rod—she often joked that it looked like toilet paper for a giant—and Murphy would simply pull the canvas down and clamp it into place. When she decided the artwork was done, she would cut the canvas from the roll and the studio would be ready for the next time. The ceiling canvas had only taken a few extra clamps, and it hung above her, covering half the ceiling.

In the centre she had rigged a standing mixed martial arts wrestling dummy, a full-sized human figure, which hung from the ceiling with its legs strapped to the floor.

Murphy put on paint coveralls, safety goggles and a respirator mask, and pulled the hood tightly around her face. She opened four of the buckets of glossy alkyd enamel paints and then grabbed four of her painting tools. She stuck the lacrosse stick head first into the yellow paint and stirred, then left it standing in the bucket. She repeated this for each bucket—a hockey stick in the white paint, a cricket bat in the blue and a baseball bat in the black.

Murphy breathed in deeply and shook her arms and legs before beginning. She quickly snatched the baseball bat out of the black paint and swung at the dummy as if she was swinging for a home run. The bat hit the dummy with a loud, satisfying smack, and black paint flew across all three wall canvases. She quickly swung again, higher, aiming for the dummy's head, and more paint flew off the bat with the impact.

Murphy quickly jammed the bat into the paint again and spun backward, throwing a line of paint onto one canvas before hitting the dummy and splattering more on the other canvases. She raised the bat over her head and brought it down on the dummy's head and shoulder, spraying the ceiling canvas with streaks of paint.

Murphy continued with each colour, dipping the tool into the paint and then hitting the dummy to cause the paint to spray onto the canvases. She had seen a similar technique used by forensic blood spatter experts and had decided to use it to create art. Wham! A spray of white flew off the hockey stick. Smack! Streaks of yellow left the shooting strings of the lacrosse stick and soared through the air. A pocket of paint had accumulated in the ball stop and hit the canvas with a gloopy thud.

The sights and sounds of her creativity were mesmerizing. The colours blended and mixed in unexpected ways, creating unique textures and patterns. As Murphy worked, the sounds of the sticks and bats hitting the dummy, then followed by the patter of paint hitting the canvas, were both rhythmic and chaotic. Bam! Bam! Bam! The splatters and drips created a symphony of sounds that were both exciting and soothing. Sweat-drenched and fatigued, she wearily swung the bat again, her determination the only thing keeping her going.

She reached for the hockey stick but her gloved hands were slippery from paint. When she swung, the stick flew from her hands, bounced off the dummy and smacked the canvas before clattering to the floor. She bent over to grab the stick, gasping heavily for air.

It had only been an hour, but she felt like it had been a day. Her mouth was dry, her throat thirsting for cold, clean water. Her arms were sore from the force with which the dummy stopped each blow. She could feel herself overheating in her coveralls, streams of sweat trickling down her legs, the inside of her goggles becoming too steamy. She was engulfed in her discomfort, fully involved in her own mental salvation. She washed away her anger in her own sweat, cleansed her body with her pain. She felt renewed and exhausted and finally satisfied. Bam! One last hit.

Breathing heavily, Murphy scraped the paint off her tools and back into the buckets as best as she could, then tossed each on the floor to dry on their own. She pounded the lids back on the paint buckets with a rubber mallet and stripped off the mask and coveralls. The acrid smell of paint was overwhelming, and she quickly exited the studio and drew in deep breaths of clean summer air. After a few moments, she locked the doors and trudged back to the house. She stopped for a moment to quench her thirst from the outdoor hose, and slipped into the house.

Murphy quietly climbed the stairs to her bedroom. It had all taken less than two hours, and she could hear Maria and Del still chatting in the living room. After a quick shower to wash away the sweat and any errant flecks of paint, Murphy crawled under the covers hoping for an early night's sleep.

"In your hands, O Lord, are humbly entrusted our brothers and sisters. Welcome them into Your paradise, free of pain and worry. Grant these souls eternal rest. Raymond Oswald, Fiona Miller, Ghalen Kilbane, Fiona Sanders," she said as the 's' trailed off while she let out a deep breath and fell asleep.

Murphy was in the office early the next morning, hoping Dr. Chen had sent the post mortem report, but she had no luck. She prepared a cup of coffee for herself and sat at her desk, ruminating over the cases. She typed up her final report on the Alexander/Battiste case, agreeing with the evidence that it appeared Battiste had shot and killed Alexander and then turned the gun on himself. She made a particular note on the watered-down crime scene and recommended a professional standards investigation by fire services, although she knew it was unlikely to happen.

A murmur of voices dragged Murphy's attention away from the computer screen, and she looked up to see Hamilton and Parker walk into the office, followed closely by Girard. With a quick glance at the clock, Murphy grabbed some papers and headed into the atelier with everyone else.

"Good morning, everyone," she said, and smiled. "Hope you all had a good night's sleep. I think today will be a busy one. What have you all got?"

Parker, who had had arranged for Search and Rescue to use ground penetrating radar, responded first. "There is no evidence of further remains found, boss. They searched a one hundred metre radius and recovered no additional human remains," he said.

"Thank God," Murphy said. "I cannot tell you how glad I am that this is not a serial killer's dumping ground. The Chief will be relieved too. Be sure to let his office know, Michael. Who's next? Cleo?"

Hamilton got up to speak and headed to the board to tack up her map. "Boss, I was right about that being a road once. Old aerial maps show there was a logging road here, starting in 1923, with logging permitted by the province until 1968, through here to here," she said, pointing out the logged area. "Protests brought the logging to an end, and the Spalding Conservation Area was set up by Muskoka. Here."

Hamilton explained that the road continued to be used as a shortcut between Highways 6 and 11 until September 1968. "In '68, there was a car crash," she said, putting a news article up on the board. "Two kids racing down the road, both crashed, both killed. It injured two more teenagers who had been standing at the side of the road, watching. Since the road technically belonged to the province—the logging company had gone out of business—the families sued the province. They lost, but the province then made the road impassable." Hamilton talked two news articles onto the board.

"They hired a local company, Waters Price Landers, to bring in deadfall, landfill and boulders on the Highway 11 end, to block off the road. At that end, they blocked more than a kilometre of road. By 1968 there were no loggers, and by 1969 no one just travelling through."

Murphy thought for a moment. "So, that means people could come in from Highway 6, but would have to leave the same way?"

"Yes boss. Until 1975. Some back-to-nature folks had set up a camp there, but for whatever reason, stayed there through winter. They were found dead the next year, all frozen to death," Hamilton said.

"Well, yeah, it gets cold up here," Murphy said as she shook her head. "What happened to the road in 1975?"

"By them the municipality owned the road. The Highway 6 entrance was closed. Concrete barriers from Harmon Concrete this time, about a half kilometre in. By 1969, you could only enter from Highway 6, and by 1975, you couldn't enter at all, at least not by car," Hamilton said. "Someone could have dumped the body here in the early 1970s, by car, but it would have had to have been a local to know about the road by then since it wasn't marked, well travelled or maintained."

"Okay, great. At least we cut our suspect pool down from thousands to, to what, Adam? You were looking at-"

Girard interrupted and spun to his computer. "It's complex, boss. Bradburn-"

"From the library book?" Murphy interrupted.

"Yes, from the library book. Bradburn was located here until 1993, when it was amalgamated into Campbellsville, which was later amalgamated into Muskoka," he replied.

"What has that got to do with 1970 to 1975 logging companies?" Murphy asked.

"The amalgamation of Bradburn, Preston, Ryder Lake, the settlement of Rockhaven and a small portion of surrounding townships formed Campbellsville in 1993. The former Bradburn covered the largest portion of Campbellsville, making up the southern half of the town, while Preston and Rockhaven covered the western side. Ryder Lake made up the most northeastern section of Campbellsville."

"Why the history lesson?" Murphy asked impatiently.

"It will make finding information difficult, boss. The logging was both local and provincial, I have not tracked down anyone who can find a list of logging companies.

I spoke with one records clerk who thinks they will all be on paper, not digitized. She thought it could take months to locate, if they kept it at all, because of all the local political changes."

"We will never identify employees if we can't even identify companies. Does it make sense? All that just to get the names of people who used to work at logging companies fifty years ago?" Hamilton asked.

"No... no. Not right now, because I have a line of inquiry going that I think will be more productive. Do we have any phone records for Smith or Price yet?"

"Smith does not have a cell phone. TechWave would not give us Price's records without a court order. That has been delivered, so we are just waiting on them," Girard said.

"Okay, keep on it. We need Dr. Chen's report," Murphy said.

"Let me call him on the phone," Girard said as he turned to his desk. Murphy and the team gathered around Girard. He dialled the doctor and hit the speaker button.

"DSS Girard! Did you know there are more than 40,000 species of snails? Gastropoda. Stomach foot," Dr. Chen said cheerfully.

"Were there snails at the site?" Girard asked, visibly confused.

"Probably, it is a forest. But that's not important right now," Dr. Chen said.

Dr. Chen summarized the report for the team. Arsenic in the bones was consistent with the femur, and he was confident it resulted from chronic poisoning. Based on a dental review, the female child was between nine and eleven years old. She stood at 125 centimetres.

The fragments of a pair of jeans and pink cotton shirt were tested for blood, but they found none. The bones had been intertwined in the roots of the tree, showing the tree was there when she was left, and that she had not been moved. Both feet were missing, and a tibia and fibula, part of the leg he had matched the femur to, likely a result of animal predation resulting in the dispersal of bones.

Dr. Chen paused dramatically, then revealed the most important news. "The skull had a defect, a gunshot wound. Gunshot."

"They shot her?" Murphy exclaimed excitedly.

"Better still, detective, a .22 round was recovered with the bones in the hollow. There is no exit wound in the skull, so the bullet likely just fell out as the body decayed. It is in excellent condition, too. If you find a gun, I might be able to make a match. Gun."

The team cheered loudly, delighted they had such significant evidence. Murphy shushed the group and asked, "Is there any way you can tell me the ethnicity of the girl?"

"DI Murphy, ethnicity or race based on skeletal remains is controversial, and it would take a forensic anthropologist, which your department would have to pay for," Dr. Chen said. Then he laughed and said, "So of course, I contacted one. Anthropologist. We are blessed to have video conferencing these days. Preliminary, inexact, et cetera, et cetera. She is Asian. North American Indian, an Indigenous person. The anthropologist used some sophisticated software to generate a sketch. I have just forwarded that to you."

Murphy was elated, as this meant her information suggesting the victim was from the Tiny Flowers Reservation became much more credible. "Doctor, doctor, thank you for the information and the sketch. Send that bill along and I'll get it sorted out," she said.

"Here is a scenario I have," Murphy said as she walked to the board and began rearranging photos. "Jose Mercado finds the femur bone of a young murder victim, who I am now going to call Lake Kelbowek Horn, from fifty years ago. The original killer finds out and murders Jose before he can reveal more. He or she did not move Lake Kelbowek Horn before we found her."

"Why that name, boss?" Girard asked.

"Ah," she said, waving a marker in her hand, "she is young, suffering from arsenic poisoning and likely Indigenous. Tiny Flowers Reservation," she said as she drew an 'X' on the map over the Goldfinch Greens golf course, "used to be here, on Lake Kelbowek. Feds came in and relocated everyone in 1971, because of arsenic in the groundwater. The adults and children were separated-"

"Wait! The government separated the families from the children?" Parker said in disbelief.

"Welcome to the Sixties Scoop," Girard said. "The government really hated First Nations, Indigenous and Metis people, so anything short of actually killing us was fair game."

"That's disgusting," Parker said, his face twisted up with revulsion.

"Try to keep yourself unemotional on this, Michael. It is going to get worse. Okay, I met with a PhD student who had been studying the Tiny Flowers Reservation, and had located all the people who lived there, except for eight people. One of the people he hasn't been able to locate is a ten-year-old girl, last name Horn."

"Our Lake Kelbowek Horn," Hamilton said, nodding.

"That's my theory. The paperwork he gave me shows three kids, including Lake Kelbowek Horn, being fostered out to a single family, but the records are coded. Whoever the employee who filled out the paperwork was a real piece of work. None have first names listed. There are codes instead of foster family names and towns. Racist comments written in. No employee name, just a number and illegible signature."

"Lake Kelbowek Horn was fostered out and murdered, then dumped, to be found decades later by some Sasquatch hunter who was murdered to hide the original murder?" Girard said. Each of the detectives sat silently, considering all the evidence they had collected so far, and whether it agreed or conflicted with Murphy's theory.

"The killer has to be at least, what, sixty-five, and still alive after all these years, and knew about the femur," Parker said.

"Cornelius Price and Phillip Smith," Murphy said as she tapped the two pictures. "Cleo, I want everything on the two. I want work history, criminal records, registered weapons, everything. Look for an association with racist or white supremacist groups, but remember, this goes way back. And check into the parents and grandparents of Emily Powell, the waitress. She also saw the femur. I would like to rule her relatives in or out of this scenario."

"Yes boss," Hamilton replied as she turned to her computer to begin the work.

"Adam and Michael, you get the Feds. Let's try to ask without a production order, because we can be very specific. They might cooperate. Go to Human Resources to get employee information on our mystery employee number from the Department of Indian Child Welfare from 1970 to 1975, including name, contact information at the time, wages and time off. If there is a pension, get a current address. Contact the Department of Indigenous Services to get names of everyone living on Tiny Flowers Reservation who was relocated, fifty-six people in all. Get birthdates, and settled location, whatever else they have." With a gleam of excitement in his eyes, Murphy scanned the board, exhilarated at the prospect of uncovering new murder suspects that could crack the case wide open.

"Find out what happened specifically to the children. Request form DICW438 for each child, those are the placement forms. And we want the identity of foster family 23DICW438. Explain that we are trying to identify a historic murder victim and the employee we believe handled her relocation."

"And if they don't cooperate, boss?"

"Then contact the Interagency Secretariat. If that fails, court order. No, in fact, go through the Secretariat first, don't bother contacting the feds directly. They can often help get the information in hours, not days."

The phone rang in Murphy's office. Chief Valencia had just read the Alexander/Battiste report, and he was not happy. "Why are you recommending a Fire Services internal review? It was a goddamn firefighter putting out a fire."

"Chief, like the report said, we could find no evidence of a fire at the scene."

"That is because they put the damn thing out. You aren't a fire expert, are you?"

"Sir, I feel strongly about them possibly destroying evidence. There was no reason to water down my crime scene," Murphy said defensively.

"No. I don't want to get into a pissing contest with the Fire Department. They use volunteers for crying out loud. The Mayor is just looking for an excuse to get rid of their volunteer positions and their contract is in the middle of negotiations. I will not pour fuel on that political fire. Take out the recommendation, keep in the fact their guys doused the scene." And with that, the Chief hung up.

Murphy groaned and sat back in her chair. She would have to remove the recommendation. She pulled up the report, searched for the recommendation, and deleted the text. Before she hit the 'Send' button, she thought she should let the team know. Murphy walked into the atelier and told the team. "The firefighters who hosed down the Alexander/Battiste scene will not be reviewed. It has to come out. The Chief thinks it will start a pissing contest with Fire," she explained.

"Boss, they need to know they can't ruin our crime scene," Hamilton protested. Girard nodded his head in agreement.

"I bet I have a better score than either of them," Parker mumbled. Murphy heard.

"Michael? What was that?"

"Nothing boss, sorry."

"Ha, not nothing. What did you say?"

Parker put his head back and rolled his eyes. Am I going to get in trouble again for making a joke? "Boss, it was just a joke. I said I bet I have a better score than either of the firefighters who were on scene." Murphy shrugged and shook her head. She did not know what he was talking about.

Girard interrupted. "Pissing contest, boss. In the men's washrooms, the urinals have targets on them. You aim for the numbers. Each time you hit a number and hold it there for three seconds, you get that number of points. It's a game, a contest. It's just to encourage men to aim because sometimes it can get a little messy in there."

"Literally a pissing contest. Where you urinate on numbers? Like stickers, or..." Murphy asked. Sometimes the mysteries of men were beyond her.

"It's a shooting target that has been painted on the inside of each urinal. The torso with the numbers reversed. The lower you aim, the higher the number. It reduces the splash. We unofficially compare numbers. There is no scoreboard, just the honour system. It's just a..."

"I get it. It's a pissing contest where you get points for aim. You casually compare piss numbers the way women might casually compare shoes," Murphy said.

Girard blushed a little and said, "Well, not really. It's human nature to aim for things. If I am watering the garden, I might aim at a bug to blast it off a plant. Three points. A fly is four points. But it's minus two if you hit a bee. That's only me, though."

"Enough. This conversation got off track and I cannot underscore to you how much I do not care about your urination practices. I am letting you know, the recommendation for an internal review is out. I will leave in something about maintaining the integrity of crime scenes." Murphy walked back to her office, shaking her head. She clicked the 'Send' button without further ado.

Murphy spent a few minutes considering her next step, deciding how she would inform the Chief about Lake Kelbowek Horn and whether to make a statement to the press. She finally called his assistant, Sandra, and made an appointment to see him in an hour. Murphy then turned to her computer and began searching, hoping to find old newspapers that might provide information on the Reservation.

She had always attempted to remain technologically literate. In today's fast-paced world, technology advances at an astonishing rate. From smartphones and tablets to artificial intelligence and robotics, the digital landscape constantly evolves, and so does evidence.

It is no longer enough to simply know how to use a computer or send an email. Detectives must now have a deep understanding of emerging technologies and how they can be applied in homicide enquiries. Murphy did not care for the old timers who scoffed at using computers and left it for others on the team—often a woman—to find digital information. A throwback, she was sure, to the idea that women and typing just go together. The Chief was a good example of that. From video doorbells to dash cams to drones, the tools Murphy could make use of were almost endless, if you knew to look.

Murphy pulled up the Internet browser and typed 'local newspapers online' and hit the Enter key. With just a few clicks, she found the Ontario Community Newspapers Portal and the Canadian Community Digital Archives. Both sites provided access to digitized, text-searchable newspaper archives. She began by searching for Tiny Flowers Reservation, then expanded her search to Phillip Smith and Cornelius Price. It was with Price that she hit pay dirt.

CHAPTER FOURTEEN

Cornelius Price was the son of a local businessman who operated Waters Price Landers, a haulage company whose name Murphy recognized from Hamilton's update earlier in the day. An October, 1969 newspaper article about the closure of the logging road included a photograph showing two men standing on a pile of rubble. The photo caption read, Franklin Price and son Cornelius stand on barrier to old logging road. Murphy printed the article, wrote the date and time on the paper, and put it aside.

She continued with every article she could find about Cornelius or his father Franklin, and she was grateful to learn Franklin died in 1970, before the Tiny Flowers Reservation scoop. It meant she could dismiss him as a suspect. She printed and catalogued his obituary and continued her search.

The next article, from March 11, 1974, shocked Murphy. Teen Dies in Tragic Ice Accident.

'Tragedy struck a family in Bradburn yesterday, when 14-year-old Oren Price fell through thin ice on a snowmobile and lost his life. The young boy was out with friends when the accident occurred, and despite efforts to save him, he succumbed to the icy waters.

Oren's parents, Cornelius and Beatrice, are understandably heartbroken by their loss. They remember their son as a bright and caring boy with a passion for adventure, who had his whole life ahead of him. The family is receiving support from their community in this difficult time.

This unfortunate incident serves as a reminder of the dangers of thin ice during the winter months. With temperatures fluctuating, it is important to be cautious when venturing out onto frozen bodies of water. Experts advise that ice should be at least four inches thick to support a person, and even thicker for snowmobiles or other vehicles.'

Murphy felt a pang of sympathy for the Price family. She had seen families torn apart by the death of a child, and it was something she would never wish on anyone.

Cornelius Price was featured in June, 1974 in a feel-good piece about fundraising for a muscular dystrophy group. He was photographed at the local fall fair later in the year. Looking forward to apple pie! the caption read. In 1979, Price became mayor of Bradburn and he suddenly began appearing in newspapers with startling frequency. She read a few articles, but nothing seemed relevant other than what they revealed about his public life.

Murphy smiled. She had evidence that Price knew about the logging road, and he was probably an egotist, although that in no way made him a killer. Combined with a false alibi and a lie about the confrontation with Jose, he was shaping up as a solid suspect. She tapped her fingers on the pages of newspaper articles she had printed, wondering, hoping her theory was the right one.

Ever diligent, Murphy also conducted a search on Phillip Smith, although it was much harder. His name was common, and she was rarely certain that any given 'Phillip Smith' was hers. She had only begun the search when her phone rang. It was Sandra, reminding her about the meeting with the Chief.

Murphy raced upstairs to the Chief's office, arriving two minutes late. "Thanks for the call, I owe you," Murphy said with a smile as she headed into the Chief's office.

"A box of chocolates would be nice," Sandra murmured as she turned her attention back to her computer.

Murphy apologized to the Chief and outlined the case so far. He listened patiently as Murphy explained how they found the body of the girl, expected a full name by the end of the day, and zeroed in on two suspects. Her detectives were contacting federal authorities for information, although she did not have an update. She wanted to hold a news conference with the sketch, asking if anyone had information.

"Jesus Christ, Murphy," Valencia said as he sat back in his chair. "Cornelius Price was a good friend, is a good friend of former Chief Lloyd Griffith. He was mayor of some little town for a while, too, a well-respected man." Valencia sighed heavily.

"This body is going to cause a problem with the Indigenous crowd. They are going to be up in arms if that is what happened to that little girl," Valencia said. "But I don't want any protests or blockades or anything. Do you know how many calls we are getting about that damn blockade to the golf course? And now, this little girl might be from the reservation that was there before that golf course? Aahh!"

"Sir, I-"

"Quiet, let me think," Valencia said, holding up his hand to silence Murphy. After a few moments, Valencia sighed heavily and spoke. "That racism report that came out. That, that... 'Hands In Unison' report."

"Hands and Voices In Unison," Murphy corrected him.

"You've read it, right? Yeah, you're probably the only one, you and me. The reporters will ask about it. How many of their recommendations have we implemented?" he asked.

Murphy cleared her throat. "As far as I know, none, sir." Her answer caused Valencia to slam his fist on the table. "But sir, I have a Liaison position posted, and I am already combing through resumes. I should have someone soon, in a week or so."

"Okay, I'll talk to Media Relations, we will set a press conference, you'll be there to answer questions. Don't answer any questions about the report, I will handle those. Keep everything vague. I'll have Tanisha Jones send you my speech, so you're on the same page. If anyone asks about those recommendations, we'll just deflect, yes? Dismissed." Murphy nodded and headed out the door.

Murphy went across the street. As she entered the busy, clean store, Jacqueline's Pâtisserie, she was greeted with the sound of soft music playing in the background and the smell of freshly baked artisanal bread. It was a wholesome change from the office. The brightly lit store was well-organized with neat display cases and a few shelves on the walls. The pâtisserie was stocked with a wide variety of products geared toward the lunch crowd; handmade individual pizzas, calzones, sandwiches, quiche, salads, and pastries.

Murphy spotted a few boxes of Fusion Chocolates, hand-crafted by a local confectioner, on a shelf near the cashier, and purchased a box. She headed back across the street to headquarters. "Chocolates, as promised," she said as she handed the box to Sandra.

"You are the only person to buy the chocolates," she said with a smile. "Today is my lucky day!"

"Buy a lottery ticket," Murphy grinned. Her phone dinged with a text notification. "Share the pot if it's over ten million, eh?" she added with a laugh as she walked away. Pulling out her phone, she saw a text message from Sun. 'Dinner tonight? Tavola. 6:30'. She texted back she would be there and set an alarm on her phone.

Murphy spent the rest of the work day reviewing her cases, typing reports, reviewing Liaison resumes and reading and responding to emails. She read over an email from the Attorney General advising that Peter Ramos, a man she investigated for double murder six years previously, was appealing his sentence of two consecutive life terms.

The investigation was solid; the conviction was solid. She doubted his appeal would get anywhere, and since it concerned his sentences, not his conviction, the appeal was not based on an investigative error. Ramos killed his two children, and as far as Murphy was concerned, he could stay in prison. Murphy crafted a quick 'thanks for the heads up' response and asked if the victims' mother and grandparents had been notified.

Beeeeeeep! The alarm on her phone startled Murphy. She had lost track of time, as she knew she would. Gathering her things, she gave a quick goodbye to the team and headed out of the office. She arrived at Tavola on time and walked into the restaurant to see The Boys waving at her. Sun was at their table. Murphy rolled her eyes, hoping they hadn't overwhelmed Sun. She headed over to the table.

"Finally! You're late!" Bob snorted with fake indignation.

"Our beautiful sister finally arrives. We kidnapped Sun, forced her to join us," Thomas teased.

Murphy greeted The Boys and leaned down to kiss Sun before smacking Thomas playfully on the shoulder. "Move over. That's my seat," she said. She sat beside Sun and took a sip of water from the glass in front of her.

"You look gorgeous, as always," Jens said. "Such a radical new choice of wardrobe. The white really brightens your pale ass skin." Everyone at the table laughed at the lighthearted joke.

"Sun, I'm sure you've noticed by now, she only wears white shirts and black pants," Bob said.

"I hadn't really-"

"Two bottles of house white," Jens interrupted. The waiter had appeared silently at the table while everyone chatted.

"She wears the same ensemble everywhere. Different clothes, mind you..." Thomas said.

"Oh yes, it's not like our dear Caitlin is a dirty girl. Well, sometimes she gets a little dirty," Jens added with a sly smile.

"For work, for play..."

"It's convenient. No having to think about how to dress," Murphy explained.

"For funerals, for weddings..."

"Oh God, she even wore that to her own wedding!" Bob explained. Sun turned a quizzical face to Murphy, but could not get a word in edge-wise.

"You looked very dapper, my dear," Bob said with a crooked smile.

"And Del looked fabulous in her wedding dress," Thomas added.

"A stunning white satin number. Designed by Jay Bloomfield, for heaven's sake!" Jens said as he held up his hand and rubbed his fingers together.

Murphy nodded. "Ha! So expensive, but it is what she wanted. It took me months to pay that off," Murphy laughed.

"That's because you're always spending your money on your wife and her friends. At restaurants?" Jens hinted unsubtly.

"Okay, I'll throw some-" Murphy cut her sentence short. Her phone was ringing, and she had to answer it. She moved away from the table, away from the loud laughter and chatter, into the restaurant vestibule. She knew she would be leaving, and as she spoke, she the small ATM machine in the entrance and withdrew $300. She figured that would cover their bill.

"Michael?" she asked.

"Boss, we have the girl's name. Can you come back to the office?" Parker asked.

"I'll be there in ten minutes," she said. She headed back into the restaurant and to the table.

"I have to go," she said apologetically. She folded six $50 bills, leaned down and tucked it into Sun's cleavage. She winked and whispered "Pour vous." Sun's mouth opened but nothing came out.

Murphy frowned, straightened up, and addressed the group. "I'm leaving. Please don't embarrass me please."

"Don't worry, Sun, we're all bark and no bite. Stay with us for dinner, please?" Thomas said.

"Well, I, I-" Sun stammered as she shook her head.

"We'll take that as a yes. Bye Caitlin!" Thomas shouted.

"Love you guys. See you later, Sun," she said as she left the restaurant. Sun had a look on her face that she seen on past girlfriends, that 'How dare you leave?' look. She hoped she was wrong. She really liked Sun. And the sex was great. But she so rarely got past a few dates that she expected the worst.

Driving back to the office, Murphy stopped in at a local fast-food joint and picked up four submarine sandwiches. She hadn't eaten, and she was sure the others had not either.

"Subs for everyone," she said, walking into the office, holding bags aloft. "Ten minutes to eat, then on to the update," she said, sitting down on the couch in the atelier. "On the couch, away from your desk. Tell me her name, and you all get to eat."

"Cardinal Horn, boss," Girard said with a solemn smile. "Cardinal Horn."

"You guys are fantastic. I should have brought a better dinner. Okay, here, Adam, turkey with extra pickles, no cheese on white. Cleo, vegetarian on gluten-free bread, extra mustard. Michael, Philly Cheesesteak on white," she said, as she handed over the sandwiches. Murphy unwrapped her own toasted tuna on whole wheat and took a satisfying bite.

Everyone was eager to talk about the case, but Murphy was worried that fallen shreds of lettuce or an errant onion would fall on the paperwork. "I don't care, boss," Girard said. "I want to discuss it now. Please."

"Okay, just wipe your hands before you handle the papers, okay?"

"Boss, we can reprint them. Okay, I contacted the Department of Indigenous Services. They have the old records from the Department of Indian Relocation and the Department of Indian Child Welfare. They refused to help, so I contacted the Interagency Secretariat. I have to tell you, they know their stuff, they really do. I explained what I wanted and why, and within an hour I had Indigenous Services calling me back, eager to help," Girard said. He took another bite of his sub, wiped his hands, and handed Murphy a double-sided printout.

"They sent over all fifty-six names. Handwritten in the original, but I took the time to type them out. This is the list."

"They didn't have the list already typed? Wh—what is wrong with these people?" Hamilton asked.

"Overworked or uncaring bureaucrats. Adam, make sure we get this list back to Indigenous Services in digital form, just to help. And so…"

"Cardinal Horn lived on the Reservation with her parents, Charlie and Mary Horn, and an auntie, Joy Horn. Charlie, Mary, and Joy all went to the Emerald Bay Reservation number 538. All now deceased, no other living relatives on record. So, Cardinal Horn, age ten years, five months, went to foster family 23DICW438 in 1971. Her official form DICW438 is like the copy you brought in boss, incomplete, full of handwritten crap. But you will never guess who foster family 23DICW438 is," Girard said.

"Oh come on Adam, no teasing," Murphy said as the others laughed.

"Cornelius Price."

"Are you shitting me? He was her foster father?" Her eyes widened in shocked delight and her body stiffened with anticipation. Her heart pounded as a mixture of adrenaline and excitement surged through her veins. Her hands trembled slightly.

"Yes. He fostered eleven Indigenous kids over the years. I am waiting for the records, should have those by tomorrow. We will know who and when and what happened with each one."

"Do we know what he said happened to Cardinal Horn?" Murphy asked.

"No. And I can't check school records. The Bradburn Grade School was closed in 1976. I have no way of knowing where those records went because of the amalgamations," Girard said.

Murphy was suddenly aware she was beginning to sweat. Her thoughts leapt sickeningly forward. Cornelius murdered his foster daughter. Then, when Jose discovered part of her body, Cornelius killed again? She felt it in her bones. There was a feeling of familiarity. It would not be the first time someone killed to cover up an older murder.

"Cleo, what did you find?"

Hamilton said she contacted Emily Powell, who said she had no idea where her parents or grandparents lived in 1972. "She made me feel old as hell when she said, 'I was born in 2007, what do I know about ancient history'. Ha ha!"

"Oh no, and I'm way older than you," Murphy laughed.

"But I got her mother's phone number and called her. She was born in 1984, ex-husband in 1980. And her parents, Emily's grandparents, are from Halifax. Never moved. She thinks her in-laws lived in Dartmouth, but they are both dead now," Hamilton said.

"Okay, they are out of the suspect pool. Next?"

"I got a court order for bank records for Price and Smith, going back two weeks. Both the CIBC and RBC are getting those records for us, including an RBC Visa credit card. It will be a few days," Hamilton said. "Nothing related to white supremacists or racist groups that I could find. Price had a parking ticket in 1994. Smith has no record on the system. Neither Smith nor Price has social media. One cell phone in Cornelius's name, records have been requested. His land line records show only a few calls to Smith, his dentist and his doctor. None on the day Jose was murdered," Hamilton said.

"Price was with the federal Department of Indian Child Welfare from 1967 to 1979. He was a placement officer as well as a foster father. He made $16,918 in 1967 and was up to $19,512 by 1979. Four weeks vacation, two in summer, two in winter. His listed address is his current one. He vetted the foster families, sent the children, and completed the paperwork. His employee ID was 43438," Parker said.

"So, is this his paperwork? With all the slurs?" Murphy asked.

Parker grabbed a sheet of paper and went up to the board. "Yes. The employee ID on the form is 43438."

Murphy nodded. She was beginning to despise Price, despite having reminded her staff how important it was to remain detached. More and more, as each piece of his terrible personality unfolded, his actions were revealed. "Michael. Go on."

"In 1979, he became mayor of Bradburn at age twenty-nine. He held that for thirteen years until the town joined Campbellsville. He then became a postmaster and worked for Canada Post until he retired in 2013."

"No criminal record," Hamilton said. "I searched gun licenses and Quit Claim forms, focusing on dates between 1960 to 1980. I found references to three gun licenses in his name and three Quit Claims. All the Quit Claims were on the same date, May 2, 1979, right before he ran for mayor in June. Price owned one .22 calibre gun, a Winchester Cooey Model 64b hunting rifle bought in 1970. He had a Smith & Wesson Model 19 revolver, which was a .357 bought in 1968, and a Colt Diamondback .38 Special bought in 1969. All turned in and destroyed years ago."

"Okay, so he had a .22 at the time we think Cardinal Horn was killed. Excellent. But it was destroyed. Anything else?"

"Phillip Smith. A Bell Canada accountant for thirty-four years, worked at an office in Toronto. Retired and moved to Muskoka in 2015 with his wife, bought the house across the street from Price. So, unlikely, boss," Girard said.

"All right, we have eliminated Violet Mercado and family, and Patrick Lambert and Norman Moreau, the tattooists, in the murder of Jose Mercado. We had Emily Powell and family who were cleared. Emily was working. Was she working? Did we check on that?"

"For some of it. Kettering Traveller Motel Café records confirmed she worked Friday until 10pm. She worked again on Saturday at noon. But we don't have her whereabouts on Friday night to Saturday noon."

"She seems unlikely, so we will put her on hold. Phillip and Cornelius. Phillip said he was with his wife all day, which she confirmed. That leaves Price in the picture for Jose. And Price is the only one in the picture for Cardinal Horn, so far. That makes the theory of related murders even stronger." Murphy said with a nod.

"Okay, go home, enjoy what's left of the evening. Get a good night's sleep. You will need it tomorrow once the news hits the media."

After the others left, Murphy logged into her computer and began scrolling through emails. Tanisha had forwarded the press statement for tomorrow. Sandra confirmed she had notified the Muskoka Tip Line to prepare them for a deluge of callers.

Murphy reviewed the list of Tiny Flowers Reservation children, sorting them into categories based on foster family code. Abigail Buffalo, aged 13, her brother Billy Buffalo, aged 16 and Cardinal Horn, aged 10, were all sent to the same foster family, the Prices. The records showed they moved Abigail to another family in 1973, Billy aged out the same year. Cardinal just seemed to disappear.

Murphy wondered if other children just seemed to disappear and read each document thoroughly. They shuttled many of the children between foster homes. One boy, Paul McDonald, was transferred five times before aging out of the system.

It was 11:30 by the time Murphy got home. Del was asleep, so she headed upstairs to her own room. She stripped and propped herself up under the covers, and started listening to her voicemail messages.

Sandra wanted her to confirm she would be at the 4:30 news conference. Someone from 'windows' called about a virus on her iPad, and Sun left a message, asking her to call. Nothing that couldn't wait until tomorrow.

Before falling asleep, she spoke more names in her prayers. "Danielle Leary, Liam Pinter, Fraserburg Road Jane Doe, Timothy Magee, Carrie Abbott."

Murphy dreamt she was walking down a cobblestone street and suddenly the nearby stores were in flames. She continued on unfettered as storefront windows exploded from the heat, shooting glass like tiny projectiles. As she raised her hands to shield her eyes, an orange car appeared on the side of the road, parked in front of a pub. It blew up, sending shards of metal ripping through her flesh. She pulled them out, but the more she removed, the more jagged and cutting each piece became.

Suddenly, Father O'Brien came and took her hand, leading her to a drawbridge toward the safety of the old stone church. The moment she stepped onto the drawbridge, it raised up, tossing her into the moat below. She clambered up the muddy embankment, shards of almost-buried bone cutting her hands as she went. After extreme effort, she dragged herself on to solid ground. She saw Father O'Brien standing at the entrance of the gatehouse, pointing at a twisted bicycle lying in a pool of blood. She heard a child call her name.

Murphy woke up frozen in place, her heart pounding, her pillow soaked in sweat. It was the first time her dream ended like that, the first time she heard Roisin call out to her. The familiar and once-finished dream had become unfinished.

In 1981, when Murphy was six years old, she and her best friend Roisin were walking along Ardan Avenue after school. But Londonderry, Ireland was not safe. The girls had been chatting and laughing when Roisin suddenly ran. "Race you!" she shouted as she headed up the street. Never one to be left behind, Murphy raced after her, scooting around people, before getting ahead of her friend. Roisin slowed down once she was caught, letting Murphy sprint ahead. Roisin stopped near an orange car to catch her breath, Murphy near the butcher's store. And then it happened. The orange car exploded, tearing Roisin apart, sending shockwaves into the surrounding shops. Shop glass exploded all around as Murphy instinctively curled up. Glass raked across her back. Murphy did not hear the screams and shouts as she lay bleeding on the sidewalk. She did not hear Father O'Brien shouting as he ran to her. The Father scooped her up and slung her over his shoulder, then ran madly to St. Mary's Infirmary three streets over.

Bouncing crazily on his shoulders, Murphy could see only the Father's black cassock and the pavement racing past under foot. Father O'Brien shouted loudly to the nuns as he ran the bell, demanding the gates be opened. A nun, Sister Anthony, came running to unlock the cast iron gate and allowed the Father and the child entry. Murphy was carefully laid down on a bed and her wounds were tended to. A dozen nuns prayed over her as she lay on the white feather duvet, numb from the experience.

The scars on her back became fainter over time, but the nightmares were growing stronger. Roisin was not the only one from Murphy's world to die during the Troubles, but she was the first.

CHAPTER FIFTEEN

The next morning Murphy rose early, showered and headed to the Goose Gas diner for breakfast, even though it was not a Tuesday. She took her pencil crayons and colouring book and, sitting in a booth, Murphy coloured a cartoon tiger while nibbling hash browns.

Out of the corner of her eye, she spotted a white van pulling into a parking spot in front of the diner. She smiled and waved at Sun as she exited the van, but could tell by Sun's reaction this would not be a friendly meeting. What now? she thought to herself as she put away her colouring book.

Sun sat down across from Murphy with an angry fire in her eyes. Paige grabbed a pot of coffee and walked from behind the counter to pour a cup for Sun.

"Well, what do you have to say for yourself?" Sun asked, her voice seething.

"Uh, I am sorry. I had to leave. I had to get back to the office for-"

Sun interrupted. "How fucking dare you pay me!" she shouted. She threw the $300 from the previous night at Murphy. At that, Paige turned on her heels and headed back to safety, and a better view of the action, behind the counter. Murphy looked at her, mouth agape, and then laughed so loudly the sound echoed in the empty stillness of the diner.

"You are laughing at me? Who the fuck do you think you are? Who do you think I am?" Sun slapped her hands down on the table, frustrated and angry at being treated this way.

"What the hell are you talking about?"

Sun stared at Murphy, mouth open, wondering if the early morning sun or the raging hangover were playing tricks on her mind. Her eyes narrowed as she watched Murphy sitting calmly, looking more like she was discussing the weather than giving her money.

"Wha—How... Caitlin Murphy, is this some kind of joke? I-" Sun's rage was building, and she was finding it hard to speak.

"Is it the money? It's that why you are giving it back? You did not want the money?" She could not understand. Maybe by offering to pay for dinner, she had insulted Sun, suggested Sun was unable to pay for herself.

Murphy looked into Sun's eyes, trying to find some clue, and saw anger and betrayal. But there was something more, something Murphy had seen before in other women's eyes. She settled back, her shoulders relaxed, her manner became casual. She knew the break up was coming next.

Sun was flustered and could only scream, "Are you seriously trying to pay me for my time? I can't believe you'd even consider doing that. I don't need your money, and it's insulting that you think you should pay me! How dare you!" she spat out. Her hands were trembling as fiery anger coursed through her veins.

"You were supposed—"

"Don't you dare try to weasel your way out of this shit!" she snarled through clenched teeth. Sun was flush with anger and embarrassment.

Murphy's face flushed. She was angry, and leaned forward as she said, "If the money insults you—"

"You are a fucking asshole!"

Murphy looked at her watch, not wanting to be late to the office, and only after, realized how indifferent it looked.

"How dare you!" Sun screamed.

"Come on," Murphy said. She was frustrated. "Stop this. I like you, I—"

"Oh my God, you just don't stop! You are conceited and shameless! And I am done. Done!" Sun shouted. "You are a terrible human being."

Murphy squared her jaw and narrowed her eyes. "Oh, grow up. It's just dinner money. If you are offended by me paying, this is not going to work out. But you never said not to. How am I supposed to know you have money hangups? Then you get angry at me? Me? I did nothing wrong. You're angry at yourself and instead of saying 'This isn't for me,' you decide to take it out on me? Not cool, Sun, not cool."

"Not cool? Not cool?! You're a jerk! A conceited, cruel asshole who took advantage of me! I'm done!" Sun shouted.

"Good! Because I do not want to date someone with the emotional intelligence of a fifteen-year-old," Murphy snapped. Sun reached over the table and tried to slap Murphy across the face, but Murphy grabbed her hand easily and stopped her. "Don't you fucking dare try to hit me! Don't you fucking dare!" she growled and then pushed Sun's hand to the side.

Sun looked at her own trembling hands, horrified. "Oh my God, oh my God, I am so sorry! I, I have never raised a hand to anyone. Not my kids, not anyone. I am so sorry, I don't know what came over me," she said. Her voice became raspy and uneven as her throat tightened.

Murphy glared at her and then turned away. "Paige, put this on my tab," Murphy said as she walked out of the diner, leaving Sun sitting speechless in the booth, staring open-mouthed at the table.

This was not the kind of morning Murphy was hoping to have.

As she drove to the office in silence, Murphy revisited the encounter. Sun was completely overwhelming to Murphy's attempt to pick up the dinner tab. She was sorry she left the money scattered about, not was sure Paige would keep it safe for her.

This was not the first time someone had tried to hit her. In fact, she was quite adept at grabbing mid-swing. That was just part of the territory that comes with being a cop. Someone, somewhere, will take a swing at you at some time or another. She did not like it, but homicide detectives walk a tightrope between peace and chaos with a precariousness unfamiliar to most people.

To work professionally in a career of other people's violence was something most people could not really understand. Some police detractors have no idea how unpredictably aggressive people could get when their emotions got out of control. Murphy knew she often appeared cold-hearted and far too pragmatic for other people's emotions, but it was rooted in the hard truths that homicide detectives endure regularly.

If there was no harm, Murphy thought, there was no foul. And conversely, if there was no foul, there was no harm.

She was sorry that Sun was upset. "Fuck! It's just dinner," she said aloud. "She manufactured that drama. I was not flaunting my money. I don't have enough to flaunt. Imagine being pissed off someone wanted to pay for dinner. She reacted like a teenager. How am I suppose to deal with that?" Murphy was more disappointed by the loss of a good lay than the attempted slap.

Murphy arrived at the office in record time. She knew she had to be in excellent form to speak with Price and made herself a specialty instant coffee from a pouch she had previously bought from Starbucks. She liked to keep a stash of flavoured coffees handy for just such an occasion.

She flipped through her file while sipping hot coffee, enjoying the slight burn in her throat as the liquid flowed down. The relationship drama faded into the background, as she had to for Murphy to work at her best. Contemplating each photograph in the folder, she looked at Jose Mercado's face, his wounds, his hands. She looked at the femur Jose had found, the crappy tattoo gun he stole and the mugshots for Patrick Lambert and Norman Moreau.

More faces, more witnesses, more suspects. There was a photograph of the book that started Jose's journey to his death, and the almost childish scrawl of 'Saskwatch sighting at Spalding near S.L. 1972'.

She flipped through more documents, newspaper printouts, employee records, initial statements, simple family trees. Murphy stared hard at the Price family tree. Franklin Price, who died in 1970, had one son, Cornelius, who had two sons and a daughter. Oren died in 1974. Everyone else was alive.

Murphy walked into the atelier and asked, "Do we have any information on the Price children? Is there any reason we can rule these other family members out?" Everyone had arrived earlier than usual. It was going to be a big day.

"Age. It's unlikely it was Beatrice for Jose's murder. An elderly woman probably could not stab a young man that deeply, and Beatrice is... eighty-one. With the children, none was old enough in 1972. Samantha would have been four when Cardinal died. Wilburt was six and Oren was two."

"Hm, does Cornelius have the strength to stab a young man?" Parker asked.

"Maybe. He seems fit enough, plays golf. How did he get the body into the lake, though? That's a haul for a man his age." Murphy said. "Okay, he's still a suspect in Jose's murder, and Cardinal's. He would have been thirty-two in 1972. That fits, but did we focus too quickly on Cornelius? It could have been any of the foster kids living with the family. Sweet Jesus..."

After her blowout with Sun—she had said a few things she wished she had not—she was having trouble concentrating, keeping the links together. She took a deep breath to calm herself before continuing. She could not afford to doubt herself.

"I am speaking with Price soon. We have to keep an open mind. Michael, Cleo, go over the evidence again. Every piece. I do not want to miss a thing. Clean up the board and make special note of anything that we have not talked about before. Adam, you are coming with me to speak to Price."

Murphy called Price's home and spoke with Beatrice. Murphy explained she needed to talk to Cornelius about some paperwork related to his old job at Indian Child Welfare. Beatrice told them to come over now as Cornelius had plans to golf in the afternoon. Murphy gathered up her government files. She took a gulp of room temperature coffee and headed out with Girard.

On the way to the Price household, Murphy gently chastised Girard. "Is everything okay, Adam? You seem a little distracted."

"You too, boss," he said.

"Pardon me?"

"I'm sorry, boss. It's just been a tough time for my family recently. Ayamis's emphysema is getting worse. The whole family is just really worried and stressed out right now."

"Adam, I'm sorry to hear about your grandmother. Is there anything I can do to help?" Murphy asked.

"I appreciate your concern. I might need to take some time off to take care of her and make sure everyone is okay. But we are right in the middle of this major investigation and it just doesn't seem right," Girard said. His voice was low and sad, as if weighted by the world.

"Of course, Adam," Murphy said, with sympathy in her voice. "Family comes first. The dead stay dead. Sorry, that came out wrong, but you know what I mean. Just let me know what you need. Take your vacation days whenever you need them. Nothing can happen to Ayamis," she said.

"Thank you, boss. I really appreciate your understanding. I'll do my best to keep up with my work, but I might need to take a few hours here and there to go to doctor appointments or the hospital, maybe. If I can convince Ayamis."

"We have a pact, you and I, since we both have vulnerable people at home. Is Ayamis in her home, or yours?"

"Hers. It will be all right. I mean, it is what it is, right?" he responded. He remained quietly contemplative for the rest of the drive. Murphy took the silence as an opportunity to think about how to seek answers from Price to questions she did not want to ask out loud.

"Okay, Adam, that's the Price house up there. You let me do most of the talking. You take notes. We are here for information on the old paperwork only. I don't want even a hint that he is a suspect in either murder. In fact, don't mention Mercado at all. Light and easy, we will see what he gives us. And overly respectful, please."

Murphy pulled into the driveway and waved at Phillip Smith, who was in his garden across the road. Beatrice greeted them at the door.

"Come on in. Cornelius is a bit grumpy this morning, but when isn't he?" Beatrice said with a chuckle. "Tea or coffee?"

"Will this take long? I have things to do," Price said. He was sitting in the living room in an old wingback chair, picking at the faded floral pattern. To Murphy, he looked like a petulant child called into the principal's office.

"Nothing for me, thank you," Girard said, answering Beatrice's question.

"I would love some water," Murphy said. "This is just a look at some old paperwork, sir. The Chief insisted I speak with an expert. Can we sit at a table? That will just help with keeping them in order, make things go faster," Murphy said.

When she called him an expert, Cornelius perked up. "Come into the kitchen then," Price said as he got up from the chair. "The Chief is right. Always get an expert opinion when you don't know something."

Murphy's choice of words had worked, and put Price at ease, stroked his ego.

"Can I join you?" Beatrice asked. "I've never sat in on a police investigation. Do you mind?"

Murphy nodded. "Of course, if your husband doesn't mind." Price gestured for his wife to sit at the large oak table. He was about to sit at the head of the table when Murphy stopped him. "Sir, it would be easier and faster if we could all just review the paperwork together. Side by side. Would you sit here in the middle, please?"

"Oh, yes, all right," Price said as he sat on the cushioned, matching oak chair. Murphy sat to his left, Girard to his right, and Beatrice sat across the table. Murphy opened her bag and pulled out a manilla file she had prepared specifically for this conversation.

"This relates to an ongoing inquiry into a historic issue. I cannot say too much about it right now. Police business. I'd like to get your expert opinion on the old paperwork from Indian Child Welfare. You were a regional manager, and I know it was a long time ago, but you are a smart man, and I am sure you will remember a thing or two. There is a big announcement coming up and I have to be there. I hope you don't mind. The Chief wants me to cross those Ts and dot those Is before he speaks to the media."

"Happy to help," Price said with a smile.

CHAPTER SIXTEEN

"Sir, I want you to know we appreciate your help. I appreciate your help, your expert memory. I need to understand," Murphy said as she pulled papers out of her file, "what is contained on Form DICW438. They completed some areas of the forms in code."

Murphy pushed a form in front of Price. "Here we have-"

"Name of child, just like it says," Price said.

"Name of child," Beatrice repeated.

"Shush, woman, let the experts talk, eh?" her husband scolded.

"And is that usually a first and last name?" Girard asked.

"No, just the last name, usually."

"And, if I can be a little indelicate, Mr. Price, is that always a Christian name?" Murphy asked. Given the racist scrawls on official government paperwork, she thought she might make him relax more if she subtly played into his prejudices.

"Yes, yes, we only used Christian names on the forms. Government policy," Price said. "If they only had an Indian name, we would make it English, you know? None of this Beaver Sitting In a Mountain Pond stuff. Someone like that would become Beverly Montaine or Bob Manfield or some such. If they didn't have a last name, we would use our own name. Government policy, as I said," Price explained as he eyed the form in front of him. "We didn't always follow the rules, but, well, it was a bit of the Wild West back then."

Murphy wanted to scream. This was 1970s Ontario, not 1870s Texas. This was not the Wild West, it was government bullshit. "Sure, yes, okay, no problem. I understand. Policy is policy, eh? Next line, Sex. Tick box, but you could just write it in, too?"

"Yes, that's right. Boy, girl, man, woman."

Murphy leaned over slightly, and delicately asked, "Same with squaw or brave?"

"Ha, yes, a bit of fun. But no one got the wrong sex. Just words you know, harmless fun," Price said as he smiled. Murphy smiled back and nodded, but Girard simply glared.

Murphy went through several questions. "Was there a standard order for entering a date?"

"It was year, month, day but some men would do day, month, year," Price said.

"That might be read as the wrong birthdate, is that right? November tenth could be October eleventh? But the year was always correct, eh?" Murphy asked.

"Yes, I guess that's true. Never thought about it. Is all this really necessary?" Price asked as he pushed away the sheet of paper in front of him. He seemed to get a little frustrated, which was exactly where Murphy wanted him to be.

"Oh, sorry, sir. Let's try to speed things up. Contact number, fine. Identification number. Was that random or...?"

"Came out of a big binder of numbers. You just take the next number in line, fill in the child's name in the binder, then put the number on the form. It might have meant something to someone, but I do not know. Just following the rules," he said as he flicked his hand casually, dismissively. He coughed slightly and cleared his throat.

"Right, right. Start date of wardship, end date, yes it looks... Oh, I forgot. What is Placement Address? That seems to be in code on almost all of them. Surely that wasn't random?" Murphy asked.

"No no. Each foster family was assigned a number. To save time, we would just enter in the numbers," Price said.

"We were number twenty-three!" Beatrice suddenly exclaimed. Murphy jumped a little, having forgotten the woman was there.

"Oh, yes? Did you foster children?" Murphy asked, trying to feign surprise.

"We did. We had several Indian children over the years. We were number twenty-three. We stopped when Cornelius became mayor of Bradburn," Beatrice said with a proud smile.

"Yes, they were a handful. I couldn't leave Bea to handle them all by herself. See this tick box here? We checked it off if the child was a problem. We took on a lot of those problem children," Price said.

"It was a good Christian thing to do. Kept those children out of the hands of Catholics. I mean, they don't even believe in sola scriptura! You cannot have children raised in that kind of house, hm?" Beatrice asked.

"Uh, yes, I understand," Murphy said, wracking her brain for the meaning of sola scriptura. Something to do with the Bible being the infallible authority for Christian faith. Something like that. Corrupt and unchallenged Church leaders was only one reason the abuses by church leaders went on for so long.

"Well, thank you Mr. and Mrs. Price. We appreciate your help," Murphy added as she gathered up the forms.

"Oh! We're done? That wasn't so bad, Cornelius," Beatrice said.

"No, not so bad," he agreed, relieved the questioning had ended.

"That means I can clear up some paperwork. Again, thank you. Oh yes, Mr. Price, one more thing. Is this your signature here on the form?"

"Yes, it is. Employees signed there to authorize the whole thing," he said.

Murphy put the documents into the folder as they walked out of the house. "I'm so glad you remember all of this," she said as she stepped out into the sunlight.

"There is nothing wrong with this noggin. I eat well, play golf, do a fair bit of reading to keep myself in good stead. My mind is as sharp as a tack," Price said, tapping the side of his head.

The detectives waved goodbye as they pulled away from the house and headed back to the office. "Adam, make sure you note his comment about his mind being sharp. Record the time for the end of the interview. Note that he said it at the end, after answering all the detailed questions."

"Boss, I have to hand it to you. That was really smooth," Girard said.

"Ha! Thanks. That bit with Beatrice jumping in with their foster family number. That was great. Call Michael, get him started on obtaining all the DICW438 forms for foster family twenty-three, from, let's say, 1960 to 1980. I want to know who else stayed with them. If Cardinal Horn was one of his, and she wasn't reported missing... Oh, ask Cleo to double-check our missing persons database, and the OPP's database. RCMP too. Any female ten years old missing from 1970 to 1975. That should give us enough leeway to find her, if they ever reported her missing, and we just did not catch it the first time."

"Yes boss," Girard said as he called the office. He told the others that he and Murphy would be about twenty minutes, and they were to rush through whatever they could.

Then, Murphy got a call from Sandra, advising the press conference was now set for noon. "Sorry, Adam, you are coming with me. You can stand there and look pretty for the cameras," she joked.

Girard hated appearing on television and dealing with the media. "Really boss? I don't have to say anything, do I?"

"No. But don't be surprised if the Chief sticks his foot in his mouth. Just grin and bare it," Murphy said. "Oh yes, Adam, do a Google search for the Tiny Flowers Reservation justice project. I need Lethabo Zibi's phone number."

Girard began searching and quickly found the contact phone number. At Murphy's direction, he dialled.

"Justice For Tiny Flowers, how may I help you?" said the voice over the phone.

"Lethabo? It's DI Caitlin Murphy. I wanted to let you know that there will be a police press conference you might be interested in."

"Oh, yes? What is it about, detective?" Lethabo asked.

"The Tiny Flowers Reservation. Noon, at police headquarters. We are expecting local television coverage. You will want to tune in," she said.

"I have no television," he responded. "Can I attend the press conference?"

"Yes, as far as I know, it will be outside HQ, open to the public," Murphy said.

"I will try to make it," Lethabo said. "But you will not tell me more about it?"

"No. This is a message directly from the Chief, so I can promise it is important. Attending might give you a chance to follow up with the media that show up. You know, give background and commentary on your work," Murphy said.

"Okay, thank you DI Murphy," Lethabo replied. Murphy pressed the 'end call' button on her dashboard display and smiled.

"Adam, this could be an enormous opportunity for the group to get noticed, get some media attention."

"Didn't you get in trouble with the Chief the last time you did something like that? Told a group that there was a press conference, and they ended up showing up with signs and a bullhorn?" Girard asked incredulously.

"Oh, he was furious. But how was I to know? I don't think Lethabo will do that. He's basically a one man show. It will be fine," she hoped. "Now, in the meantime, I have one stop I want to make. I need to go to Fire Station 8."

Murphy had retrieved the names and fire station for the two firefighters who had contaminated her murder-suicide scene. Since she could not recommend a professional review of their actions in her report, she was going to speak to the Fire Captain. Station 8 was just a five-minute drive from headquarters.

Murphy told Girard what her plans were, and they agreed he should stay in the vehicle when they arrived. He could update the others on the press conference. It would make the stop look casual, coincidental. She parked her Brawler to the side of the station and walked in. "Detective Inspector Caitlin Murphy, Muskoka Municipal Police. Is the Captain available?" she asked the first firefighter she saw.

"Yes, ma'am, this way," he said, chaperoning her to a back office. "Captain Flannigan? Someone to see you," he said, knocking on the door.

"Captain Flannigan, I'm Detective Inspector Caitlin Murphy, with the Muskoka Municipal Police. Can I have a few minutes of your time?"

"Certainly. Please have a seat. Please call me Flannigan. What can I do for you?"

Murphy explained to the Captain that two of his men had contaminated her crime scene, claiming they were putting out a fire. "Of course, I had to document the reason, for my homicide report. A grass fire. But then I left a junior detective in charge. She noted there were no signs of fire. No signs. And now, that is also in the official report. You see the problem here, don't you? They hosed down my crime scene and lied about the reason."

Flannigan burst into laughter. "I'm sorry detective, my lads can be a handful sometimes. They meant no harm."

"No, of course not. But if my report is reviewed by a... well, a certain kind of liberal person. Well, your men, your lads, could be held to account. You see?"

"Are you recommending a disciplinary hearing?" he asked warily.

"Oh no sir, that is not in my report. But someone could read it, and, well... Why did they do it? Do you know why? I might be able to work that into my report."

Flannigan shook his head and looked out the office door. He leaned toward Murphy and she leaned forward to hear him as he lowered his voice. "Some lads like to give homeless people a shower, right? Just a joke, it's just a game. It's harmless."

Murphy nodded and smiled, but felt a pit quickly form in her stomach. She had already had her fill of noxious people. "So some of the lads spray people sometimes?" She could feel the bile in her throat building. She knew this stunt, had even experienced it back in Ireland. Firefighters would hose down protesters, Catholics, anyone they felt like. It was humiliating and painful. "Flannagan. Irish?"

"Yes, Belfast. You?"

"The family stayed in Ireland until 1994, when we moved to Canada."

"Ha ha!" Flannigan said. "Aye well, some people are just a little dirtier than others, right? Just need a little help. Now, these lads told me what happened. They didn't know the couple was dead. I swear on my sweet mother's grave, they thought it was just a couple of alkies passed out on the grass."

Murphy's hands quivered, and she quickly put them on her lap so Flannigan could not see them. When she was fourteen, a jet of water had knocked her over. It was so strong, she broke her wrist when she landed. It was a vile form of attack, one heartily enjoyed by petty men with cruel hearts. They probably had a point system. She smiled sweetly, said she could probably get it all straightened, but could he please keep them away from crime scenes. She thanked Captain Flannigan for his time. Walking back to the Brawler, Murphy was seething.

"Everything okay, boss?" Girard asked as they peeled out of the parking lot.

"No Adam. No, everything is not okay. But that's for later. Right now I, I just need to focus on Cardinal Horn."

Minutes later, Murphy and Girard were standing to the side of a podium while Tanisha Jones introduced Police Chief Valencia to reporters. He nodded his head, walked to the podium, and began reading a prepared statement. Beside him was a large printed copy of the forensic sketch of Cardinal Hope.

"On Wednesday, shortly after 11:00 AM, Muskoka Municipal Police followed up on a tip advising them of skeletal remains in the Spalding Conservation Area near Sunny Lake. Police arrived at the scene where they located human remains. The area was sealed off and the Forensics Unit was called. A determination was made by pathologist Dr. Chen that the remains had been there between fifty and fifty-five years. We launched an investigation to determine the circumstances surrounding the girl's death. We have taken the remains into custody where they underwent further forensic examination.

"Based on a post mortem examination and further investigative work, it was determined that the remains were those of a young girl, approximately ten years old, from the Tiny Flowers Reservation. In 1971, this Reservation was determined to have arsenic in the groundwater, and all persons were relocated. Hank Miller from Crown-Indigenous Relations and Northern Affairs Canada can speak further on that issue," Valencia said as he pointed to a young bureaucrat in an ill-fitting blue suit. The man awkwardly waved hello.

"We have a forensic drawing available from our website. We are attempting to contact relatives before releasing her name. I appreciate we are talking about the early 1970s, but I encourage anyone with information related to this case to contact the police tip line. Any details, no matter how small, could assist in the ongoing investigation. Thank you," he said as he stepped back from the podium.

"Robin Markmann, Channel 3 News. Chief Valencia, how did the little girl die?" shouted Markmann from the crowd. It was protocol for a reporter to announce who they were, and what their association was, before asking their question.

"We are not releasing that information at this time," he replied. Valencia used this phrase a dozen more times as reporters continued to pepper him with questions; 'Where she was found?', 'Who reported the remains?', 'Is the death considered suspicious?'

"Chief Valencia, who on your team is investigating the death?" Markmann asked.

Valencia gave a wry smile, knowing that was just a tricky way of asking if they considered it a natural death or a homicide. "Detective Inspector Caitlin Murphy," Valencia answered as he gestured toward Murphy to come to the podium. He stepped back as Murphy took to the microphone.

"I am Detective Inspector Caitlin Murphy, Homicide Unit. I am leading the investigation into the death of this young girl," Murphy said.

"Karen Fraser, CNA News. So is it a murder?"

"It is a suspicious death. We need more information right now to determine cause of death. That is why we are appealing to the public to come forward with any information," Murphy responded. Technically, she was not lying, since it could have been a murder, suicide or accident, and she was okay with that technicality.

"Why do you think she is from the Tiny Flowers Reservation?" Markmann asked.

"The remains contained levels of arsenic consistent with chronic arsenic exposure over a period of time. The Tiny Flowers Reservation was determined to have arsenic in its groundwater, and its people were relocated in 1971. The pathologist's office can respond in more detail," Murphy said.

"How did you determine her age?" Markmann asked.

"The pathologist's office can respond in more detail."

"Lyle Fraser, Muskoka Crime blog. Where in Spalding was she found?"

"We found her remains in a hollow some distance from the entrance. I can't give you a more exact location," Murphy said. She was trying to keep it vague, just as Valencia had requested.

"This question is for Chief Valencia." Murphy stepped aside while the Chief took the microphone again. "It's about the costs of this investigation so far," said the reporter. The Chief held up his hand to stop the man.

"DI Murphy can answer your question," Valencia said as he ceded the podium. "I told you this was getting expensive," he whispered as she stepped forward. Murphy felt like a setup was coming.

As she stepped up to the microphone, she heard Tanisha ask the reporter to state his name and affiliation.

"Kevin Bonham, Pecuniary Association of Canadian Taxpayers. On average, last year, the law enforcement cost of a homicide investigation was $182,211. I have heard from a reliable source that this particular homicide investigation has already cost Muskoka taxpayers $187,922, and will double before its solved. No offense, but it's a person who died over fifty years ago, a cold case. No offense, but how do you justify that expense to the taxpayers?"

The Pecuniary Association of Canadian Taxpayers was a right-wing individualist market-oriented group that rejected the collective political, socioeconomic and health solutions Canada was world-renowned for. Their goal was to stir up fear and hate under the guise of economic panic. And it pissed Murphy off.

"No offense? Are you kidding me? The greatest racial disparity in the Municipality of Muskoka is who gets killed. Indigenous people represent maybe five percent of the Canadian population, but accounted for thirty-four percent of all homicide victims in our municipality last year. Thirty-four percent of my homicide victims every year are Indigenous. Thirty-four percent, not five percent. Five percent of the population, thirty-four percent of the victims."

Murphy was on a roll. "Now you don't get fired up about costs whenever an Indigenous person kills a white person, you say the cost of policing is justified. But there's not one of you who can name one of the latest three Indigenous homicide victims. Not one of you. The taxpayers, the community, are at risk, and it's not because Indigenous men and women are running around killing people. It's at risk because Indigenous men and women are being murdered and only the police and the families seem to care. The community has become indifferent to these deaths, indifferent."

Murphy was fuming. She could not understand why he would think that attacking the investigation into the death of a little girl was going to get him anywhere. And there was no way he knew about the link to the Mercado investigation. Unless his goal was to foment racial division, he was just making himself look stupid, and aggravating Murphy.

"Now I'm leaving here to go to the office and keep working on the death of this little Indigenous girl. And I take it personally, OK? I take offense. I... Look, we went up there to Spalding and there were a bunch of cops and forensic analysts who processed the scene of a dead child. A. Dead. Child. We had used ground penetrating radar and expensive forensic tests and DNA tests and consulted with experts, paid forensic experts, to identify who she was and what happened to her. My team and I are the ones that are going to take the responsibility for finding out what happened to her. The fact is that the people out here — some of them, not all — the people who have the most criticism about the costs of this investigation are absolutely MIA when it comes to the true threats facing this community, and frankly it gets a little tiresome when we get yelled at for putting the same effort and resources into the murders of Indigenous victims as any other victim. So, I take it personally, my team takes it personally, and I just wish to God that everyone else took it personally. Now no offense to you, but I'm going back to the office, I'm going to find out what happened, and I am going to solve this death."

Murphy was fuming. She knew Valencia and Bonham were friends. Valencia had been hounding her about expenses on the Horn case, but could not be too overt. In this case, she was not sure who was the taskmaster and who was the flunkey.

Valencia stepped up to the podium again, gently nudging Murphy aside. "Once again, we are appealing to the public for assistance in finding out what happened to this little girl. I ask you to call our tip line with any information. Thank you," Valencia said as he walked away from the podium. She knew Valencia would have nothing more to say. How could he? To suggest using any fewer resources would not look good politically. Murphy and Girard quickly followed Valencia's lead and distanced themselves from the reporters. This left Miller to answer questions about the reservation and relocation.

As she was heading to her car, Murphy spotted Lethabo Zibi talking to a reporter. She caught Lethabo's eye and nodded discreetly. Lethabo smiled and nodded back while continuing to talk to the television crew.

The announcement of this discovery of the skeletal remains rocked the community and prompted a tsunami of phone calls to the police hotline. A clip of Murphy chastising Bonham was going viral online. Calls poured in non-stop, with concerned citizens and individuals from all walks of life calling in with tips, information, and their own theories about the case.

Many were either condoning or condemning Murphy. Some anonymous threats were logged, and while none were deemed credible, they were passed on to Murphy, regardless. Some callers were emotional, expressing their sadness and shock at the tragic news. Others were angry, demanding justice. Many callers shared their own experiences with violence while others went on racist diatribes.

The hotline operators were fielding, evaluating, rating and cataloguing a wide range of calls, from individuals who claim to have seen suspicious activity last month in the area where the remains were found, to those who have information about potential suspects. Some callers even claimed to have witnessed the crime. One caller claimed to have overheard a conversation between two individuals in a local bar, where they discussed the strangulation of a child.

The police hotline also received calls from concerned family members of missing Indigenous women, who fear that their loved ones may have fallen victim to the same perpetrator.

Murphy and her team spent the next ten hours going through the high priority tips passed on by front-line staff. It meant follow-up phone calls and in-person interviews. Four people under the age of forty confessed. Each had to be interviewed in person, although Murphy refused to do more than a cursory interview.

"Were you involved in the murder and or disposal of the Spalding body?"

"How old are you"

"How do you account for not being alive in 1972, when the murder occurred?"

The psychics were not any better. One woman was so convincing that her phone call was passed on to Murphy. It was 2:30 Saturday morning and Murphy had sent the team home long ago. She had fallen asleep on the couch in the atelier when the phone woke her.

"DI Murphy, I think you need to talk with this woman. She knows some information about the case," said the voice on the other end of the line. "May I patch you through?"

Groggily, Murphy agreed. She pulled out her notebook and pen, and after hearing the click caused by the line transfer, said, "Detective Inspector Caitlin Murphy."

"I heard about the young child found today in the conversation area. I have vital information on what happened." Murphy noted the woman referred to a conversation area, and not the conservation area. The woman explained she went into a psychic trance shortly after seeing the news on television, and remained in that trance for hours.

"I see a man, Black, a black man. I hear screaming, high pitched like a child. I'm running across the grass and into the forest. My head... someone bounces my head on a tree or rock. I see more trees-a forest? By a lake, but green. There is a deer watching the chase. Did this person run there? What does the number five mean? It is important. I get a bad, bloody taste in my mouth. The names John or Joseph or something like that. It begins with a J, or G, or CH. I am running through the field like crazy. This is a very serious crime. I, I have to release this vision!"

Murphy mentally cursed the officer who thought this was remotely important. "Thank you so much for the information," Murphy said, trying to sound as nice as possible.

"How much is the reward money? You know, for helping you catch the killer?" she asked.

"There is no reward money," Murphy said.

"What a waste of my fucking time!" the woman spat before hanging up. Murphy groaned, tossed the phone onto the table, and fell asleep again.

The rest of Saturday morning provided no better results. A few trolls were submitting false and baseless allegations, naming murderers and providing made-up details from their own sick minds.

It was exhausting work, and Murphy thought that on more than one occasion, she could arrest a tipster for obstruction of justice, or even just public mischief. Person by person, her team arrived. She assigned them various follow-up calls and inquiries for whatever was passed on to the team, and retreated to her office and away from the din of conversation.

CHAPTER SEVENTEEN

After a long and exhausting twenty-four hours, a hot shower was just what Murphy wanted to relax and unwind. She knew she would have to settle for a deluge of lukewarm water blasted out from the shower in the staff change room. She grabbed an overnight bag holding a change of clothes and a towel she stored in her office—kept there for just such an occasion—and headed to the showers.

On the way, she checked her personal cell phone. Sun had texted, 'Sorry. Want to apologize face to face like an adult. Pls call'. Jens had called but left no message. Del had texted 'caught u on tv u r awesome!' Bob texted 'U R hot TV babe'. Her business cell phone had one message from Sandra: 'Dr. Saunders 16:00 today'. Unlike many of her colleagues, Murphy carried a personal cell phone and the official police issued cellphone so that if she had to produce her phone as evidence at a trial, her dating habits, criticisms of her boss and calls to her friends, would never be revealed.

The women's change room was carved out of the existing men's change room, with a wall of lockers splitting the two genders. Murphy pushed open the heavy door with a misspelled femail chainge room sign on it, and walked in. Discoloured white grout separated the square brown floor tiles. Only the tile in the three shower stalls was non-slip, so Murphy avoided the small puddles of water. An acrylic brown wall separated each of the stalls, and each had a shower area, bench and clothes hooks. A white shower curtain could be pulled across the stall opening for privacy.

Murphy stepped into the stall, and pulled the curtain. She pulled a towel out of her bag and hung both on hooks and then disrobed, tossing her dirty clothes onto the bench.

Turning on the taps, a painfully high-pressure jet of water shot out. Murphy waited a few moments until the water had finally reached its lukewarm hottest and stepped under the blast. She pivoted to her back, letting the torrent massage her back and neck. As water ran down her face, she thought suddenly of Sun, sweat dripping down her face. Murphy's muscles contracted instantly, uncontrollably. She opened her eyes, shook her head, and continued her shower.

She turned off the water after just a few minutes and was drying off when her phone rang. "Murphy," she said.

"Boss, we have someone who called into the hotline. They know who the girl is, so it might be reliable," Girard said.

Murphy slipped her bra on, transferring the phone from ear to ear. "Did the caller use her name specifically?" she asked. They had withheld the name from the press purposefully.

"Yes boss, by name."

"Two minutes," she said as she quickly hung up the phone and finished dressing, sprinting up the stairs to the office.

"That was three minutes, boss," Girard joked as she rushed into the atelier.

"Smart ass," she said with a grin. "Where is the call?" When Parker waved his handset in the air, she responded, "Transfer it to my office," and headed into her office.

"Detective Inspector Caitlin Murphy. To whom am I speaking?"

"Dan-Elle Fox. I'm calling from Victoria, but I used to live in Muskoka."

"Dan L? How do I spell that, please?"

"D-a-n, dash, capital E-l-l-e. Pronounced 'Dan-El'. Last name f-o-x. They/them pronouns, please," Dan-Elle said.

"Yes, absolutely. My pronouns are she and her. Please call me Caitlin. Do you mind if I put the speaker phone on? I would like the other detectives to hear," Murphy said. With a yes, she waved to her team, and they rushed in to listen to the conversation. "Okay, we are listening. What would you like to say?"

"I lived on Franklin Bay Reservation. My parents both died in 1975, and I ended up in the foster system. I was sixteen, and I already had a couple of arrests for theft. They flagged me as a troubled kid, so I got moved around a lot. In June 1976, I ended up being fostered by some guy named Price. Can't remember the first name but it was a kind of old-fashioned white man name. Like Finster or Abraham, or..."

Murphy wanted to jump in, to tell him the name, but she dare not, for fear of later being accused of directing them with a name, directing the witness's statement. She motioned to Parker and mouthed 'Is Dan-Elle on Price's list?', sending him into the atelier for the list of known foster kids for Price.

Dan-Elle continued. "Anyway, they had one other foster kid, Samuel, when I got there." Silently, Parker slipped into the office with a pile of papers and held one up, nodding.

"Samuel had the names of all the kids before us. I haven't seen that before in any other foster home, but the first night I was there, he said I had to memorize all the names. He said, so nobody would ever get lost. I remember he was just a young kid, but he was so serious," they continued.

"Billy Buffalo, Abigail Buffalo, Cardinal Horn, George Davis, Samuel Cloutier and me, Dan-Elle Fox. I was Daniel then. If you talk to the others, they will know me as Daniel. There might have been more after me, but those are the names I learned. He told me to say them every night, before bed. Ha, all these years later, I still say them. Billy Buffalo, Abigail Buffalo, Cardinal Horn, George Davis, Samuel Cloutier."

Emotions welled up inside Murphy, causing her to choke up and blink back tears. She was usually composed, but this time, she fought to contain the overwhelming emotions. Anger simmered within her towards the reporter and the firefighters, her heart yearning for Sun, now on the verge of tears herself. Just like them, she had her own list of people, names she whispered at night, praying so none of them were lost. Taking a deep breath, she cleared her throat, attempting to regain her composure amidst the tumult of feelings.

"Should I go on?" Dan-Elle asked. When Murphy asked them to continue, they said, "The Prices forced all the foster kids to sleep in the garage on a couple of dirty mattresses. One night, Mrs. Price started screaming that someone ate a cookie. I mean, we didn't get cookies. It was the Price kids, not us. Mr. Price came in with this rifle, and he had such a cold, dead stare in his eyes. Fuck! I remember he reached up to get a bullet off the shelf in the corner and I was terrified. I remember it was an old yellow box of bullets and he carefully put in the bullet and snapped it shut, staring at us the whole time with such hate. Mrs. Price was in the doorway screaming about her fucking cookie. 'It was one of the dirty Indians' she said. Mr. Price just aimed that gun and cocked it, and I thought he would shoot me. I almost pissed myself. But then Oren, one of the guy's sons, he yelled he took the cookie, and Mrs. Price was like Jekyll and Hyde, you know? She suddenly smiled and just walked back into the house, telling him he could have another. Then Mr. Price ejected the round, and put it back in the yellow box and said 'next time,' and he walked out."

Dan-Elle's voice quivered, choked with emotion, as they recalled the haunting memories of the terror and cruelty of the incident. "Just give me a minute," they pleaded, needing a moment to compose themselves. The detectives could hear the quiet sobs escaping from their trembling lips, followed by the sound of them blowing their nose. After a moment, Dan-Elle took a deep breath and bravely resumed the conversation, despite the emotional toll the recollection had taken on them.

"Ugh, I mean fuck. Who does that? Well, a psycho does that, that's who. That was the Price family. Psychotic. I left that night, no way I was staying there. Sam stayed. He didn't have anywhere to go. Me either, but I left anyway, went to the highway, hitched a ride to Toronto, and eventually hitched across the country to B.C. I'd like to say I never looked back, but I say those names every night in my prayers. Billy Buffalo, Abigail Buffalo, Cardinal Horn, George Davis, Samuel Cloutier."

Murphy's heart broke as she listened to their story, listened to the kind of life they had, the fear those kids felt, the terror Cardinal would have experienced before being shot. She needed to get Price and make him pay.

"Can you explain why you think you can identify this body in Spalding? And who do you think it is?" she asked.

"It's Cardinal Horn. The story Samuel told me was that the Buffalo kids—they were brother and sister—and Cardinal, were taken from Tiny Flowers and that in the summer of 1972. Billy told George who told Samuel who told me. He said, Cardinal pissed the bed one night. He, Samuel, said Price flipped and kicked her out of the garage. He threw the mattress and the girl into the backyard and told her to sleep there. Next day, Billy woke up, and she was gone. Price said she ran away into the forest. Billy asked where she went because the house is nowhere near a forest, and Price backhanded him and said to never mention it again. And he never did. But Billy told George who told Samuel who told me. And now I am telling you. I think they girl you found in the forest is Cardinal Horn."

"Okay, so you think Mr. Price fostered Cardinal Horn from Tiny Flowers, and she wet the bed and then ran away to a forest?" Girard asked.

"Yes. I guess she got lost? I do not know how she got there. Or even how far away it is. But I think that's who you found," Dan-Elle said.

Murphy thanked Dan-Elle for their help and, after hanging up, sat back heavily in her chair. She sighed and rubbed her face.

"Boss, do we think he might have shot her for wetting her bed?" Parker asked quietly.

"If Dan-Elle's story is to be believed about threatening kids over the cookie, then yes. That was decades ago, but they told it like it was yesterday. What do you all think?"

"I... How can we prove this?" Hamilton asked.

"Ask Beatrice Price?"

"Beatrice seemed like a sweet old lady in the interview," Girard said. "I can't see her hurting anyone, losing her temper like that. I think there are two living Price children. And we know the Buffalos are dead. And we could find the other foster kids to see if they remember."

"Beatrice has no criminal charges. We checked the database, right? Adam, you ask the neighbours. Maybe she is the neighbour from hell, but it never gets recorded by the police. Be discreet."

"Yes, boss."

"They mentioned bullets in a yellow box. I'm sure they meant cartridges, not bullets. Cleo, find a .22 cartridge that came in a yellow box before 1975. If we can locate that, it will lend credence to their story."

"Yes boss," Hamilton said.

"What can I do, boss?" Parker asked, eager to help.

"Double check the names of all foster kids that went to the Price household. You are looking for all the people they mentioned. Find out if anyone is missing. We do not actually know if anyone else is missing from the Price home. Do not contact them yet, just try to locate them."

"Yes boss," Parker said. Murphy waved them out of her office. There was a soft silence in the atelier as detectives turned their attention to assigned tasks. Murphy's body was drained, feeling as if she had just completed a grueling marathon. The weight of loss wrapped around her like a heavy shroud, leaving her utterly exhausted and fragile, a feeling she despised. She loathed the vulnerability that crept into her being. When her phone buzzed a notification, she ignored it. She simply did not have the energy. It buzzed again, and a third time. Then it rang.

"Murphy."

"You have two minutes until your appointment with Dr. Saunders."

"Right, thanks for the reminder, Sandra. Leaving now," she said. Murphy walked into the atelier and asked if everyone had their appointments scheduled. Girard and Hamilton had already gone, and Parker was scheduled for later that day. "Okay, I'm going home afterward. You two, don't stay late. Parker, go home from your session. We have to be fresh tomorrow. We have a lot of work to do. Okay?"

A chorus of 'Yes boss' rung out, and Murphy left the office. She hated these mandatory sessions. Twenty minutes of talking to someone who liked to hear their own voice. It was of exceedingly little value.

Murphy went up to the third floor, walked directly into the waiting room for psychiatrist Dr. Troy Saunders, and sat down. It was only a few minutes before Dr. Saunders's current client walked out of the counselling room and into the waiting room. As was tradition, Murphy gave him a low-five as she passed by, and walked into Dr. Saunders's office.

"Hi my name is Detective Inspector Caitlin Murphy. I am a homicide detective. I am here because we found the skeletal remains of a ten-year-old girl."

"Hello Caitlin, welcome." Dr. Saunders said. "What's been on your mind lately?"

She wondered if the doctor had heard her. "It is policy to talk to a therapist if a homicide victim is under the age of 16. Yesterday we found the skeletal remains of a 10-year-old girl."

"I'm so sorry to hear that, Caitlin. It's understandable that this kind of thing would be difficult for you. As a homicide detective, you're often exposed to traumatic events, and it's important to take care of your mental and emotional well-being. I hope you don't mind that it is mandatory. This shows that your department recognizes the importance of addressing the potential emotional impact of these types of cases," Dr. Saunders said.

Murphy knew that was a lie; it was policy so the police department could avoid liability when cops blew their brains out.

"I want you to know this is a safe and confidential space where you can express your thoughts and feelings about the situation. By your body language, I sense you are uncomfortable."

"Huh? No, I am quite comfortable. This is how I sit at home, slouching, relaxed. I can sit up if you'd like," Murphy offered.

"I'm glad that you feel comfortable talking to me, Caitlin. It's difficult to talk about traumatic experiences, especially for the first time. It's important to recognize that it's completely normal to have a range of emotions in response to a traumatic event like this. You might feel sad, angry, anxious, or even numb. It's okay to feel these emotions, and it's important to give yourself permission to feel them. One helpful strategy for coping with traumatic events is to practice self-care. This might include getting enough rest, eating well, exercising, spending time with loved ones, and engaging in activities that you enjoy."

Murphy was getting bored listening to his rote advice, and it wasn't her first time. He was going to talk about getting a more permanent therapist, ask what aspects made her feel whatever way she was feeling, and then suggest engaging in positive energy.

"Remember that I am here whenever you want, and you are always welcome back, but you can also find a therapist of your own. Police benefits cover up to $1,000 a year. Now, I know some people pretend it does not bother them, but seeing death all the time can cause a range of intense emotions. What are your emotions right now?"

"I am angry and frustrated," she said honestly. There was no way she was going to address any of it with this talking Wikipedia page. Not her childhood, not her job, not this murder. Nothing.

"Talking about your anger can be a helpful way to process your emotions. You might find it helpful to talk about what specifically makes you angry about this case. Is it the senseless violence against a child? That the perpetrator might still be out there? Failing to prevent the crime from happening?"

Murphy tuned out, waiting for him to get to the part of how important her job is and how she should take care of herself. As if on cue, Dr. Saunders began talking about self-care.

"It's also important to remember to take care of yourself throughout the process. Coping with the trauma of a violent crime can take a toll on your mental and emotional well-being, so it's important to seek support when you need it."

Murphy thought for a moment before responding. "Well, I've always turned to my faith for guidance and comfort in times like these. Prayer and reflection help me find a sense of peace and hope amidst the darkness." She knew what was next. It was always next whenever she used the word 'darkness.'

"It's understandable that you feel a darkness, Caitlin. Coping with the trauma of a violent crime can be emotionally and mentally draining. I would suggest you continue reflecting, practice mindfulness. Mindfulness is being fully present and engaged in the moment. You might find it helpful to engage in mindfulness practices like deep breathing, meditation, or yoga to help you relax and reduce stress," he said. Murphy wondered why he was repeating himself.

"If I am at a crime scene, looking at a dead body, I can't really do yoga, can I? And I don't know how much more engaged in the scene I can be, I have to keep an eye out for every clue, every detail, every scent and sound. I have to talk to grief-stricken parents and nosey media. I am incredibly mindful, incredibly present."

Dr. Saunders repeated himself, suggesting that meditation in a quiet place, perhaps behind a building, would help. "Spending time with loved ones or supportive colleagues can be a great way to reduce stress and feel more connected. You might talk to trusted colleagues or friends who can provide a listening ear and support."

"Oh yes, thanks, I hadn't thought of that," she said sarcastically. Murphy resented talking to the automaton. She knew she was not smarter than the doctor, but she was stronger. And sometimes, strength meant endurance, not action.

"Yes, you'll find it helpful. Engage in physical activity, take breaks, consider taking a short walk. One approach to managing anger is to understand where the anger is coming from. Anger can be a natural and understandable response to an unjust situation. However, it can also be a response to feelings of helplessness, frustration, or fear. Understanding the root of your anger can help you better manage and cope with your emotions," Dr. Saunders said. It was what he always said.

"Mindfulness, rest, relaxation, taking breaks, understanding my feelings. Get help when I think I need it. Thank you doctor, I appreciate your insight," Murphy lied.

"You are most welcome. Now, our time is up. Would you mind sending in the next person?"

"Sure thing," Murphy said, as she got up and walked out. She gave a low-five to the next person in the room and left the office. It was close enough to quitting time, if such a thing existed, and she headed home.

On the drive home, she said the prayer of St. Augustine. "O Lord our God, grant us to trust in your overshadowing wings. Protect us beneath them and bear us up..." Pulling into the driveway, she recognized Thomas's car. She hoped Del might be available for a chat.

CHAPTER EIGHTEEN

"Hi everyone," Murphy said as she walked into the kitchen. She received a chorus of greetings in reply. Del and Thomas were sitting at the kitchen table chatting quietly while Maria stirred a pot of sauce on the stovetop.

"Maria is making dinner, can you join us?" Del asked.

"Bucatini with mushroom ragu, there is plenty," Maria said. Her sauce was rich and aromatic. The onions and garlic sizzled and smoked when she added vermouth to deglaze the pot. The cremini, maitake and porcini mushrooms absorbed the liquid as Maria used a wooden spoon to scrape up the browned bits at the bottom of the pot.

Murphy plopped into a wooden kitchen chair and smiled. "It smells great Maria, yes please and thank you."

"Anything for the TV star," she said with a smile, eliciting light laughter from everyone.

"You are becoming viral," Thomas said as he poured a glass of unoaked chardonnay for Murphy. "That was quite the dressing down you gave that reporter."

"Not a reporter, a jackass. I was so mad. The only place he could have gotten those figures was from someone in accounting. I thought at first it might be Valencia, but anyone with access to our budget could have passed that on," Murphy said. She took a sip of wine, it was bright but hearty. "Mmm, good choice," she said to Del holding up her glass.

"That's me, thank you," Thomas said. Murphy raised her glass to him.

"Is that the group of people from the pamphlet?" Maria asked as she wrangled the boiling pasta into a strainer.

"Yes, it is."

"And you found a little girl from there? Someone killed a sick little girl?"

"Hmm, yes. But I think I will resolve it in a day or two," she said.

"You do the Lord's work," Maria said as she began filling bowls with pasta.

Del laughed, and Thomas snorted causing Murphy to smile wryly. "A bit of wolf in sheep's clothing," Thomas said

"Did you know, legally I can lie to a suspect during questioning? Everyone assumes I can't, and while I am usually so well-prepared I don't need to, I can," Murphy said.

"I don't think lying is the Lord's work, is it?" Thomas asked, looking at Maria as she placed a bowl of bucatini in front of him.

"Well, the greater good is being done," Maria said. She paused and added, "If us Catholics are good at anything, it's gaslighting." Everyone cheered and laughed, and the conversation around the table became lighter. Maria sat beside Murphy but close enough to Del to pass the parmesan, pepper or whatever she asked for. The pasta had a rich umami flavour, the mushrooms were soft, with crispy browned edges. Everyone got quiet for a moment until after the first few bites. And then came the flurry of compliments.

"Maria, you make damn good food," Thomas said.

"It's been a long time since I've had something this good," Murphy added.

"Since the last time you ate one of her dinners," Del teased.

Murphy agreed with a "True, true," and raised her glass in a toast to Maria.

"Oh, before I forget, Sun called for you," Del said as she ate another forkful of pasta. Murphy nodded her head but said nothing. "Ah. Are you going to ghost her?"

"I thought you liked her," Thomas said, then added, "Oh shit, did one of us say something to offend her the other night? We were out for dinner, me and Bob and Jens, and we saw her come in, so we invited her to sit with us before Caitlin showed up."

"Let me guess, you showed up and left immediately," Del said.

"She did. And did not even offer to pay this time," Thomas agreed.

"That was the problem. I have Sun the money, and she thought I was lording it over her or something."

"You gave her money for dinner and she didn't pay?"

"Yeah, well, she seems to have taken offense. She found me at the Goose Gas and threw the money back in my face this morning. How dare I, blah blah blah," Murphy said.

"That makes no sense," Del said with a frown.

Murphy sighed and took another sip. "I said that. Then I said she had the emotional intelligence of a fifteen-year-old, and then she tried to slap me."

Maria crossed herself. "Oh, my!" she said. "I took the message. That explains why she said she wanted to say 'sorry' face-to-face. So she could try to hit you again!"

"Yeah maybe. No, no I doubt it," Murphy said. "She's left a couple of messages apologizing."

Thomas stared at his fork thoughtfully and asked, "Are you going to contact her?" Murphy simply shrugged and took the last bite of her pasta.

"Forget her. No one should get away with hitting someone," Maria said.

"She didn't hit me, she just tried to. She apologized immediately," Murphy said.

"I want to hear more," Del said. "Living room?" she asked. Thomas and Murphy followed her into the room while Maria cleared the table. "She doesn't seem the type to strike out," Del said as she transferred herself from her wheelchair to a recliner.

"Frankly, she's too small for that, isn't she?" Thomas asked.

"Size doesn't matter."

"That's what you women always say," Thomas teased with a grin.

"You know," Murphy said, refilling her glass from a fresh bottle of wine, "I deal with what happens when people lose their temper. On purpose, by accident, it doesn't take much to go way too far. And you have to live with that. You have to be held accountable and reap what you have sown. But where is forgiveness in that? I mean, geez, this is going to sound corny, but I believe in redemption. I believe in the power of redemption. Not that bullshit that the churches spew, but on an individual level. Remorse and redemption."

Murphy paused for a moment, took another drink, and continued. "I know killers who have zero remorse. I remember one guy, when I was in Ottawa homicide, an older guy, had served his time and was out. He killed a gay guy in a park back in the eighties. He called my partner, who was the detective who put him away. After he got out, called to say he was innocent. He said he had been protecting himself against a 'fag' and how my partner had stolen years of his life. No remorse, no responsibility. No redemption."

"But Sun, I mean, I don't know if she believes in redemption, but I am seeing remorse. I am seeing her trying to apologize," Murphy said as she swirled the wine in her glass.

"Why the hesitation?" Thomas asked.

"My relationships never work out, anyway."

"Ahem," Del said, clearing her throat.

"Ha! Everyone but you, honey bunch," Murphy took another drink and said, "If it isn't one thing, it's another. If we get past this, then the homicide life will tear it apart. The crazy hours and sudden departures."

"Way to stop it before it ever happens. Coward. Do you like her?" Del asked.

The coward comment stung Murphy, but Del wasn't wrong.

"I do. She... She just does something to me that..."

"And maybe you do something to her, something that's freaking her out. Maybe she's in love and it's scaring her," Del said.

"But you are so unlovable," Thomas protested with a laugh, breaking the seriousness in the room.

"Fuck you," Murphy said with a chuckle.

"Totally unlovable," Thomas said.

"Unbearable," Del added playfully.

"Unfuckable," Murphy added herself. Everyone began shouting, playing the word game. Odious. Abhorrent. Unpleasant. Abominable.

"Abominable? Like the snowman? Hah! Sasquatch! It all comes back to Sasquatch!" joked Murphy.

"Call the woman back, meet her. Put your Christian mouth where her money is," Del said. She then opened her eyes wide and gaped in jest at her own joke. Thomas joined in, but Maria's faith would not allow her. She sat silently, but desperately wanting Murphy to call Sun. Despite all else, love is love, and she thought Murphy was in love.

"You guys are animals," Murphy laughed. "I'm going to bed."

"Call her. Bow chicka wow wow," Thomas sang out, poorly imitating music used in old porn movies.

"Animals," Murphy said over her shoulder as she walked out and headed upstairs.

In her room, Murphy changed into an undershirt and pajama bottoms and sat in her reading chair. It was a worn brown leather club she bought in an antique store when she first moved to Muskoka, and she loved it. She considered whether she should call Sun and arrange a meeting, but opened The Grace Diaries 1570-1598 to page 103 as she found comfort in the words of long-forgotten poet and diarist Grace Hathaway.

'Oh, sinne, the mark upon our soul so deep,

That staines our hertes and maketh conscience weep,

A burthen heavy, hard to beare alone,

A wounde that festers, hard as stone.

So let us leave our past behind,

And seeke the peace that we may finde,

In mercy's arms, we shall be free,

And walke the path of purity.

Oh, sinne, the burthen we must beare,

But in redemption, we shall finde a way to repair,

And through forgiveness, we shall be made whole,

And finde the joy that filleth the soule.'

Murphy ran her fingers over the words 'And through forgiveness, we shall be made whole' as she slowly re-read the line. She picked up her phone and called Sun.

"Caitlin?" came a quiet voice from the other end of the line.

"Yep," she answered casually, and waited. Give her space, Murphy thought, give her a path that is open.

"I'm very sorry. I'd like to apologize to you. Properly, face to face. To explain. Explain, not excuse. Can we meet? Tonight?" Sun asked. Murphy could hear a note of desperation, a hint of pleading.

"For apology sex?" Murphy hoped.

"No. No sex. An apology, an explanation. Pete's Coffee? Just across the street from my store? In thirty minutes?"

Murphy agreed, hung up, changed into a pair of jeans, and walked downstairs. "Going out this late?" Del asked.

"Yeah, I-"

"Apology sex?" Thomas asked excitedly.

"That's what I said! But no. I think she needs to confess something. That's the vibe I get," Murphy said as she pulled on her boots and grabbed a leather jacket.

"Well, if anyone knows about confessions, it's a Catholic detective," Del said.

"I'm all about the confession," Murphy laughed and walked out.

Twenty minutes later, Murphy pulled her Brawler into a parking spot on the street outside Pete's Coffee. There was a cool night wind and Murphy was glad she had her jacket as she got out of the Brawler and peered inside the coffee shop. Sun had not yet arrived, so Murphy leaned against her Brawler and waited. She struck a pose she called the 'James Dean'. One leg bent, resting on the running board, her worn white t-shirt peaking out from the unzipped jacket, her thumbs hooked into her pockets. All she needed was a cigarette to finish the look.

This was a town that was home. She had a wife and good friends here. She lived and worked in a place where distances were measured by the time it took to get there, and where the streets were named after the thing they took you to. Church Street led to the first church in the area, built in 1801. Garden Street led to the public gardens. Mill Street still led to the old gristmill, though now it was a Canadiana shop and bed-and-breakfast.

But the quaint names belied the truth. As she looked down the street, Murphy could see the laneway where Ashley Tatlow was raped and murdered, and the bar where Hugh Wyatt lost his life after getting into a fight over which beer was better: Canadian or Moosehead. In the other direction, Murphy could see a drunk yahoo screaming at his girlfriend outside Brad's Barworks. She wondered if that would be the next murder scene to attend, or if they would make it home before he killed her. Homicide permeated the soul of the town and filled in its dark corners.

Sun saw Murphy and crossed the street, walking up behind her quietly. She paused for a moment before saying, "God, you are beautiful."

Murphy turned to greet Sun and smiled. "You too."

"I'm glad you came," Sun said. "I am sorry. I am so sorry for what I did. I need to apologize and tell you, I never meant to hurt you, certainly never meant to hit you. I can tell you it will never happen again," Sun said. She tucked $300 in Murphy's pocket.

"Hmm," Murphy said, then remained silent. Most people hate silence and will try to fill it. Sun was one of those.

"I thought you had looked me up in the police database," Sun said.

"Wh—why would I?" Murphy's senses tingled with wariness after hearing Sun's words, sensing something was amiss. "Ah. Got it. Drug trafficking or sex work?" Murphy asked.

Sun drew in a deep breath, gathering her thoughts, and then began to speak. "Sex work. I started in 2003, when I was twenty-four year old. I had two small kids, my husband had just left me. I needed money. But look, do not get me wrong. I enjoyed it. I made money. A lot of money. I saved enough for both kids to go to university, although who knows if my son will ever go. I had enough for a house, and to start my own business. And I enjoyed the sex. I was really good at it, and it was incredibly fun. I specialized in couples. I did sex work for about twelve years, and stopped. Just like that." As she shared the revealing details of her past, she felt a rush of nervousness, fearing judgment or misunderstanding. Vulnerability washed over her like a tidal wave, leaving her feeling exposed and anxious about how Murphy might perceive her.

"So no one forced you? Just you, no pimp?"

"Just me. By the end I was pulling in $5,000 a night."

Murphy's eyes widened. "Five thousand?"

"Shhh. Yes. Why is that hard to believe?" Sun said, a little insulted.

"For one... session? Or was that like, dozens a night?"

Sun was definitely insulted. "One night, one couple. I was really, really good. I earned my money."

"Hell yes you did. Let me think...Did you quit before or after Bill C-36?"

"Before. They made prostitution legal just after I stopped. Well, kind of legal. And I had been arrested a few times in the early days. I thought you would have checked the police records for—" Sun stopped herself when she saw Murphy glower.

"No. That would be immoral and unethical," Murphy said. "And I could lose my job. So, you made bank, had fun, saved your money and just went on with life?"

"We aren't all trafficked you know. A lot of us go into the trade voluntarily. I know what I am good at, and I got paid for it."

"So when I gave you money..."

"I thought you were paying me for sex. But then I ran into one of your friends. Jens, I think. And he was complaining about that night. You told him you would pay for dinner, but then you did not. And I...Well, I put two and two together. You gave me the money to pay for dinner. Not to pay for sex."

"Yes, of course dinner. I had no idea about the other stuff."

"And now that you do?"

"Well, let me ask. Were children involved?"

"Oh God no."

"Are you still in the business?"

"No. I've been out for a decade."

"Have you been tested?"

"Have you?"

Murphy was taken aback by the question. "No. No I haven't."

"I have. I'm clean. I get tested at the start and end of every relationship. Have you never been tested for any STDs?"

"Well, no. It.. I..."

"Damn, well, get yourself tested. If I have, you should."

"I only sleep with women, though. And not all that often," Murphy countered.

Sun tilted her head and stared at Murphy. "Get. Tested. You only have to do it once, if you aren't sleeping with anyone else."

"I barely have time for you," Murphy grumbled. "No. No one else."

"Me neither. Get tested and that is the end of it."

Murphy took a deep breath and leaned back. Somehow the conversation went from apology to revelation to admonition. It was hard to believe that the woman capable of controlling the conversation so adeptly was also the one who got so out of control she tried to slap an armed cop. Murphy put her hands around Sun's waist and pulled her closer. They had never even made it inside the coffee shop, and she doubted they would.

"Sun, I apologize too. What I said was cruel."

Sun laughed. "Ha. You were probably right that I was acting like a teenager. And I should never have raised my hand. I am sorry."

"Okay, we can get through this. If you want to." Murphy ran her hand down Sun's cheek.

"Oh, I do, I really do. But do you? I mean, are you okay dating a former sex worker?" Sun asked.

"You would not be the first." Murphy hugged Sun tightly, then turned her around. She leaned herself tightly against Sun's back and said, "Tell me what you see."

"You mean the street? The store?" she asked as she looked down the same street Murphy had been contemplating earlier.

"Don't tell me what's there. Tell me what you see."

"What I see. Well, I see some beautiful Lady's Mantle blooming in that planter. Alchemilla mollis, a nice fresh scent. Over there is Catananche caerulea, Cupid's Dart. They are herbaceous plants and see the blue-purple flower heads? So pretty. They belong to the daisy family."

"What's the tall one there?" Murphy asked as she pointed to a green plant with stalks of pink-white flowers.

"Gas plant. Dictamnus albus, it is a species of flowering plant in the family Rutaceae. It is called burning bush, dittany, or fraxinella. You know, the town has done a pretty good job with planters. Bee friendly, too."

Murphy turned the two of them around, so they were now looking in the opposite direction. "What is that thing on the building?"

"It's a climber called Virgin's Bower, Clematis virginiana, from the Ranunculaceae. Beautiful, hardy. It will flower in July. Why? Why are you asking about plants?" Sun asked as she turned in Murphy's arms.

"I didn't ask about plants. I asked what you saw, and you see plants. You see flowers and leaves and greenery and things growing and blooming. I can hear in your voice how much joy plants bring you. I can see it in your eyes. You see beauty, you see nature. You smell like flowers, you smell beautiful and fresh and alive. That's what I want, what I need. I need someone who is alive and kind and who sees flowers when they look down the street. I need you to see that, to remind me that beauty and light and joy exist." A soft calm came over Murphy as she talked. Her eyes sparkled and her smile warmed.

"That is not what I see when I look at the world. I could never see the world like that, I haven't for a long time. But you see it and maybe you can share that. Maybe we can go to a restaurant and you can tell me about the flowers on the table. Or out for a walk and you can show me some..." Murphy choked up and her voice became strained. "Show me some stupid bush that smells sweet in winter, you know? I need that, I need you, and I think I could love you."

Murphy hugged Sun tightly and stopped talking. She looked up and saw a pocket of stars.

CHAPTER NINETEEN

As the homicide detectives sat in the atelier, going over the evidence and the plan to bring in Cornelius Price, Murphy swirled a spoon in her instant coffee, enjoying the light clinking of the spoon against the cup.

"I checked with the Price neighbours," Girard said. "As we know, there have been no official police complaints, but some neighbours had things to say. The neighbour two houses down, a single mom with three kids, claims Beatrice has been harassing her kids. It started a year ago when Beatrice knocked on her door to ask if she could please stop her children riding their scooters past the Price home. It's continued with almost daily complaints. Beatrice most recently said they should not ride on the sidewalk outside her house. Says she's concerned the kids are riding their scooters near her car."

"Hm, not exactly the end of the world," Murphy said.

"But the backyard neighbour on Whitlock Avenue, they have a bigger complaint. Apparently, Beatrice hates their dog. They actually reported a suspicious person in December. The resident said his dog alerted him by barking at someone in the yard. He said he saw an elderly woman, dressed in black, walking along his property line, on the other side of the fence. I pulled the police report. It says the man recognized his neighbour from Old Brown Road. I do not know why it doesn't name Beatrice, but the Prices live at 17 Old Brown Road. They share a backyard fence with this guy. He said he saw the woman throw a small round item over the fence into their yard. When he checked, he found a half dozen treats. Said they looked like cream-filled chocolate-covered candy, but when he broke it open, he discovered a mothball hidden inside and became concerned the woman was attempting to feed the thing to his dog. Boss, mothballs are toxic. He thinks she was trying to kill his dog for barking."

"Okay, that goes to the criminal nature of the woman, disregard for life. Animal life, but children could have found them. The search warrant won't cover mothballs. It will be even more important to have her permission to look around for signs of a crime. As soon as you are there, ask if you can check the backyard, get officers out there to look for any of those treats. When we look in the garage, same thing, keep your eye out for mothballs. I mean, who the hell uses mothballs anymore? Anyway, try to get permission to look for signs of a crime," Murphy said.

"Yes boss. We have the treats in the Evidence Room from the original complaint, so we can... we can compare mothballs?" Girard said.

"Good enough. They don't much matter, but good to know, it goes to character. Any other complaints? No?" With so many moving parts in this investigation, Murphy momentarily paused, holding up a finger to silence everyone. As if a light switched on, she suddenly continued. "Okay, what about the DNA on the ropes? Can we confirm it was Jose Mercado's?"

"No boss. Too degraded," Parker said. "I have printouts from the Emily Powell video. They aren't great, but they show Cornelius and Phillip in the background while Jose is holding the femur."

"Excellent. Michael, we are going to record this interview, so you set that up. Cleo, you can be with Michael in the observation room until we get permission to search his house. Then you take the warrants and go to the Price home. Remember, friendly. I would rather have some cooperation. I will give you the signal for when to go. I want you, Michael, to have a paper copy of all the evidence sorted and tabbed so that as we talk, you can follow along with the evidence. Not everything, but any time I need some piece of evidence I don't have with me, you are to get it. Adam, you will be with me. Bring your laptop. You will email Michael to bring in whatever evidence I ask for. Cleo, feed Adam any information you find when you search the Price home. Good so far?"

Her detectives acknowledged they were all good. The preparations were typical for any interview conducted by Murphy where she wanted a confession, although this one was potentially going to be much longer than most. She always aimed for a confession because they had great sway with judges and juries, and she wanted Price to admit to two murders.

"Boss, TechWave just came through with Price's cell phone records. In the last month, he has made fifteen calls to his home number," Girard said. "And... Let me see, uh, yes! His phone pinged off a tower at Highway 11 and Old Brier Road on Saturday at 7:35am. That's the closest tower to Sunny Lake. Not great, but puts him in the general area at the right time."

"Fantastic. I've let the Chief know, and he is not happy about the idea of arresting Price, and wants us to get him to agree to come in on his own volition. And I think he will," Murphy said.

"Boss, what if he doesn't?" Parker asked.

"I think Price is too arrogant not to want to talk to us. I have already consulted with him once as an expert. Michael and Cleo, you are going to head to the Baptist United Church. When they get out, ask him if he can help us with the investigation. He will ask why, tell him you don't know for sure, but it includes old paperwork. Tell him it's important to the case. If he balks, ask him when he can come down to the station. Tell him it's important...tell him it's important for a Monday press conference. But don't let on in any way that he is a suspect. I think in front of the other churchgoers, he will accept. Maybe even boast. Are we good?"

The detectives all nodded and then each got onto their respective tasks, with Hamilton and Girard helping Parker organize the evidence file as requested. In the meantime, Murphy retreated to her office and prepared her own paperwork. At 8:30, she instructed Parker and Hamilton to head to the church for the end of mass at 9:00, while she and Girard went over strategy again.

Shortly after 9:00, Murphy's phone rang. "Boss," Hamilton said, "Price wants to stay for church breakfast. Says he will be by around 11:00."

"Okay, are you with him now?"

"No, we're back at the car, I can-"

"No, that's perfect. Let him come in on his own, let him think he is in control. If he's as narcissistic as I think he is, he will not bring a lawyer. I sure hope not, anyway. Okay, come on back," Murphy said. She suddenly felt butterflies in her stomach. It was unusual for her to feel nervous at all, but she got light-headed and anxious. This was a man she was about to get a confession from for two murders, decades apart. Would he walk into her trap? Or had he wised up, delayed his arrest? Was he spending time with his wife because this would be the last time they saw each other outside of the legal system? He wasn't likely to flee, but even that scenario flashed quickly into Murphy's mind. She felt like a ten-year-old about to take a math test she had not studied for.

"Hah," Murphy said aloud as she stood up from her desk.

"You okay, boss?" Girard asked.

"Yeah yeah. Just psyching myself up, trying to go through all the scenarios. We have enough, more than enough, evidence. We are good. We are good."

Beatrice Price dropped her husband off at the police station and headed off to pick up his dry cleaning before heading home. Cornelius walked confidently into the police station and strode right up to the front desk. "Cornelius Price. I'm here to see Detective Caitlin Murphy," he announced.

The officer behind the desk smiled until she caught sight of the pocketknife in a sheath hanging on Price's belt. It wasn't that unusual in the district for people to carry knives, as there were many hunters and farmers. She nodded at Price and reached down to grab a numbered basket. "Sir, if you wouldn't mind, there are no knives allowed in the station. Best if you just put it in your car, or use this basket. Everything in, sheath included, so no one needs to worry if I missed it on your way in. And you'll have to sign a release form." The officer held out a metal tag with the number fifteen stamped into it, matching the basket.

Price sighed and nodded. "I've never been in a police station," he said as he undid his belt and slid the sheath off.

"No worries, sir, happens all the time when people are reporting crimes. Thank you. Here's a release form you have to sign. Just read it over carefully, write down 'knife' or 'Buck knife' in that box, date and sign at the bottom. Then hand in the metal tag when you're done and you will get your knife back."

"Good, I thought you were going to tell me I couldn't own it," Price said.

"Oh no, it's fine. It looks like a pocket knife. My granddad wears his all the time, he even eats apples with it! Now I'll call up the detective."

Price put his knife into the basket, quickly scrawled 'Spitfire Buck knife' into the box and signed and dated the form before pushing it back toward the officer.

"Someone will come down to get you in a moment. Please have a seat," the officer said as she slipped the basket into a numbered storage slot. It reminded Price of the old hotel key cubby system. He nodded and smiled and sat down. It was just a moment before Girard came down.

"I'm Detective Staff Sergeant Adam Girard. Mr. Price, thank you for coming to speak with us today. I'll take you to Interview One," Girard said.

"I remember who you are," Price said. "I'm not senile, you know."

"Sorry sir, I didn't mean to imply anything. One moment please," Girard said. He reached into his jacket pocket, withdrew his notebook and pen, and made a notation that Price said he remembered meeting the detective, and was not senile. Then Girard and Price were on their way.

Parker stopped Murphy in the hallway. "Boss, front desk reports they checked in a knife for Price," he said. "He signed the release form." Murphy smiled and asked that it be sent to the Forensics Unit to test for human blood and, eventually, DNA. Nobody ever read the form, even though it clearly stated that by signing, you authorized your weapon to be forensically tested if they reasonably suspected it to be related to a crime.

"Okay, everyone, he is in Interview One. Let's give him a minute to settle, and we will go in."

The room was brightly lit, tidy, and in good repair. The hum of air conditioning was low, providing calming white noise that many people failed to notice. When she first arrived in Muskoka, Murphy had spent thousands of dollars from her budget on renovating and styling the interview rooms. It often caught people off guard; too many cops used dingy, dark rooms where detectives yelled at people and slammed their fists on the desk. Her rooms offered a jug of water, pleasant lighting and good air circulation. Sometimes she even put out the coffee maker. After all, she would always interview more witnesses than killers in any murder investigation. Why not be decent about it? The Chief hated it but could not argue with Murphy's high confession rate.

After a few minutes, Murphy announced, "Okay, we are on."

CHAPTER TWENTY

"For the record, this is Detective Inspector Caitlin Murphy, here with Detective Staff Sergeant Adam Girard. We are speaking with Mr. Cornelius Price, former mayor of Bradburn. As you can see, everything here is being videotaped and audio recorded. And behind the glass, I have my detectives, Detective Constable 2nd class Cleo Hamilton and Detective Constable 2nd class Michael Parker. Have you ever been interviewed by the police, Mr. Price?" Murphy asked.

"No, the police have not interviewed me. I did interview Lloyd Griffith for the position of Chief of Police," Price said. Murphy nodded. "And of course, I am familiar with talking with the press. Newspapers from all over the world, actually." Price seemed relaxed, confident, as if he was in control. Murphy wanted to keep him that way, at least for a while. She put a thin folder of papers in front of her and waited for Girard to set up his laptop before continuing.

"Right. Well, Mr. Price, Cornelius if I may, I appreciate you coming in. You've had a lot of experience with reporters, so you know how they are. This is big news. The media are all over it, the finding of the historic body, dubbed Spalding Doe by the media. We have to fast forward everything a little bit, you know, just get things out of the way. Keep my boss happy, keep the press happy, keep the politicians happy, keep the Internet happy."

Murphy joked with Price about podcasters and Internet investigators before explaining that the interview would be thorough and would take some time. A coffee maker was set up in the corner with a dozen cups, and sugar and cream were available; after giving him his first cup, Murphy invited Price to get up and get his own refills. "I treat everyone with respect, and so does DSS Girard, of course. I'll just ask that you do the same for me. Have you ever been read your rights?"

"Of course not. Never had any problem with police," Price said. "I mean, I've seen the Miranda Rights thing on TV so often I could recite it with you," he laughed.

Murphy laughed with him. "Well, that's America. Things are different here. But I want to be clear, we are trying to determine who Spalding Doe is and what happened. Paperwork, eh? Now, you aren't under arrest, you can leave at any time. Feel free to leave at any time, the door isn't locked. Adam will walk you down to the lobby any time. And any time you want to talk to a lawyer, your lawyer, you just let me know."

Murphy explained they were looking into the death of Spalding Doe, "Just one of the many things we have to investigate, you know how it is when these old bodies come up. A big commotion, lots of fuss, and then it calms down and we can get back to our regular jobs," she reassured him. "We just need to know who she was, what happened to her and how she got to Spalding Conservation Area. The pathologist said there was a wound in her skull, so we need to know how that got there and who did it or if it was accidental. I want to be clear, to make sure you understand. This is literally our job to find out who is responsible and make sure we charge them with the right offense, no matter who it is. It's due diligence, you know, because we have eyes on us."

She did not see any reaction from Price when she mentioned the head wound. Price simply nodded his head. "Reporters."

"Reporters, exactly," Murphy said. "And Chief Valencia does not want to look bad, so I have to cross all my Ts and dot all my Is. This is so much about old paperwork, you know, federal forms and... Oh, I forgot. Do you have a lawyer? No? Okay, if you want to call someone to get advice or anything, we have a list of lawyers who will give you advice over the phone, free of charge, legal aid, eh? You can call now if you want."

Price declined to call a lawyer. "I hardly need legal aid," he said. He felt insulted, and Murphy was delighted.

Murphy got him to agree to be interviewed, told him he should not feel pressured by media coverage, and that prosecutors could compel her to testify in court. "It is not a big thing, being called for evidence. It's just part of the legal system." Price seemed blasé about everything, and that was exactly what Murphy wanted. He was being advised of all of his legal rights before he said anything incriminating.

One of the most successful interrogation techniques is minimization, playing down the significance of the crime or the suspect's involvement during the initial stage of the interview. Murphy considered using this tactic, offering Price a potential excuse for shooting Cardinal—You just meant to scare her. She looked into Price's smug face and knew she could never minimize what he had done.

Murphy vaguely outlined the case so far, getting Price to agree that he had been an employee at the Department of Indian Child Welfare from 1967 to 1979, when he became mayor of Bradburn. Price said that, as a federal employee, he was responsible for arranging for the fostering of Indigenous children identified by the department. He checked out the foster families, moved the children, and finished the paperwork. "Typical office worker bee stuff," he said.

"Worker bee, yes. Boy, I sure understand that," Murphy said as she gestured at the papers in front of her on the table. "And people were well-paid, weren't they? The foster families?"

"Yes, very generously. About seven dollars a day to the foster families. Very generous back then. About fifty in today's money. The per-diem was higher for Indian kids than normal kids because they were so much trouble," Price said. "Native kids. Back then it was Indian, but the term is Native now, right? Anyway, I advocated for a higher per diem back in 1970, and in 1971 it was raised to fifteen dollars. Plus, extra for school supplies and sports equipment. More if a social worker tagged the kid as a problem."

"Substantial money even by today's standard," Murphy said casually as she pulled out a notebook and wrote it down. She was trying to convey a sense of interest in fostering so Price would stay cooperative, and to set him up for the next line of questioning. He kept talking, humble bragging about the money he brought in both as a federal employee and as a foster parent himself. Price told Murphy his family had fostered seven children over the years, from 1971 to 1978.

"What was it like, fostering kids?"

"Not just children, but Indi—I mean Native children, ones with behaviour problems. At least at the start. My wife was a saint with those kids. We treated them just like our own. A little structure and discipline were all they needed. We started out taking Indian kids with problems, but after a few years, we realized they were a bad influence on our real kids. I mean, my William still hasn't left home because he learned how to be lazy and greedy. Of course, now he helps around the house and whatnot so we need him home. But he made nothing of himself because of the uh, Native kids."

It was everything Murphy could do to hold back her anger at the man. But she was well-practiced at appearing disinterested; it often disarmed suspects. Girard simply kept his head down, tapping lightly at the keyboard of the laptop, though not actually pressing the keys. It was imperative that she not lose focus for a moment and that the pressure for Price to move forward never ceased. She must always push, and he must always respond.

"Troublesome children, eh?" Murphy said as she wrote in her notebook.

"The first three were the worst. A boy and two girls. Those kids really needed our help. They were neglected, they all had skin problems. I remember my wife had to clean them with an old wire brush. I'm sure their parents never cared for them. The boy was smart, but the two girls were slow, you know, a little retarded. Well, whatever that's called now. They were always forgetting where they lived, getting lost in the woods. We caught one of them walking down the side of the highway one time, swearing she was trying to go home! Heck, we lived in town. She did not know where she was going."

"Which one? What were their names?"

Murphy already knew the answer, having tracked down every foster child who went to the Price home. Billy Buffalo, Abigail Buffalo and Cardinal Horn showed up in 1971. George Davis in 1973, Samuel Cloutier in 1975, Dan-Elle Fox in 1976 and Mary Two Feathers in 1977.

"Well, let me think. There was Billy Buffalo, he was, I don't know, fifteen maybe? Boy, that was such a long time ago. Billy Buffalo, hah, what a funny name. Then the two girls, Abigail Buffalo, they were brother and sister, her and Billy. She was thirteen or fourteen and, gee, what was the other girl's name? A bird name... Cardinal! Cardinal Horn, I think. My wife knows better. She spent time with them. I was the dad, you know, kept a roof over their heads and food in their bellies; the one who disciplined the kids. There were more kids, but we stopped taking problem kids like the first three. There was Sam Cloutier, George Davis, Dan Fox and Mary Two Feathers. We stopped fostering kids when I ran for mayor."

Murphy noticed the effort Price appeared to put into trying to remember Cardinal's name. It seemed forced to her, and she knew he was pretending he was having a hard time remembering. "What happened to all those kids?" Murphy asked.

Price said Billy, Abigail, George and Sam aged out of foster care and left the area. Mary and Dan-Elle had each been incarcerated. He was ignoring Cardinal.

"And what happened to the other girl, Cardinal? Did she get arrested? Age out of the system?"

"No, she ran away. She stayed with us for about a year, but she just ran away."

Murphy nodded. "Do you know what day?"

"Gosh no, I can't remember. It was a long time ago. I reported it to the police, though, so you should have a record of it. I spoke with Chief Griffith directly," Price said.

"So you aren't sure..."

"No."

"Which day you..."

"No, no idea."

"Reported Cardinal missing?"

"As I said, Chief Griffith was told. If he didn't write a report, that's not my problem."

Murphy knew he was lying again. If he really had reported a missing girl to the Chief of Police, not only would there be a record, but there would have been a search and some media coverage. "We'll follow it up. Did you report her missing under her name, or as Price? I remember you said-"

"Horn. She was no Price. A problem kid, always trying to run away, vulgar, talking back. Not my child," Price said.

"Ok," Murphy said as she nodded. She knew introducing incriminating evidence progressively, rather than all at once, was far more likely to make a liar slip up, and that was exactly what she intended to do. "Let's keep going. I want to talk a little more about those remains we found. We know that with a body that's been buried for so long, there's probably not going to be the killer's DNA or fingerprints on clothes."

"She was killed? You said something about a wound or something. No, I imagine you won't find any DNA or fingerprints." He smiled.

"But there's trace evidence. Here, our victim was shot. In the head. Whoever shot her just dumped her into the hollow. They didn't take the bullet from her skull. We found it with her," Murphy explained.

"Oh, I see. Well, I'm sure you can test bullets or something, can't you?"

"Yes, we think so if we have a gun to match it to. Do you own any guns, Cornelius?" Murphy asked.

"I got rid of my guns years ago. 1979. I was running for mayor, my advisor said I had to get rid of my guns. Bad optics," Price said with a smile. "It worked. I won."

"Did you sell them, or...?"

"No, no, turned them over to Chief Griffiths for destruction. As mayor, not only do you have to be responsible, you have to be seen to be responsible. The newspapers took photos of me handing my rifles over to the Chief, and of my empty gun safe. There was even a photo of my wife trying to unlock the safe. I was the only one with the combination, you see, so we did it for laughs. No one else could get in and get the guns. No one. It played well with the more liberal voters."

Murphy quickly scrawled 'get newspaper photos' in her notebook and angled it surreptitiously toward Girard. He shot off an email to Parker to look for the exact newspaper article Price was referring to. She wanted a newspaper article that declared only he had access to the guns.

"You gave the guns to the Chief through Quit Claims?"

"Yes. In front of reporters, and even a local TV crew." Without being prompted, Girard emailed Hamilton asking her to find news footage.

"For due diligence, do you give us permission to check your home for weapons? I mean, if we don't check for them, the defence lawyer for the killer might try to use it to create doubt. Another suspect, eh?" Murphy said. Her heart was pounding. It was a make-or-break moment for the investigation.

Price's eyes turned dark. She found it disconcerting, but then in an instant he blinked, smiled, and the darkness was gone. He got up to get himself another cup of coffee. As he stirred in the sugar, he grinned and leaned toward the video camera recording the interview and said "I Cornelius Price hereby grant Detective Murphy and the Muskoka Police the right to search my home of any guns, ammunition, weapons of any kind."

Murphy liked his confidence. In Homicide, a successful interrogation can be the difference between a conviction and a cold case. She nodded and smiled. "Okay Cornelius, thank you, I-"

Parker knocked on the door to Interview One. "Oh, do you have any questions for me right now? No? Okay, I'm just going to step out. Make sure my crew tracked down your Quit Claim forms and whatnot. Adam will stay with you. I'll just be a minute," Murphy said as she headed out of the room.

Murphy stepped into the atelier to speak with Parker and Hamilton. Since Price had given his consent to search his home, Hamilton and Parker were told to search for weapons and ammunition, in particular, any .22 calibre weapons and cartridges, and any knives, and to report back as soon as possible. "Let Beatrice know Cornelius has given permission. Make that clear. Tell her she can call him if she would like. Don't forget what Dan-Elle told us about the yellow ammo box. Yellow. It might still be in the house or garage somewhere. And don't forget the damn dog treats, it's a weapon, poison." They headed out while Murphy went back to Interview One.

"Boss," Girard said as he turned his phone toward Murphy, showing Dr. Chen's email. The test for human blood on the knife was positive.

"Right, well, that should clear things up. Let's talk about something more recent. Let's talk about Jose Mercado. Do you know Jose?"

"Mercado you say? No, never heard of him." Price shifted in his chair slightly and failed to meet her gaze. Long ago she realized that lack of eye contact was not a sign of deception, and in fact could have medical, psychological or cultural reasons. However, a switch from making eye contact to not making eye contact, was informative.

"We found his body last Sunday. A young Toronto man. Is there any reason at all you can think of that during our investigation that, um, well, we're investigating how he died. Found him floating in a lake," Murphy said.

"Mm hmm, drowned then?" Price said as he sipped his coffee.

"I'm not at liberty to give details, but we're looking at his manner of death."

"Sunday you found him? I was at church on Sunday morning, then helping at the church picnic that afternoon. A few dozen people saw me, including the minister. Go ahead and ask," Price interrupted.

"I wouldn't doubt the minister's word," Murphy said, as she tapped the cross around her neck and smiled. "I'm not worried about Sunday, but I think you saw him on Friday night? You and I spoke about him on Tuesday afternoon."

"Ah, the guy with no name. That idiot with the deer bone."

"Yes, he's the one. Jose Mercado. Tell me again about seeing him?"

Price was bothered. "As I said, he was making some kind of a video about Bigfoot, talking loudly, disrupting everyone, so I told him to shut up. The waitress asked if I could get him to quiet down. I grabbed that stupid phone out of his hand and slammed it down on the table, and told him to pack up and get out. He sure did. And, well, some people clapped. That's how much he was annoying people."

Murphy was incredulous. People clapped? "Did you speak to him again?"

"No, that was the end of it."

"Right. You see, Cornelius, we never found his phone."

"I sure didn't take it. I already have one. I never let it out of my sight. No one needs more phones. Maybe he lost it, or he lent it to someone," Price said dismissively.

"Kids today never let it out of their sight, or lend it out. I bet you always have yours. Do you have it now?" Price reached into his pocket, waved his phone at her, and put it back. "I do not think he lent his. No, we don't think that's what happened. Personally, I think it's at the bottom of Sunny Lake. We may never find it. But you see, the thing about today's young people is, they live on their phones. This guy especially. He recorded videos, took photos. His wife told me he even created music on it. So, we really wanted to find that phone. But, like I said before, I have to cross my Ts and dot my Is, so we had to figure out a way to get access to the phone, without having the phone. It was my youngest detective who showed me. Today, everything is saved to the cloud."

"Young people spend too much time on their phones, if you ask me. Hmph," Price said as he took a sip from his cup. "Ugh. Cold. Mind if I use your facilities?" Girard showed him where the washroom was and escorted him back to Interview One. Murphy knew he was trying to control the pace of the interview and did not mind letting him think he was.

Price arrived back in the room but suddenly balked at being there and walked around rather than sitting down. Murphy refused to consider the possibility even for an instant that he would leave. It was her interview and she would begin the fight for exclusive control of it. "Cornelius, was it something I said?" she said lightly and friendly.

"Ha ha! No no, just stretching my legs. This is a pleasant room, isn't it?" Price said. Murphy explained that this was for interviews, not interrogations. There was no difference to her, but she understood the connotations each word carried.

"I interview far more witnesses than suspects, so I like to make the room nice." Satisfied, Cornelius sat down. "Now, honestly, I had to wrap my head around this cloud thing a little, but it's just like saving your computer files to the network instead of your hard drive. If there's a copy on the network, I don't need the hard drive. And if there's a copy on the cloud, I don't need the phone. Since Jose travelled all over hunting Sasquatches, he always saved everything to the cloud. Photos, videos, even draft videos on his phone. And you broke it." Murphy tapped her pen on her notebook.

Price shifted slightly in his chair, and his eyes went to her notebook. He relaxed a little when she put her pen down. "Yes, I told you I did that. With the phone."

"And that was the last time you saw him? You didn't see him again? Talk to him, give him a lift somewhere?"

"No. Absolutely not."

There was a knock at the door, and Parker stuck his head into the room. "Excuse me," Murphy said, as she got up to speak with Parker.

"I brought the phone data, boss, is that what you wanted?"

"Yes, thanks Michael," she said before sending him back to the observation room. She waited another two minutes before re-entering the room with paper in hand. She sat down, looked at her suspect, and cleared her throat. It was time.

CHAPTER TWENTY-ONE

"Cornelius, I told you when you came in here that I'll treat you with respect and I've asked you to do the same for me. I know your reputation in the community matters. Reputation with others in your church, the media. We've approached you, trying to be as discreet as possible. But the problem is, every time I get more information from my team, there's another issue that comes up, and it's not issues that point away from you. It's issues that point at you, and I want you to know. No tricks, just respect."

Murphy laid out the location data she received on Price's TechWave phone. "Your phone, which you said earlier you never lend out, your phone was with you on Saturday morning."

"Hmm, yes I was, uh, I was home gardening."

"Oh, I thought you were playing golf. I'm sure that's what you said earlier," Murphy said as she looked at Girard. He looked back at her and nodded.

"Oh yes, well I was gardening then golfing, I went golfing afterward."

"No Cornelius. Look at this map. This is the golf course, this is your home and this, way over here, is the Spalding Conservation Area. Your phone was near Spalding, not Goldfinch Greens, not your home, at 7:25 on Saturday morning. You see?" Murphy asked as she tapped the phone data report. Price remained silent, staring at the map. She gave him just long enough to let the information sink in before she put the phone logs and map back into her file.

"You dropped off a knife when you arrived and..."

"Uh huh, my fishing knife."

"You signed a release form. We have tested the knife for blood and-"

"It's a damn fishing knife. Of course there's blood."

"The presumptive test for human blood was positive. There is human blood on your knife."

Price frowned. "I don't like where this is going. Oh, of course. I cut myself or something."

"Hold out your hands. Do you have any recent cuts?"

Price laid his hands out on the table, turning them over and revealing a minor cut on his left thumb. "See, mine."

"Okay, but of course I have to double check. Can we get some DNA from you, a buccal swab, so we can compare? That will clear this right up." When Price reluctantly agreed, Murphy left the room and spoke with Parker, but he was a step ahead.

"The Forensics Unit should be here in-" A member of Dr. Chen's team arrived, put on some gloves and accompanied Murphy into Interview One.

"This is harmless sir," said the tech, as he peeled open the sealed buccal swab test. "I am going to swab the inside of your mouth, both cheeks. Please open your mouth. That's it, thank you sir," the tech said while putting the swab into a tube and then sealing it. After writing on the label, the tech left the room to process the swab.

Murphy pulled out a transparency line map of Mercado's walk through Spalding, and a paper map at the same scale of Spalding. "This is Jose's walk on Friday afternoon. He had a phone app that let him track his walks using GPS. His phone automatically uploaded to the cloud, so he had his trips mapped. This is Friday, when he found the bone. This little mark tells us exactly where it was found. It is amazing what software can do. If you look here, you'll see a ruler. That gives us distance travelled. Now, let me overlay this on the map of Spalding. Same ruler here, same scale.

"You see here, you can follow Jose's walk through the Conservation area right up to here. Then you can see, he heads back to where he came from. We followed that route, Adam and I. Right where Jose stops and doubles back, is where Adam and I found more bones. Human bones, not deer."

"Human." An intense sinking feeling came over Price and his shoulders slumped. Murphy resolutely watched him, knowing she had him.

"The Spalding Doe. Jose found the Spalding Doe femur. He didn't realize it. He planned to go back and find more, but he never made it. And this," Murphy said as she pulled out another transparency, "this is his Saturday morning route. Right back to Spalding, well, the north section. He never went into the Conservation Area proper. See? The route stops here, at Sunny Lake. It just stopped, and there was no more movement. Jose travelled nowhere after that. That's where his body was found, where his phone last recorded his location. Do you see the time here? Saturday morning at 7:21."

Price pulled the maps toward him for a closer look. "Mmm," was all he could muster.

"Do you see this here, and here?" Murphy asked as she tapped on each transparency. "This is the average speed. A fitness thing, so you can track running and walking. He had an average of two and a half kilometres per hour on Friday's trip when he was walking. But Saturday, you see, he's travelling at an average of thirty-five kilometres per hour. He's in a vehicle, driving into the area. It wasn't his car though, his car was back at the motel. We have security footage, it never moved. Someone drove him there."

Girard's phone buzzed softly while Murphy spoke. He scribbled a note to Murphy—'Found yellow box .22s.' Murphy nodded and continued as calmly as she could, although her stomach felt like an iron ball.

"Cornelius, essentially what we're talking about here is when you start adding in other pieces of information, and evidence gets into the hands of the experts. Well, it's pointing in a particular direction. My team headed to your home, with your permission, remember? They spoke with your wife. We found no guns but. Well, excuse me for a minute," Murphy said as she stepped out.

Murphy stepped into the atelier momentarily to read Hamilton's email. It showed that Beatrice voluntarily led her to a yellow cardboard box of Canuck 22 LR Greased Ammo, and asked her to please dispose of it. It had been on a top shelf in the garage, just as Dan-Elle had said. Her team kept searching, in case they might find more, but this added credence to the oral history Dan-Elle had provided. Murphy quickly shook her head, neutralized her face, and walked back in.

"I told you there would be no guns," Price said.

"But you gave permission for us to look for ammunition. My team, led by DC Hamilton, searched your home, your backyard, your garage. She spoke with your wife, Beatrice. Very helpful. How, uh, how long have you two been married?"

"Uh, I don't know. I think we are celebrating sixty years this year. I'm old, you know, my brain just doesn't work well some days. I forget things," Price said.

"No sir, you do not. Just two days ago you could go through decades old paperwork. You told me your mind is sharp as a tack. You are still driving, no speeding tickets and one citation, we checked. Your memory, your mind is sharp, as sharp as a young man's. Now look, we were respectful with Beatrice, we only asked about weapons and ammunition. She surrendered an old box of ammo. They were..." she paused, looking at Girard.

"Canuck 22 LR Greased Ammo," Girard said.

"They were .22s, you had a .22 rifle and-"

"A million people had them."

"Yes, but you had a Winchester Cooey Model 64b hunting rifle. We have copies of both the license and the Quit Claim. The ballistic expert we have will confirm that the bullet found in Spalding Doe was a Canuck 22 LR. Like what your wife handed my detectives."

"Mmm," Price sighed. "Beatrice."

"The box is on the way to the lab. The .22s will be identical, okay? You had a .22 Winchester Cooey and .22 Canucks. And the bullet we found with Spalding Doe was a .22 Canuck. And Jose found a femur that led us to Spalding Doe and we dated her to 1971, 1972, when you had the Winchester and the Canucks. Cornelius, you want respect and discretion. I can give that, sir. We need to, well, we need to have some honesty, two-way honesty because it's mostly been one way, from me to you. But it needs to be two ways, because this is getting out of control really fast Cornelius, really, really fast. I asked you to come in to give you the benefit of the doubt, to show respect."

Murphy pulled out the printed screenshot from Emily Powell's video. "You and I both know you were listening to Jose talk to his wife, saying where he was, holding up that femur. You are a smart man. You knew right away what it meant, and you couldn't let him find the rest of that girl. You had to stop him. I need to hear you right now because they are drawing up a warrant to tear your home apart, okay, so your home will have a dozen police cars out front and a big Forensics Unit van, and your vehicles will be seized. I am trying to be discreet, for Beatrice's sake. You and I both know we are finding evidence that links you to these situations, blood on your knife, blood where Jose was stabbed, mapping and tracking that puts you with him, and the femur ties him to skeletal remains. We know who she is, we know where she came from, we know where she was, and we know how she died. This is a major investigation for the Forensics Unit, and we are getting provincial and federal help with this. Cornelius. Cornelius?"

"Yep, yes, I'm listening."

"Those experts are going to go through your life piece by piece and they are going to tie your knife with human blood to Jose, and him to Spalding Doe, who we know, we can prove, is Cardinal Horn, who you fostered and you said ran away. And the bullet expert will link the bullet found in Cardinal's skull to the cartridges from your home. I don't think you want the press to call you a cold-blooded psychopath. I don't think you want your wife and children to think that about you. I don't see that in you. If I saw that in you, I wouldn't even be in here talking to you."

"Cardinal goddamn Horn," Price said with a heavy sigh.

Murphy nodded. "Cardinal Horn. It's Cardinal Horn. Why do you think that happened?"

Price sniffed, his eyes misting over. "I don't know."

"Have you thought much about that?"

"No. I haven't thought about her for years. I mean, it was a long time ago and I'm pretty sure the answers don't matter."

"Let me ask, is it that you hated her because she was trouble? Did you maybe like her in the wrong way? Did…"

"No! Not that! She was a problem, running away and talking back and stressing my wife. She wasn't worth the money. I mean, I don't want to sound cold, but she just wasn't worth the money. And then she pissed on the bed like a goddamn animal. I just, I just picked her up and drove. I used the old logging road. There were no houses there then, no Nature Centre. We drove into Spalding and I tried to shoot her, but I couldn't at first. She ran a little way, and I raised the gun really quick and shot. I… I shoved her body into a hole. Into a…" Price's shoulders slumped and his head bowed.

"When? When did this happen?"

"I don't remember. August '72, I think."

"There is no missing person's report."

Price burst out laughing, surprising Murphy and Girard. "No, I claimed the foster fees until 1978, when I decided to run for mayor. I just marked her as a runaway in '78 and signed off on her paperwork. I couldn't have any damn reporters sniffing about, wondering why she wasn't around and ruining my political career. I was just, you know, just beginning my political career."

Murphy waited for a moment before prompting Price to talk about Mercado.

"Why did you do that to Jose?"

"What bad luck. Bad luck he found the bone, worse luck for him. I overheard him. I spent all Friday night figuring out what to do. I went to the motel and waited for him. And there he was, coming out of the motel. I just honked and rolled my window down, said I was sorry and how I'd seen something years before in the Conservation Area, a Sasquatch. I promised to go looking with him, as a way of saying sorry for the night before, to take him to where I saw something. I'm an old man. I don't look threatening. He jabbered the entire way to the Nature Centre. He had no clue. That idiot let me get close to him, out on the beach. He didn't see it coming. I just slipped that knife right in, so smooth. Shk shk."

Price did not seem disturbed by his words. Rather, he seemed almost relieved to say them. He looked concerned, but only until Murphy next spoke.

"Why did you tie the rope around his neck?" Murphy asked.

Price's sly confidence flickered across his face again. "Mmm, ha, to make it look like a drug hit or some such. A mind trick, if you will," Price said, tapping his head.

Murphy put her hand under the table and tapped Girard, who dutifully noted that he had attempted to cover his crime. The act spoke of his competence and understanding of what he had done. "You hoped he would just disappear into the water? And that would be the end of it?"

"Mmm," Price said.

"How did you get him in the water?"

"I just rolled him in. Used a couple of tree branches as a lever." Price pushed house hands up in the air, mimicking raising a lever.

"Why didn't you move the girl's remains before he could find more? Wouldn't that have been easier?"

Price let out a soft groan and leaned on the table. "It has been fifty-one years. Do you know how much that area has changed? I couldn't tell where she was. The logging road is gone. There's a residential area, a Nature Centre. And believe me when I tell you, the forest can change a lot in fifty years. I never went back after her, ever. After I, after Jose went into the water, I looked at the trees, and the forest just looked like a jungle. It was like I had never been there in my life. I thought, if I don't go in, does it really exist?"

Murphy's face hardened. "Yes Cornelius, yes, she really exists. She, not it. Cardinal Horn exists, and we have her safe now. She exists. Okay, okay, Adam, we are done now. Read him his rights. First degree murder of Cardinal Horn. First degree murder of Jose Mercado. I'll leave you to it."

"Cornelius Price, I am arresting you for first degree murders of Cardinal Horn and Jose Mercado. You have the right to retain and instruct counsel without delay. You also have the right to free and immediate legal advice from duty counsel..." Girard began. Murphy got up and left the room, feeling satisfied but exhausted and dirty. Parker had summoned two Detention and Transportation officers who walked into Interview One to handcuff Price and take him to the municipal jail where he would be held pending a bail hearing.

EPILOGUE

Murphy called Chief Valencia, who congratulated her on the confessions for both murders and told her to advise the prosecutor's office. "Yes sir, DC Hamilton is on that. There will be additional charges, sir. Indignity to a human body, two counts; discharging a firearm with intent: grievous bodily harm. I will let the federal government know about the fraud in relation to falsely claiming payments for Cardinal Horn."

"Don't kill his good will trying to get every little charge, Murphy. He won't live long enough to serve the murder sentences. I will speak with former Chief Griffith since you will have to follow up with him, and notify Media Relations. Good job with the confession, Murphy, good job."

"Thank you, sir," she said, and hung up. The next call was to Violet Mercado. "Violet, it's DI Murphy, Muskoka Municipal Police. I'm calling to let you know we have made an arrest in the murder of your husband."

Violet burst into tears. She was overwhelmed with relief and a surge of emotions, sending shockwaves through her heart. "Who? Why did somebody kill him?"

Murphy provided Violet with a broad update on the investigation. "Jose helped us find the little girl, Cardinal Horn, and find her killer. In my eyes, he is a hero."

"Thank you for letting me know. I... Tell Cleo I will send her an email, okay?" she asked.

"Yes, I'll let her know to keep an eye out for it," Murphy said.

Murphy's next call was easier. She rang Lethabo Zibi and let him know an arrest was made in the death of Cardinal Horn. She advised him it might never get to a public trial, as more than forty percent of all homicide cases were resolved with a plea agreement.

She sat at her desk, wondering how to handle Cardinal Horn's remains. Ordinarily, the municipality would bury unclaimed remains in a common grave in a local cemetery. But hers were not ordinary remains, whether or not a relative was alive to claim her. Murphy called the Indigenous Association of Central Ontario but hung up when she got their voicemail. Asking the association if they would formally take custody of Cardinal to bury her, could wait until the next day.

She was about to make the next call when Parker walked into the atelier. She joined him, shook his hand. "Good job Michael." She thanked Hamilton and Girard the same way, with a handshake and congratulations. "Tomorrow, we need to prepare a more complete list of charges. Then the recording, reports and evidence for the Crown Attorney, and the defence lawyer gets a copy once one is hired. But tonight, we get to celebrate. Dinner on me?" Murphy offered.

"Sorry boss. I would love to, but I have to get home to my family," Girard said.

"Of course, Adam, no problem. Michael? Cleo?"

"I still have to finish cataloguing what we picked up at the Price house. Which, by the way, included some sketchy looking dog treats," Hamilton said.

"I promised to help Cleo," Parker said. "Looks like you are on your own, boss."

"Okay, maybe tomorrow then. Great work everyone, great work."

With that, Murphy headed out to her Brawler. She sat for a moment, window open, engine off. There was still daylight, glowing softly like polished gold. It fell across the sky and glimmered on the Brawler's hood, making it shine like new. Cicadas were louder than the slow traffic as it passed by the parking lot. She was sure she heard a woodpecker tapping on a tree nearby. It was all part of the quiet that was never silent. She wanted this to last forever. She wanted this contentment, this peace, to go on.

Murphy pulled her personal phone out of her pocket and dialled. "I'd really like to see you tonight."